Praise for Mark de Castrique

SECRET LIVES MYSTERIES

Secret Lives

★ "Another wise, experienced senior sleuth... Quirky characters and offbeat twists."

—*Library Journal*, Starred Review

"De Castrique's uber-twisty narrative consistently entertains... A taut and crisply told thriller whose charmingly shady protagonist triumphs over a labyrinthine plot."

—*Kirkus Reviews*

"A high energy foray into cryptocurrency and government corruption. Yes, wise-cracking Ethel is highly entertaining, but to de Castrique's credit, she's no cutesy stereotype of a gun-wielding grandma. She's got her own story, and it's a complex one."

—*First Clue*

THE BLACKMAN AGENCY INVESTIGATIONS

Murder in Rat Alley

"Nicely plotted... Intelligent, kind protagonists, and an eye-opening historical background help make this one a winner."

—*Publishers Weekly*

"Mark de Castrique fabricates an elaborate, multi-layered mystery that employs espionage elements to deepen the intrigue. The author's skill in creating divergent clues that he deftly connects makes for a fascinating read at a compelling pace."

—*Reviewing the Evidence*

"*Murder in Rat Alley* is definitely a very compelling mystery with some surprising twists and unexpected connections!"

—*Fresh Fiction*

"Someone trying to bury the past kills again and threatens Blackman and Robertson before the full, convoluted scheme, involving more decades-old murder and espionage, is revealed."

—*Booklist*

Hidden Scars

2018 Thomas Wolfe Memorial Literary Award nominee

"With its strong sense of place, depiction of racial tension that still lingers in the new South, and appealing sleuths, de Castrique's well-plotted mystery is a winner."

—*Library Journal*

"De Castrique combines an examination of the South's troubled racial history with a smart probe of current political-financial shenanigans."

—*Publishers Weekly*

"De Castrique's sixth delivers a vivid gallery of suspects, lively dialogue, and an attractive pair of sleuths."

—*Kirkus Reviews*

A Specter of Justice

"A good choice for anyone who enjoys small-town mysteries and ghost stories."

—*Booklist*

"An entertaining whodunit with colorful characters, swift-footed plotting, and a confident narrative voice."

—*Kirkus Reviews*

A Murder in Passing

"This solid whodunit offers readers a glimpse into a curious chapter of cultural history."

—*Publishers Weekly*

"This fascinating mystery, merging past and present, brings some little-known history to light and shows that laws change much faster than attitudes, as Sam and Nakayla, an interracial couple themselves, discover."

—*Booklist*

The Sandburg Connection

★ "Stellar… A missing folk song, a buried treasure from Civil War days, and a pregnant goat all play a part in this marvelous blend of history and mystery seasoned with information about Carl Sandburg's life…"

—*Publishers Weekly*, Starred Review

"A suspicious death on top of Glassy Mountain turns two laid-back private sleuths into prime suspects."

—*Kirkus Reviews*

"Folk songs, Sandburg, and Civil War history—what a winning combination!"

—*Library Journal*

The Fitzgerald Ruse

"An excellent regional mystery, full of local color and historical detail."

—*Library Journal*

"The warmth of Sam and Nakayla's relationship and Sam's challenged but determined heart make for a great read..."

—*Kirkus Reviews*

"Readers will hope to see a lot more of the book's amiable characters..."

—*Publishers Weekly*

Blackman's Coffin

★ "A wealth of historical detail, an exciting treasure hunt, and credible characters distinguish this fresh, adventurous read."

—*Publishers Weekly*, Starred Review

"Known for his effortless storytelling, de Castrique once again delivers a compelling tale blending fact and fiction..."

—*Library Journal*

"In the struggling Sam Blackman, de Castrique has created a compelling hero whose flinty first-person narrative nicely complements Henderson's earnest, measured, and equally involving account."

—*Kirkus Reviews*

Also by Mark de Castrique

Secret Lives Mysteries
Secret Lives

The Blackman Agency Investigations
Blackman's Coffin
The Fitzgerald Ruse
The Sandburg Connection
A Murder in Passing
A Specter of Justice
Hidden Scars
Murder in Rat Alley
Fatal Scores
The Secret of FBI File 100-3-116

The Buryin' Barry Mysteries
Dangerous Undertaking
Grave Undertaking
Foolish Undertaking
Final Undertaking
Fatal Undertaking
Risky Undertaking
Secret Undertaking

Standalone Thrillers
The Singularity Race
The 13th Target
Double Cross of Time

Mysteries for Young Adults
A Conspiracy of Genes
Death on a Southern Breeze

DANGEROUS WOMEN

DANGEROUS WOMEN

MARK DE CASTRIQUE

Cover illustration and design by Andrew Davis

Sourcebooks, Poisoned Pen Press, and the colophon are
registered trademarks of Sourcebooks.

Published by Poisoned Pen Press, an imprint of Sourcebooks
P.O. Box 4410, Naperville, Illinois 60567-4410
(630) 961-3900
sourcebooks.com

Cataloging-in-Publication Data is on file with the Library of Congress.

Printed and bound in the United States of America.
SB 10 9 8 7 6 5 4 3 2 1

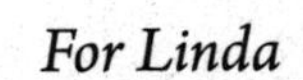

For Linda

Fight for the things you care about,
but do it in a way that will lead others to join you.

—ASSOCIATE SUPREME COURT JUSTICE
RUTH BADER GINSBURG

Chapter 1

Chief Justice Clarissa Baxter meticulously cleared the surface of her desk. The drafts of memos compiled by her clerks and relevant research documents were refiled and locked in the steel-lined drawers of her expansive oak desk. What was left, her random musings jotted down on legal pads, were quickly reviewed and a few pages kept while she fed most of them to the shredder in the back corner.

Chief Justice Baxter took no chances that anyone other than her four clerks had access to arguments she formulated during her process of deliberation. She knew the eight associate justices didn't consider her a team player, a throwback to the Burger court. Not only was she reticent in their weekly Friday conferences, she instructed her clerks to be tight-lipped until she was ready to voice a position.

Well, she wasn't a team player. She wasn't part of the club—the Harvard or Yale law school grads who dominated the bench. She felt an affinity with the other two women justices, but they also were products of the northeastern elite schools. Clarissa Baxter had attended law school at the University of Wyoming, her native state. She had graduated at the top of her class, and her judicial career had kept her close to home as she rose from district judge to sit on the U.S. Court of Appeals for the Tenth Circuit. When the former chief justice retired, the president had made her his surprise nominee, claiming it was time for a woman to hold the top judicial position in the nation. Forty-eight-year-old Clarissa Baxter had issued no polarizing rulings and gave heavy weight to legal precedent. She had won senate confirmation by a comfortable margin. That had been six months ago and toward the end of the court's last term. Now this term would be hers and she was eager to make her mark.

She stood and grabbed her raincoat from the coat rack by the door. The weather forecast called for a light drizzle to last into the night. She wanted to get home, start a fire, and finish the bottle of pinot noir she'd uncorked the night before. Just her and Max. Max the German shepherd. Her sole companion. Her husband, Jackson, lay in the family plot back in Laramie. Twenty years of marriage, and then pancreatic cancer stole the love of her life six weeks before the president called. It wasn't fair. But if life wasn't fair, she would work to see that the law was. She knew that goal wasn't easy, not when the possibility of bad consequences existed no matter how a ruling came down. That was the dilemma she found herself in now. A dilemma she'd take home with her despite the warm fire, fine wine, and comforting presence of her husband's beloved Max.

She went to her desk phone and lifted the receiver. Before she could dial, her secretary, Nicole Cramerton, spoke through the intercom. "Marshal Ventana is here to see you."

"Send him in."

A middle-aged white man with close-cropped gray hair and tired brown eyes entered.

"What is it, Daniel?" The chief justice dropped the receiver back on the cradle.

"Sorry to interrupt." Supreme Court Marshal Daniel Ventana held out a sealed manila envelope. "Got a minute?"

Chief Justice Baxter draped her raincoat over the back of her chair and then walked to meet the man rather than invite him in. "What is it?"

"The scenarios you asked me to play out—if protests turn violent like the January 6th insurrection at the Capitol. I got input from the U.S. Marshals and the FBI, as well as construction estimates. I thought you might want to review my recommendations over the weekend."

"Construction?"

"Mostly reinforcing windows and doors. And creating more defensive positions for my team in case there's an actual breach."

The chief justice took the proffered document. She knew it was a priority for Ventana. His title of Supreme Court marshal could be confusing because he wasn't a U.S. Marshal but rather the head of the Supreme Court police and chief administrator. Court security was his responsibility.

"Thank you," she said. "I'm sure you've thought of everything."

"There's always room for better ideas. But if you've got a big weekend planned, don't feel like you've got to read it right away. I just wanted to give you the option."

"It will be a quiet weekend, Daniel."

"Have you called for your car?"

"I was just about to." She returned to her desk and reached for the phone.

"I'll contact them for you." He retrieved a cell phone from his pocket and punched in a number. "The chief justice is on her way down." He disconnected and watched her pick up the raincoat. "Can I carry anything for you?"

"I'm just taking your report. Everything else can wait till Monday."

Ventana chuckled. "I'm sure everything you need is in your head." He followed her to the outer office where Nicole was locking up her desk. She was in her early thirties, but with her burgundy cardigan sweater and blond hair pulled up in a bun, she looked like a stereotypical librarian ten years older. She smiled at Clarissa. "Have a nice weekend, ma'am."

"You too. Since we're not hearing arguments next week, we'll have a chance to catch up on current cases. So, rest up."

Ventana nodded to the secretary and then stepped into the marble hallway behind the chief justice. One of the clerks was waiting for her. The tall African American man. The basketball player who could have turned pro. Robert Finley was his name, Daniel recalled.

Clarissa smiled. "Robert, do you need something?"

"No, ma'am. I was checking to see if you had anything else for me before I go."

"No." She eyed the backpack by his side. "I believe I've given you enough."

"Thank you for your confidence."

"Try to have a little fun," she said. "You too, Daniel."

The two men watched her walk down the hall.

"Is she always tight-lipped?" Ventana asked.

"She weighs her words, sir. She knows every ruling has consequences for both sides."

"Well, I hope she weighs her words in the light of something I don't think they teach you in law school."

"What's that, sir?"

"Common sense."

Robert laughed. "Maybe it's not all that common."

"So, what are you doing for fun other than work?"

"I'm allowing myself one drink at the Dubliner. I'm afraid that's the extent of it."

Ventana's cell phone rang, and he glanced at the incoming number. "Sorry, gotta take this. Enjoy that drink." He briskly walked away. "Hold up a second," he whispered, and said nothing more until he was out of earshot.

Robert found Brooke Chaplin pacing by the elevator.

His fellow law clerk shook her head dramatically, her long blond ponytail swinging side to side. "What took you so long? I thought all you had to do was change out of your gym clothes. Jake's asked me three times why I won't get on."

"Sorry, I had to see the chief. Besides, you could have ridden up and down with him till I got here."

Brooke pressed the button to summon the elevator cage. "I don't know which surprised me more. The fact that the Supreme Court is topped by a basketball court or that it still has manned elevators."

With a squeal, the door opened. "Are you finally getting on, young lady?" Jake Simmons waved her in. He looked at Robert. "Don't tell me you were waiting on this giant. How's the air up there, my good man?"

"Clear enough to see the bald spot on the top of your head."

The elevator operator let out a raspy laugh. He was in his early forties, broad-shouldered with an even broader stomach. He perched on a cushioned stool with his legs dangling just above the floor. Most people got on and off without noticing the metal visible between his left trouser cuff and his shoe. Jake Simmons was an amputee with a prosthetic leg, and, when asked, he would simply say his military career had been cut short by a roadside bomb in Afghanistan. Despite his horrific injury, his outlook was cheerful and positive. His good-natured banter made him a favorite of the law clerks.

"Hold up, please." Nicole Cramerton hurried to the elevator, her raincoat draped over one arm.

"Train's leaving, Nicole." Jake started closing the door to

tease her. "Oh, come on in. If you can fit beside Robert." He looked at the bulging backpack in the clerk's hand. "That's not a promising start to the weekend."

"You're telling me. But Brooke's going to buy me a drink at the Dubliner, aren't you, Brooke?"

"A sympathy drink," she told Jake and Nicole. "I just beat his butt at basketball."

Nicole looked at the tremendous height difference between the two clerks. "Really?"

Jake closed the door and the elevator descended. "You were playing HORSE, weren't you? She got you with her backward foul shot."

"You've played her?" Robert asked.

"Oh, yeah. I'm on an amputee team, and she found me practicing one day." Jake laughed. "She was ruthless, even to a wounded warrior."

"Who are you kidding?" Brooke said. "You wouldn't want it any other way."

"You're right. There's a fine line between sympathy and pity. I can accept the first but not the second."

Jake's sudden serious tone drew silence until the elevator came to an abrupt stop. "Sorry," Jake said, "not my best landing." He opened the door. "See you all Monday. And, High Pockets, try not to burn the midnight oil."

"It's not about burning oil."

"Right." Jake winked at him. "So, try not to drain your batteries."

—

One drink at the Dubliner turned into two. Then an evening shower began, and Brooke suggested they each have the pub's famed Capitol Hill Burger since Robert had to eat sometime and neither wanted to leave during the height of the storm. When he'd devoured his last french fry, Robert glanced at his watch. Brooke caught the gesture and wasn't offended. It wasn't like they were on a date.

"Listen," she said, "if you've got to split, don't let me hold you up."

"No. I can wait."

"Well, then tell me what Chief Justice Baxter has you working on all weekend. I can keep a secret. It's the mining case, isn't it?"

Robert looked around the pub from their corner booth. No one was paying them any attention. He leaned across the table. "Like I said, I've been her sounding board. For some reason, out of her four clerks, she chose me to play devil's advocate for both sides."

"Why? Can't she make up her mind?"

"She's made up her mind that there's not a good outcome, no matter how the ruling goes. She knows the other justices are split, and her vote will create the majority. And she'll assign herself to write that majority opinion with a caution about consequences. Maybe even include an appeal to Congress for legislative action."

"I could be your sounding board," Brooke said. "I know my justice will be voting to overturn the lower ruling. Parker's logic is very sound."

"Thanks, but Baxter gave the task to me. I shouldn't have said as much as I did."

"Don't worry. It stays with me." Brooke looked at the half burger and scattering of fries on her plate. "I'm done. You can go ahead. Dinner's my treat."

"You were buying me a drink, not dinner. Let's split it, and you can leave the tip. Then I'll walk you to the Metro. You're going back to Arlington, right?"

"Back to Ethel's Dormitory for another exciting weekend. So, if you change your mind about help, call me."

The rain had stopped, although the uneven sidewalks still captured small puddles and water trickled down storm drains. As they walked along Massachusetts Avenue, Robert began to regret his dismissal of Brooke's help. His three roommates were out for the evening, and what he'd thought would be welcomed silence for his work devolved into just another lonely night. He'd enjoyed the impromptu dinner and the company of an attractive woman—especially one who could make a backward foul shot.

His steady girlfriend was in her third year at the University of Michigan Medical School, and so far she'd only been able to come to DC once since he'd started his clerkship year. They agreed Robert's opportunity at the court was the career chance of a lifetime and were committed to making a long-distance relationship work.

However, a voice on the phone or a face on Zoom could only go so far. Not that he considered breaking up or having an affair. He just missed nights of good conversation and companionship like he'd had tonight.

"You're not listening to a word I'm saying, are you?"

Brooke's question snapped him out of his thoughts. "Sorry, I...I was thinking maybe I could use your help, at least on assessing Parker's arguments. I don't live too far from here, if your offer's still good. I insist on paying for an Uber, and no later than ten thirty."

She looked at the heavy backpack he'd slung over his shoulder. "How much do we have to read through?"

"Oh, most of these are documents that Baxter references

in her notes. It's those notes plus the ones she made after this morning's conference that she wants organized into cogent arguments."

"Do you want me to help with the writing?"

"No. Just debate the merits of both sides. Otherwise we'd need to have every volume of the Oxford English Dictionary on hand just to read your opening paragraph."

They walked another ten minutes until the street buildings became residential town houses southeast of the Capitol. Robert stopped in front of a white brick home with a stoop of six steps leading up to the front door. He fumbled through a front pocket for his key while Brooke stood two steps below him.

Robert threw the dead bolt and pushed open the door. He crossed the threshold. "Let me get the light."

Brooke stepped into the dark interior. Suddenly, she heard rapid footsteps, not from inside, but from behind her. She turned as the sound ascended the stoop. For a split second she saw a blur of motion, then an explosion as bright as the sun.

Then nothing.

Chapter 2

Ronald Drake itched all over. The layers of old clothes he wore scratched from the frayed collar to the threadbare wool socks. Yet, he couldn't argue with the plan. The week's worth of stubble, fingerless gloves, and twine belt completed his transformation of appearance into nonappearance. Just another homeless man, someone to be avoided—even down to eye contact.

Drake's only misgiving was the demand not to conceal a gun. He understood carrying a blackjack could be considered a necessary weapon of self-defense to protect what little possessions a homeless person hauls around. But if he were picked up with a gun, then he'd be thoroughly questioned and probably arrested. The people who hired him definitely wouldn't like that.

He'd made his way over to North Capitol Street, where some of the homeless people camped in front of Gonzaga College High School. He'd blend in with the others. The backpack was scuffed from where he'd dragged it along the sidewalk, but the woman's designer shoulder bag would have stood out. So, he'd tossed it in a dumpster, but not before rifling through the contents, discarding cosmetics and keys, but holding on to a wallet with credit cards, cash, a REAL ID, and a surprising business card. Lieutenant Frank Mancini, Robbery-Homicide, Arlington Police Department. The name on the other cards was Brooke Chaplin. The photo on the ID matched the woman he'd attacked. Why would she have a connection to a police officer?

Drake ditched the blackjack down a storm drain. He sensed he'd made a mistake not waiting to get the Black man alone. His employer had mentioned nothing about the woman, but made it clear he wanted the backpack tonight. Well, every operation risks collateral damage.

Drake shuffled through the tent city, dropping credit cards when no one was looking. He first wiped them down front and back to eradicate his prints. If someone had noticed a homeless man near the vicinity of the mugging, then who better to be found with the woman's cards than a homeless person?

But he'd hold on to the policeman's card. His unknown employer might find it to be important.

His cell phone vibrated in his front pocket. Drake turned away from the tents, using his body to shield the screen. The one-word readout: "UNKNOWN."

"Yes," he whispered.

"Is it done?" The voice was muffled but intelligible.

"Yes, but one complication. He had a woman with him."

The command was short and sharp. "Report."

"I followed them a block or so back, expecting them to part company. They didn't. While the man sorted his keys, I figured no one was home and caught them just as they stepped inside. They each went out cold with one blow. I was standing in the open doorway so I grabbed his backpack and her shoulder bag, closed the door behind me, and hoofed it around the next side street before slowing down. The shoulder bag's in a dumpster, the blackjack's in the sewer, and the woman's credit cards will be found here at the tents."

"And no one saw you?"

"I'm ninety-nine percent sure, and the other one percent only saw another homeless man."

"Anything else?"

"The woman's name is Brooke Chaplin. She had a policeman's card in her wallet—-a Lieutenant Frank Mancini, Arlington Police Department."

The phone went so quiet Drake thought maybe his caller was on mute.

"That's not good," he finally said. "We don't want any more attention than a routine, unsolvable mugging."

"Well, I could have aborted the operation," Drake said.

"No, you did the right thing."

"So, we'll still meet, up the street from the tents? You know the deal is I see the second half in my account before the handoff."

"Stay put for now. I'll be back in touch." The connection died.

Ronald Drake sat down and leaned against the fence surrounding the school, wondering what was in the backpack by his side worth his fee of ten thousand dollars.

—

Jesse Cooper's hands were shaking. He'd been trying to pick the Yale dead bolt for fifteen minutes and the night chill only made the task more difficult. He needed the steadiness of a brain surgeon, but instead, his trembling fingers kept slipping the probes off the pins.

"Utt am I ooing ong?" The garbled words resulted from the pencil-thin flashlight clutched between his teeth.

Ethel Fiona Crestwater bent over Jesse's shoulder and peered at the resistant lock. "You're trying to force it. You've got to coax it." The gray-haired woman reached into a pocket of her canvas jacket. "Try giving it a shot of graphite. Might loosen it up."

Jesse withdrew one of the picks and gave the lock a couple of squirts of the lubricating powder.

"Now, start again with the back pin," Ethel instructed. "Don't try to turn the lock yet."

Jesse reinserted the tempered steel pick, bent-side up, to lift the pins into an unlocked position. He felt the back one give. "Yay," he managed to say. The cold was forgotten as he found a fresh boost of energy.

"Good," Ethel said. "Work your way forward. When you're at the fifth pin, use the inserted wrench to start trying to turn the lock. It should yield as soon as the last pin moves into place."

A faint click and the lock turned so quickly Jesse opened his mouth in surprise. The flashlight fell and rolled across the plank floor of the back porch. He didn't bother to retrieve it but stood, opened the door, and stepped inside.

"Stop right there! Police!"

From behind them, the bark of a command came simultaneously with a powerful beam that illuminated Jesse and Ethel like the porch was a stage.

"Hands where I can see them and turn around to face me."

Ethel, still crouching down, raised one hand over her head while pushing herself upright with the other. Then she lifted both hands and Jesse followed suit.

"I can explain," Ethel said. "It's not what it looks like."

"Sit on the edge of the porch, please, ma'am. You too, sir."

Ethel and Jesse obeyed, squinting against the harsh light still trained on them.

"Gloria, take my cuffs along with yours. You can do their hands in front."

Ethel dropped her arms. "That's not necessary, Officer. I'm

seventy-five years old and live next door. This is my double-first-cousin-twice-removed. He's not going to run off and abandon me."

"You've been caught breaking and entering. You've said this isn't your house. We can continue talking here or at the station, but either way you're going to be cuffed."

"This is bullshit," Jesse said.

Ethel squeezed his thigh as a warning. "Let them do their job. We'll get this sorted."

The man with the flashlight lowered the beam. A female officer took a set of handcuffs from her partner's utility belt and approached them along an arc so as not to block his line of sight. Ethel and Jesse could now see that although the light had been lowered, the patrolman's Glock semiautomatic hadn't been. His line of sight was also his line of fire.

When Ethel and Jesse sat with their cuffed hands in their laps, the patrolman approached. "I'm Officer Greg Tillman. This is my partner, Officer Blankenship. Now before I read you your rights, tell me why we shouldn't arrest you."

"I have Schlage locks," Ethel said. "Mr. Frederickson has Yale. This is his house. Mr. Frederickson is in Florida for the month, and I'm collecting his mail."

"So, you were breaking in to deliver his mail?"

"No. I have a key. But Jesse hasn't picked a Yale lock before. I was letting him practice."

"At ten o'clock at night?"

"Who picks a lock during daylight?"

Tillman didn't have a ready answer. Instead, he said, "So, if we go next door, we'll find Schlage locks and Mr. Frederickson's mail?"

"Exactly. But only the few pieces of mail from today. I've already put a week's worth of mail in Mr. Frederickson's foyer yesterday."

"Do you have a contact number for this Mr. Frederickson?"

"Yes, but he's asleep by now. We shouldn't disturb him."

"Would you rather disturb him or spend the night in a cell?"

"Neither. But I have a better idea, if I can have my one phone call."

"Your lawyer?"

"No, a friend. Like on that TV show. I need to phone a friend. If you or Officer Blankenship could reach in my pocket and give me my phone, I think I can dial."

Tillman nodded at his partner, who did as she asked.

"He's on speed dial," Ethel said, and punched one button. She managed to turn the phone and lift it to her ear.

After a few rings, she heard a groggy, "Hello?"

"Frank. It's Ethel. Did you fall asleep in your chair again?"

"What time is it?"

"Time to get over to Mr. Frederickson's backyard. His house is to the right of mine. I want you to meet two of your colleagues before they arrest me."

"Tell them to go ahead with my blessing."

"You know it'll just create paperwork. And it could interfere with my ability to fix you breakfast now and then."

"All right. Who's got you?"

"Officers Tillman and Blankenship."

"Both hardly more than rookies. Put me on speaker."

"Okay. Just a minute." She handed the phone to Officer Blankenship. "He wants to talk to you both on speakerphone."

"And just who is he?" Tillman asked sarcastically.

"Frank Mancini. Senior Homicide Detective Frank Mancini."

The two police officers looked at each other.

"Well, speak up," Ethel told them.

"This is Gloria Blankenship, sir. Greg's with me. Do you know an Ethel Crestwater?"

"I'm afraid all too well. Here's what you're going to do. Escort Ethel and Jesse back to her house. Have her show you how to brew a fresh pot of coffee."

"Shouldn't she make it, sir?"

"She can't because you're going to keep her handcuffed. I wouldn't miss seeing this for the world."

Twenty minutes later, Ethel and Jesse sat beside each other on the sofa in Ethel's living room. Officer Tillman stood at one end, holding a mug of coffee rather than a pistol. Frank Mancini sat in a wingback chair, a steaming mug on the end table beside him.

The veteran Arlington detective smiled at his two handcuffed suspects. He was in his mid-fifties, five-nine in height and thirty pounds too heavy, but as he liked to say, "I'm not overweight, I'm under-tall." He wore an extra-large, logo-free black sweatshirt and wrinkled blue jeans. He looked like he'd quickly grabbed his clothes from a hamper and not a drawer.

He lifted his mug and took a healthy sip. "Ah, perfect. I'd offer you some, but I need to make sure your story checks out first."

Ethel lifted her hands and rattled the metal cuffs. "Glad you find this so entertaining, Frank. I guess a man your age has to get his kicks however he can." She looked at Jesse. "He's been wanting to get me in these love bracelets for years."

Jesse looked at Frank with a deadpan expression. "Really?" He turned back to Ethel. "Then maybe those are the locks you should be teaching me to pick."

Ethel howled with laughter. Even Officer Tillman's stony face broke into a smile.

Frank waggled a finger at the young patrolman. "What's so funny? You should know Ethel's ex-FBI, going back to the Hoover days, and she knows every trick in the book. I'm surprised not to find you and your partner the ones in handcuffs."

Ethel nodded. "Could have happened. A word of advice, if I may, Officer Tillman. Always cuff behind the back unless your suspect is injured and the position would aggravate his condition. There was a second or two when your partner was in front of me. Her holster was unsnapped. You and she saw a little old lady. I saw a chance to shoot both of you."

Officer Gloria Blankenship entered. Her bloodless face showed she'd overhead the last bit of Ethel's criticism.

"But that wasn't the only mistake," Ethel said. She raised her hands, shook them, and one of the cuffs slipped free of her wrist. "Officer Tillman, you were too distracted watching her make the coffee while I stood in the kitchen, a veritable hardware store of tools ready for improvising." She bent her fingers under the wristband of her jacket and extracted a thin, short metal rod about the size of a toothpick. "But I already had what I needed. When you told us to raise our hands, I pretended to need my arm to lift myself up. Actually, I grabbed one of Jesse's picks. I've practiced on every handcuff made, so it wasn't much of a challenge to unlock, then re-cuff much looser so I could slide my hand free whenever I needed to."

Frank nodded appreciatively and turned to his colleagues. "Lessons learned?"

"Yes," they replied in unison.

Officer Blankenship held up a set of keys. "I tried the doors at the Frederickson house. These opened them, and I found mail on the table in the foyer where Ms. Crestwater said it would be."

"So, we have an approved entry by a suspicious means," Frank said. "Did some witness phone in the report?"

Blankenship shook her head. "No. I noticed the flashlight shining on the back porch between two houses on the next street over. We radioed we were checking it out and then cut through the yards in darkness to come up behind them."

"And you get an A for stealth," complimented Ethel. "Well done."

"How did you leave it with dispatch?" Frank asked.

"That you were coming to interview the suspects and it might be a false alarm."

"Good. Anybody have a problem writing it up that way?"

Neither officer objected. They were all too happy to be done with the affair.

"Then I suggest you get your cuffs back. Just make sure Ethel doesn't pick your pockets."

An old-fashioned ringtone sounded. Frank stood, retrieved his cell, and checked the number. "It's my niece. I'd better take it." He turned away and walked toward the kitchen. "Hey, sweetheart. What's up?"

"Sir, could you tell me your name, please?" The male voice was flat. Emotionless. Too emotionless.

A cold numbness began to spread from the pit of Frank's stomach. "No. Tell me who this is."

"Glenn Meadows. I'm a detective with the DC police."

Frank's knees went weak. He leaned against the wall. "Oh, God," he murmured. He caught movement from the corner of his eye. Ethel stood about a yard away. She'd sensed something was wrong.

"I'm calling on the cell phone of a woman who has been injured," Meadows said softly. "I first tried a number marked Mom but got no answer. This number is identified as Uncle Frank. Would that be you, sir?"

"Yes. My name's Frank Mancini. I'm a detective with the Arlington Police Department. The phone belongs to my niece, Brooke Chaplin. What's her condition?"

"The victim has been transported to the emergency room at MedStar Washington Hospital Center. I understand she was unconscious at the time. Can you give me a brief description so we know we're talking about the same person?"

"Twenty-five, blue eyes, blond hair usually in a ponytail."

"That matches."

"Do you know how badly she's hurt?" Frank asked.

"Just that it's serious. Does she know a Robert Finley?"

"I've never heard her mention the name. Is Finley a suspect?"

"No. She and Mr. Finley were found just inside the front door of his house. Looks like they'd just entered when a person or persons attacked them from behind."

"Mugging?"

"That's certainly a possibility. We're hoping when your niece regains consciousness, she can tell us what happened."

Frank took some small comfort that the man said when and not if.

"Is your niece a student?" Meadows asked.

"No, she's a law clerk for Supreme Court Justice Roland Parker."

"Then that's the connection. Finley was a clerk for Chief Justice Baxter. He and your niece were colleagues."

"Were?" Frank knew the answer as he asked the question.

"I'm a homicide detective. Robert Finley died at the scene."

Chapter 3

Ethel, Frank, and Jesse stood up as the young surgeon entered the small conference room where the three had been waiting. To Ethel, he looked to be barely out of his teens, but then she thought most doctors now looked like they'd just graduated from high school.

Ethel had insisted that she and Jesse drive Frank to the hospital. "You're too upset and rightly so. Besides, Brooke is my roomer, and you know how I feel about them." Frank hadn't argued. He too had once been one of Ethel's roomers.

"How is she, Doctor?" Frank shifted on his feet, bracing for bad news.

The surgeon closed the door, dropped his mask below his chin and forced a faint smile. "I'm Jeremy Cohen. Brooke is out of surgery and in recovery. She's stable. But she's suffered a severe concussion. In addition to the surface gash and associated contusions, there was some damage to the skull. We expect cranial pressure to rise because of the trauma, so we're keeping her in an induced coma as a measure against brain swelling. The next twenty-four hours will be the most critical."

"Can I see her?" Frank asked.

"Let us get her settled and monitored in ICU. Then you can go back for a short visit. The staff would like only one at a time."

Frank ran his tongue over his dry lips. "Don't sugarcoat it. What are her chances?"

"I don't speculate, but she's young and came through the surgery without initial complications. Let's just say I'm guardedly optimistic. My advice is to be patient."

"I'll be patient when I know she's out of danger," Frank snapped.

"I understand," Cohen said. "And I'll have someone come get you when we're ready."

A knock sounded from the door behind him. Cohen stepped aside as it swung open.

An African American man wearing a wrinkled navy sport coat and equally wrinkled gray slacks stayed on the threshold. Like Frank, he looked to be in his fifties. He also shared Frank's pudgy physique.

"Excuse me, Doctor. When you're finished here, I need to speak with them. I'll be in the hall." He started to close the door.

"Wait," Frank said. "Are you Detective Meadows?"

"Yes. You must be Detective Mancini."

Frank turned to the surgeon. "I think we're done for now. Thank you for all you're doing for Brooke. Sorry if I got a little testy."

"No problem. Don't give it a second thought." Cohen slipped past Meadows.

The DC homicide detective entered the room. He focused on Frank. "Could we have a word, sir?"

"You bet. But they stay with me. This is Ethel Crestwater. She's ex-FBI, and Jesse Cooper is her double-first-cousin-twice-removed. She can explain that later, but what you need to know is they're like family, so I want them to remain."

"All right. Why don't we all sit down? We can dispense with formalities, so please call me Glenn."

"And I'm Frank, and I'd appreciate any professional courtesy you can offer a thirty-year veteran of the Arlington Police Department."

Ethel and Jesse sat down on a small sofa. Frank and Glenn pulled chairs closer to form a circle.

Frank leaned forward, elbows on knees. "So, what do you know at this point?"

"Well, I'm really hoping you can tell me. Charlie Gardner, a roommate of the deceased, found your niece and Robert Finley when he returned home a little after nine. They were lying just inside the front door."

"Was the door closed?" Frank asked.

"Yes. But he found it unlocked. When he pushed it open, he discovered it was partially blocked. He was able to slide through the gap and discovered them on the floor. Gardner works as a congressional aide and has no medical training. He called 9-1-1 and EMTs were there within ten minutes. Two uniformed officers arrived five minutes later."

"Had the roommate tried to help them?"

"He was afraid to move them. The gash on your niece's head had created a pool of blood that seemed to have stopped. Gardner could tell she was breathing. Finley showed no signs of life."

"How much did the EMTs contaminate the scene?" Frank asked.

"Well, they had to negotiate the blocked door, and the priority was getting your niece to the hospital. Finley was dead at the scene. The uniforms said his body had to be moved, but they kept it as close to the original position as possible."

"You examined the body?"

"I left that for forensics, but I did see marks of a severe blow to the base of the skull."

"The base," Frank repeated.

"Yes. I think it broke his neck. Your niece was struck on the crown."

Ethel cleared her throat. "Mind if I ask a question?"

"No, ma'am. What is it?"

"How tall was Finley?"

The detective pointed a finger at Ethel. "Yes. A very significant question. Finley had to be at least six-five or more. I think his assailant had to swing upward with something like a blackjack." He turned to Frank. "Your niece is how tall?"

"I'm not sure. Five-four, five-five."

"Closer to five-three," Jesse volunteered.

"I suspect she was struck by a downward blow," Glenn said.

"Does that tell you the assailant's height was midway between Brooke and Finley?" Jesse asked.

"Yes. But it also suggests the blow to Finley wasn't meant to be fatal. The attacker had to swing upward and hit the back of the neck instead of the skull. The force was so great that instead of knocking Finley out, it broke his neck."

"It's still murder," Frank said.

"Of course it is," Glenn agreed. "But it might alter motive. Both your niece and Finley were struck only once. This wasn't an act of rage."

"So, we're back to a mugging," Frank said.

"Except Finley's wallet was still in his pocket with a hundred and twenty dollars in cash—his hip pocket, which was easy pickings when the victim lay facedown."

"And Brooke?" Ethel asked.

"We don't know what she might have been carrying."

"But you found her phone," Frank said.

"In the front pocket of her slacks."

Jesse looked at Ethel. "She usually had a backpack or a shoulder bag, didn't she?"

"That's right." Ethel thought a moment. "Did the roommate say if anything in the house seemed to be missing? Or had he seen Brooke before?"

"No to both questions. Brooke had never been to the house. At least to his knowledge. He said Finley didn't socialize much. He had a serious girlfriend back in Michigan."

Frank shook his head. "Then why was Brooke there?"

"Could it have been work-related?" Ethel asked. "You say the signs are Brooke and Finley were attacked right after they entered."

"Yes," Glenn confirmed. "In fact, Finley's keys were found by his body. He must have had them in his hand."

Ethel looked at Frank, expecting him to follow up. He said nothing.

Ethel shrugged. "So, if they were coming to the house from work, then where was his backpack or briefcase?"

Detective Glenn Meadows stared at the septuagenarian. "Good question. I don't know; and I didn't ask."

"Then I suggest we backtrack Brooke and Finley's movements." Ethel looked at a clock on one of the walls. "It's after one. Frank, your sister's on the West Coast, right?"

"Yeah. Oregon. It's only after ten there. I was hoping to get more information on Brooke's condition, but I'd better call her now. I don't know why she didn't answer your call, Glenn. She would have recognized Brooke's number."

"I think her phone was turned off," the DC detective said. "I went straight to voicemail. I didn't want to leave a disturbing message if I had other contact options. You were my second call."

"You might have to phone a neighbor," Ethel said. "When you do reach her, ask about Brooke's credit cards. If your sister doesn't know, maybe I'll find a monthly statement in her room." She looked at Glenn. "I assume you can trace activity."

"Yes, I'll also ask the roommate about whether Finley should have had a backpack or briefcase. And I'll notify the head of the Supreme Court Police."

"Daniel Ventana," Ethel said.

"Yes. You obviously know your way around DC."

Frank managed a genuine laugh. "Ethel helped Pierre Charles L'Enfant design the place."

He stood, and his somber mood returned. "Well, I guess I shouldn't delay the call any longer."

"No, you shouldn't," Ethel said. "But stay here. We'll wait outside and give you some privacy."

Glenn Meadows got to his feet. He passed out his business card. "You know I'm limited regarding what I can share about an ongoing investigation. But let's keep the lines of communication open."

Frank gave his DC counterpart his own card. "Thank you for your understanding. I hope I would be as accommodating if the situation were reversed."

The detectives shook hands. "Frank, as far as I'm concerned, we're on the same side. I'm too old to get territorial. Shoot, I'll even take help from an ex-FBI agent and her double-first-cousin-twice-removed, whatever the hell that means."

—

Ronald Drake shifted uncomfortably on the ground. The chill had penetrated the layers of his shabby clothing, and he felt his muscles stiffening. What was taking so long? It had to be well past midnight, although he hesitated to pull out his phone to check the time. Even the do-gooders who came bringing food and water and played guitars like they were on some church retreat, even they had returned to the comfort of their warm homes.

A few old men sat up, their conversation now only the sounds of phlegm-laced coughs. No one tried to talk to him.

His phone vibrated. A text. He stood and stretched. Then cradling his phone in both hands, he read:

> You killed him.

Drake froze. Was this some ploy to renege on the second half? He knew that the speed and desperation of his attack had put extra force behind his swings—especially the man towering above him. But kill him?

Another vibration:

> The woman is the policeman's niece. We need to get you out of town. Start heading up North Capitol toward L. A car will pick you up around the corner.

Drake abandoned any semblance of a homeless man's shuffle. He threw the backpack over his shoulder and started walking. He'd turned onto L and gone about fifty yards down the desolate street when headlights cast his moving shadow out in front of him. A black Lexus sedan passed and then stopped at the curb. The right rear passenger door swung open. Drake ran toward it, slipping the backpack off his shoulder. He clutched it to his chest like a life preserver.

The interior of the car remained dark. None of the courtesy lights were on. Drake bent down to look inside. An arm extended from the shadows. Too late Drake saw the glint of metal as a streetlight caught the smooth finish of the pistol's suppressor.

A cough only slightly louder than those of the old men signaled a bullet was tearing through Drake's forehead and blowing out the back of his skull. The gunman angled the shot to avoid bloody splatter striking the inside of the open door. With his free hand, he snatched the backpack as Drake's body tumbled to the sidewalk.

A voice from the front seat ordered, "The street's clear. Get his burner phone but be quick about it. He was told not to carry anything else."

A silhouetted figure leaned out of the car and patted down the body. He pulled the phone from Drake's front pants pocket.

"Got it." He withdrew into the rear seat and closed the door. With a soft purr, the Lexus eased away from the curb.

The entire event had taken only fifteen seconds.

Chapter 4

Jesse and Ethel followed Detective Glenn Meadows out of the conference room and into the hospital hallway. Ethel mouthed the words "good luck" to Frank as she closed the door.

Glenn looked up and down the empty corridor. "Why don't we go to the cafeteria? At this hour it will be only staff, and any coffee there will be better than the swill from a vending machine."

Jesse looked at Ethel. "What if someone comes with an update on Brooke? If it's bad news, Frank shouldn't hear it while he's talking to Brooke's mother."

"I'll stay here," Ethel told Glenn. "Jesse's spoken to Brooke as much if not more than I have. You can call me later if you still have questions, but right now it's better I stay with Frank as long as necessary. Who knows how things are going to go here?"

"All right," Glenn agreed. "Jesse, I'll be quick. I left my partner at the scene and want to get back to hear what Finley's other roommates have to say."

Ten minutes later, Jesse and Glenn sat down at a small table in the corner of the cafeteria, each with a cup of black coffee.

Glenn took a long swallow and then shook his head as if

trying to send the caffeine directly to his brain. "So, let's get one thing cleared up. I come from a family whose attendance at reunions numbers in the hundreds. We've traced our ancestry all the way back to the slave market in Charleston, South Carolina. I know what a first cousin is. I know what being once or twice removed means. It's a relationship between different generations. I'm twice removed from my grandmother's first cousin. My mother is once removed. My children are three times removed. But what the devil is this double business?"

"It's really simple once Ethel explained it to me. There were two families, each with a son and a daughter. The sons married the daughters. In other words, a brother and a sister married a sister and a brother. Nothing creepy or incestuous about it. But Ethel was the daughter of one couple and my grandmother was the daughter of the other. My grandmother and Ethel were first cousins, not just through an aunt or an uncle but through both. They had a double connection."

Glenn smiled. "Well, I'll be. I'll have to go back through my family tree and see if I can find our own double branches. So, you've got a big family?"

"No, you've met the entire family tonight. My mom died back in May; Ethel's mother died in childbirth. Her father named her Ethel in memory of his wife, which is why her name sounds a little old-fashioned, even for a seventy-five-year-old. He was an FBI agent, so Ethel grew up in the Bureau. Her father was murdered when she was twenty. She tracked down his killer. She won't tell you that, but I want you to know she's special. She's also relentless in her pursuit of justice. The prisons are full of people who underestimated her."

Glenn whistled softly. "Thanks for the heads-up. How does Detective Mancini figure in this?"

"When Ethel's father died, she continued working for the

Bureau. Hoover didn't allow women to be special agents, but Ethel was one in everything but name. When Hoover died, the new director changed the policy, and Ethel had a stellar career. But she also kept the house she'd lived in with her father and started renting out rooms to law enforcement. Some were FBI, some were Secret Service, most were on temporary assignment in DC and needed a place to stay. Frank was at the police academy and was one of her roomers. He stayed on till he married."

"I take it they're close."

"Yes. That's why she rented a room to Brooke while she's in DC for her Supreme Court clerkship."

"And you? Are you in law enforcement?"

"No. I'm a grad student at AU. Computer science. I'm another exception because—"

"Because you're a double-first-cousin-twice-removed," Glenn said with a laugh.

"There are two other roomers. Douglas Gray is Secret Service and Lanny Childress is FBI. Douglas is traveling with the vice president on his Latin America trip. Lanny's away from Arlington for the weekend."

"Any famous alumni I need to know about?"

Jesse shrugged. "Depends on what you consider famous. Rudy Hauser and Cory Bradshaw come to mind."

Glenn's eyes widened. "Really? The head of the FBI and the head of the Secret Service? I'd call them famous."

Jesse leaned across the table and in a mock conspiratorial tone said, "I'll let you in on a little secret. They're both afraid of Ethel."

Glenn's cell phone rang before he could reply. He glanced at the screen. "It's my partner. I need to take this."

Jesse started to stand up.

"No, keep your seat. He's probably just checking where I

am." Glenn accepted the call. "Hap, I'm still at the hospital. The young woman's out of surgery, but in a coma. I'm finishing up with the family now."

"You're with the uncle?" Hap Rodriguez asked, his voice animated with excitement.

"Yeah. I told you I expected to find him at the hospital. And I did."

"His name's Frank Mancini, right? An Arlington detective?"

"Yes. Why? What's going on?"

"I just heard radio chatter that a homeless man was shot and killed about thirty minutes ago. Near that tent city on North Capitol. No ID, but they did find a business card and are now wondering if he was undercover. The name was Frank Mancini of the Arlington police."

Jesse read the confusion on the DC detective's face. Then Glenn got up from the table and waved for Jesse to follow.

"I can assure you our Frank Mancini is here at the hospital. Maybe the victim got that card directly from him. Maybe he's Mancini's CI."

CI, Jesse thought. He knew it meant Confidential Informant. Frank's niece was struggling to survive in intensive care, and now his informant's been murdered. Whatever happened, Ethel would be keenly interested. That was one fact he was sure of.

"Look," Glenn said, "I'm not dragging Mancini away from his injured niece to ID a body. Call the officer in charge and have them take some photos, assuming the body hasn't been moved. Email them to me, and I'll see if Mancini can make a positive ID."

"All right," Hap agreed. "I'll get them to you as fast as I can."

Glenn disconnected. "Well, Jesse, I'm afraid I'm going to have to cut Frank's call short. To quote Alice in Wonderland, things just got 'curiouser and curiouser.'"

They found the door to the conference room closed but no Ethel outside.

"I guess the call's over," Jesse said.

Glenn gave a soft rap.

"Come in," Ethel said.

She and Frank were seated on the small sofa. He looked up, surprised to see Glenn Meadows enter. "I thought you were headed back to the crime scene."

"Something's come up."

Frank got to his feet. "We've had a break in the case?"

"I don't know what we've got. Maybe you do. A homeless man was shot and killed a little while ago. He had no ID. All that was found on him was a business card. Your business card."

Frank's mouth dropped open. "My card? Was this in Arlington?"

"No. North Capitol Street. A couple of blocks from a tent city that pops up now and then. Could it be one of your CIs?"

"I don't think so."

Ethel stood up, stepped closer to the DC detective, and asked in a soft, measured voice, "You're sure this killing happened after the attack at Finley's?"

"My partner says it went down within the last hour."

"That's plenty of time to walk between the two locations." Ethel turned to Frank. "You gave her your card, didn't you?"

Frank nodded. "As soon as she hit town."

"I assume you're talking about your niece," Glenn said.

"Yes. She called it her Uncle Card. In case she needed to reach me, or show it to another police officer if she was in immediate trouble."

Not to be left out, Jesse offered an explanation. "What if the attacker flipped through her wallet and threw the card away? Couldn't the homeless guy have just found it?"

"And then just happened to get shot?" Ethel answered her own question. "No. There's a link. This shooting victim played some role, and whoever killed him either wanted him silenced or wanted something he had."

"Or both," Frank said. "What's your next move, Glenn?"

"I'd like you to try and ID him. I'm not asking you to leave your niece, but I hope to get some photos sent for you to examine here." His phone vibrated. "This might be them." He checked his email and downloaded an attached file. "Yep." He handed the phone to Frank.

The photo showed a man from the chest up, lying on a concrete sidewalk. Dirt caked his cheeks and darkened unshaven stubble. His mouth hung open in what might have been surprise but was probably a result of gravity and a slack jaw. An ugly red circle marred the center of his forehead.

"I've never seen this man in my life." Frank handed the phone to Ethel.

The rest of them watched as Ethel brought the screen close to her eyes. Then she used two fingers to make the image larger. "You can wear old clothes, smudge your face with dirt, but you can't change your teeth. I can see only a few of the ones in front, but they look capped to me." She passed the phone back to Glenn. "Ask someone at the scene to check his hands. If the nails are manicured, then, gentlemen, I think we've found our killer."

Chapter 5

A little after one thirty in the morning, Detective Glenn Meadows left the hospital, promising to share what he could if Finley's roommates offered any new information or his partner, Hap, had an update on the identity of the murdered homeless man.

As soon as he'd gone, Ethel asked Frank, "Do you need anything? Jesse can get coffee or some packaged food from the cafeteria."

Jesse started for the door. "I can be back in five minutes."

Frank scowled. "What I need is to work the case, but being an uncle doesn't give me any leverage with DC's investigation."

"Detective Meadows seems competent," Ethel said.

"Yeah, but there were over two hundred murders in Washington last year. Cases pile up. Leads dry up. You know how it goes, Ethel. I don't doubt Glenn Meadows's sincerity, but he's only one man. And if I get involved, the complaint will soon come from across the Potomac for me to butt out. I'll be issued the edict by my sympathetic superiors to respect the jurisdictions and back off."

Ethel gestured for Frank to return to the sofa, and then she sat beside him. "So, what you need is someone who doesn't give a rat's ass for jurisdictions. A person or persons who can color outside the lines." She looked at Jesse, who still stood by the door. "Know anybody like that?"

"You mean other than you and me? No. Not a clue."

Ethel laid a hand on Frank's arm. "We're not asking permission, Frank. Your niece lives under my roof, and somebody hurt her. I'm not going to stand on the sidelines, and I'm not going to follow the rules of the game. Are we clear?"

Frank's lips drew tight for a moment and his eyes teared. "Thanks, Ethel," he managed to whisper. "You too, Jesse."

"I'm glad to help," Jesse said. "Did you reach your sister?"

"Yes. Her phone had been charging in another room. She's upset, of course. She plans to take an early morning flight that will get her to Reagan around three this afternoon. I'll pick her up. I'm going to take some personal time off till Brooke's out of danger. We'll go straight to the hospital from the airport."

"Does she need a place to stay?" Ethel asked.

"I've got room. It's just her. Her husband died of prostate cancer three years ago."

"I remember," Ethel said. "If you need anything on the home front, just ask." She shifted her attention to Jesse. "And I have an assignment for you."

"Get coffee?"

"No. We need to start our investigation. There might be a link between the attack on Brooke and Finley and the murder of this supposedly homeless man. In my experience, good dental care is rare among the street people. Not unheard of, but not the norm. They just don't have access to dentists. So, if our mystery man proves to be someone assuming an identity, what can we deduce?"

"That his attack wasn't just spur of the moment," Jesse said. "He'd gone to the trouble of being in disguise."

"What else, Frank?"

"If mystery man was then shot by someone else, we're looking at other players. We're dealing with a conspiracy."

"Yes. But for what purpose and how wide is it spread? Jesse, I need you to go to the house and search Brooke's room. Take a taxi or an Uber, whichever is faster. I don't care if you go through files marked confidential or top secret, and I doubt if she'd have anything like that, but I want to see everything before we're descended upon."

"You think Detective Meadows will move that fast?"

"No. But the Supreme Court police might take an interest, or the U.S. Marshals, especially if evidence confirms this was not simply a mugging. We need to be out in front because once they seize evidence, we'll be shut out."

"Ethel's right," Frank said. "I hadn't considered the court police. There might be multiple investigations after all."

Ethel waved a finger at him. "You're not here. Understand? Some on your side of the fence could accuse us of obstructing justice rather than aiding it. I don't want you tied to anything we do."

Frank smiled. "Then I haven't heard a word you've said."

—

With headlights off, the black Lexus crept down the narrow alley to the rear of the red-brick, five-story apartment building. In contrast to the front, with its circular driveway off Connecticut Avenue NW, its oversized double-door entrance, and a bronze plaque proclaiming its listing on the National Register of Historic Places, the rear entrance was a pocked, gray steel door between two dumpsters.

The Lexus idled while a white man wearing a black sweater and slacks emerged from the rear seat. He held a manila envelope in one hand and a key in the other. The pistol remained on the seat. His two handlers would take care of its disposal.

He immediately moved into the deeper shadows, inserted the key into the dead bolt, and disappeared inside the building. The two men remaining in the car hadn't asked his name nor had he volunteered it. Anonymity was prized in his business. Especially when his broker had refused to say who was hiring him. It could have been a mob, a corporation, or a country. He'd had to be assured it wasn't a terrorist front. He had standards, including ample planning. A rushed job too easily became a botched job. But he had to admit, a rushed job paid very, very well. Whoever hired him wasn't an amateur. The hit had come off like clockwork.

He took the stairs to the second floor and walked softly to his apartment at the end of the hall. The decor was devoid of any personality or personalization. Functional but sterile. That was fine. His work could take him anywhere in the world at any time. Pets, plants, and lasting relationships had no place in his life.

He figured he'd stay out of town for a week or two. In fact, his client had insisted that he leave DC till things settled down. *What was to settle down?* he thought. It was only a dead homeless guy. But he'd been provided with an airline ticket to Miami and some travel cash in the envelope, and confirmation that eighty grand had been wired to his offshore account. Not bad for a job contracted fewer than five hours ago. He'd catch a few hours of sleep, pack a suitcase, and then take a cab to the airport.

He stripped to his underwear and stretched out on top of his king-size bed. For a moment, he wondered who the homeless guy was and what made him a target. What was in the backpack? Why had the contract been issued on such short notice? He didn't dwell on those thoughts for long. He knew asking too many questions would put him in the sights of one of his competitors. He planned to leave the business on his own terms, not in a body bag.

—

Jesse wished the Uber driver a good night and then corrected it to a good morning. Despite his words, he thought two o'clock was an awful time to be up, no matter how you categorized it. As the car pulled away, Jesse patted the front pocket of his jeans and remembered he'd left his keys in his room along with his lock-picks. Fortunately, Ethel kept a spare key in a small, magnetized box attached to the metal inside the breaker panel mounted on the side of her home.

Ethel's house was a rambling two-story on North Highland Street in Arlington. Over the decades, she'd made some improvements such as a main-floor master bedroom and bath for herself, and she'd added a small bathroom to one of the four bedrooms upstairs. That room was usually occupied by a female agent while male agents shared a larger communal bathroom off the hallway.

The breaker panel squealed loudly as rusty hinges protested being moved. Jesse found the magnetized box adhered to the top inside cover, took it to the back porch, and used the key to open the door. Instead of entering, he returned the box with the key to its hiding place so he wouldn't forget to replace it.

A light still burned in the living room where Frank and the patrol officers had sorted out the earlier lock-picking incident. That seemed like days ago.

The steps creaked as he climbed the front stairway. He switched on the hall light, knowing that the other two roomers, Secret Service Agent Douglas Gray and FBI Agent Lanny

Childress, were out of town. He passed his room and went straight to Brooke's door. He turned the knob and pushed. Locked. For the second time that night, he needed his picks. This time springing the lock took less than a minute. He flipped on the overhead light and studied the room before entering any farther. A single bed lay under the window of the longest wall. The spread was forest green with two burgundy pillows leaning against the headboard. A small nightstand stood beside the bed.

On the narrow wall adjacent to him were a flat-top desk and chair. An HP laptop was closed and pushed to one side. A legal pad and pencil were beside it.

On the opposite wall were two doors with a dresser in between. Jesse had been in the room before Brooke moved in and knew the left door led to a closet and the right to a bathroom with a sink, toilet, and shower. For the first time since receiving Ethel's instructions, he felt uncomfortable going through Brooke's things—an invasion of privacy while she lay in a coma. But Ethel had her reasons, and he trusted her judgment more than he did his own.

He went first to the computer, raised the screen, and discovered it had been in sleep mode. A photo of the Supreme Court building materialized with a password inset block and flashing cursor. Jesse's graduate studies in computer science gave him sophisticated programming skills but no surefire way to bypass a password. He turned his attention to the legal pad. The top sheet was blank, but he could see that the pad wasn't new. He flipped up a sheet and uncovered writing on the page beneath. Brooke evidently used an empty sheet as a makeshift cover.

Letters were listed under two column headings: OVERTURN and REAFFIRM. Written one letter per line under OVERTURN were A G L P. Matching the layout under REAFFIRM were C H S W. In between the columns was the letter B with a circle of question marks around it. Was it some kind of anagram? Jesse thought. Maybe in code? No. OVERTURN and REAFFIRM had to be court cases. This was about Brooke's job and a tally of how the justices were ruling. The letters stood for their names. Under OVERTURN were Abernathy, Gomez, Levine, and Parker. Under REAFFIRM, Carlton, Haley, Sinclair, and Wang. The B had to be Chief Justice Baxter and her position was unknown.

Jesse didn't understand exactly how the court's deliberations proceeded, but they must meet in conference and defend their positions. Discussion, debate, and persuasion would fuel dynamic exchanges of ideas and legal interpretations. Jesse remembered Brooke said she was assigned to Justice Parker. He was listed under the OVERTURN heading. Was this a scorecard of staked-out positions or simply Brooke's assessment of how the justices were leaning? An assessment she might share with Justice Parker as they set strategies for the most effective arguments?

Jesse pulled out his cell phone and took a photo of the page. Then he flipped to the next one. Brooke had labeled its single heading PARTIES. It wasn't social events. Like the previous page, there were two columns but with a line drawn between them. First on the left list was BLM. Black Lives Matter? Jesse wondered. Then DOD, Senator Hathaway, Progressive Mining Coalition, Auto Industry, Climate Advocates, and President Tarleton. The right column began with NAC, then F&R United, Brine Extractors, People for the Environment, Auto Industry, and Senator Mulberry.

What did the two lists signify? The auto industry appeared on both. Environmentalists were on both. Jesse photographed the page. He flipped through the remaining sheets. They were blank.

He moved to the desk drawer. All he found were extra legal

pads, two pencils, three ballpoint pens, a box of paper clips, and a small stapler. He checked the nightstand. A Louise Penny mystery and a charging cable for her phone.

Carefully, he raised the mattress to see if anything had been tucked underneath. Then he dropped to his knees and peered under the bed. He saw a suitcase and a backpack, the items along with a hanging bag that he'd help her unload when she'd arrived at Ethel's. He opened each and found them empty.

The top drawer of the dresser held her underwear. Now Jesse really felt creepy sorting through her bras and panties. Would he be able to return them to their original positions? Maybe there was some kind of system she used for arranging her clothes that he'd not noticed.

His hand touched a book tucked in the rear of the drawer. He saw that it was a journal closed by a strap and with a pen lodged between the pages. Standing at the dresser, he thumbed through it and realized he was holding something far more personal than her underwear. Her diary.

Chapter 6

Detective Glenn Meadows studied the three men squeezed together on the beige sofa in the small living room of their town house. Robert Finley's roommates seemed bewildered. Bewildered that their friend had been killed. Bewildered that the police had taken over their house. Bewildered that they individually had to give statements as to their whereabouts that evening. Glenn was sure that their shock was genuine, but they had to be considered suspects until their alibis checked out and the medical examiner established a time of death.

After interviewing them, Glenn's partner had gone to the tent city to learn what he could about the murder of the homeless man. Although it wasn't their case, the discovery of the card of the Arlington detective, Frank Mancini, on the body potentially connected the two murders. Glenn wanted to re-question the roommates together for anything they could share about Finley's habits.

"If Robert were coming in from work, would he have had more than the keys and wallet we found on him?"

Glenn focused his attention on Charlie Gardner, the

roommate who had come home first. The two others, sitting on either side of him, waited for his response.

"He should have had a backpack," Charlie said. "He took it yesterday morning."

"Is it possible he didn't bring it home because it's the weekend?"

"I guess it's possible. But that makes no sense because he told us he'd be working this weekend. That's why he didn't go out with us tonight."

"Do any of you know what was in it?" Glenn asked.

Charlie shrugged. "Usually his laptop and hard copies of documents he was working on. Robert actually preferred writing and editing on legal pads before transcribing a draft into a Word doc. And I don't know about the woman. The other detective said she was a law clerk too. I assume she was here for work rather than, well, you know."

"Did he sometimes work here with his colleagues?"

"No. Never. And he never brought girls here. He has a girlfriend back in Michigan."

"Do you have any idea what he was working on?"

"Robert? No way," Charlie said. "You'd think he generated the nuclear codes. He claimed if he told us, he'd have to kill us." The young man paled. "I'm sorry. I didn't mean any disrespect. It's just that he said he couldn't share anything about the justices' deliberations."

Glenn Meadows knew what had to happen next. The head of the Supreme Court police would need to be informed. Glenn's case could involve a Supreme Court case, and Daniel Ventana wouldn't want some DC detective nosing through Supreme Court documents. A jurisdictional confrontation loomed, and all Glenn wanted to do was keep his head down, avoid the politics, and pursue his investigation wherever the evidence led.

Avoiding the politics meant calling the DC police chief and letting her deal with Ventana on a more equal footing.

He checked his watch. Two fifteen. Chief Yolanda Collins wouldn't like it, but better a wake-up call from him now than possibly being blindsided by Ventana at dawn. He'd phone her from the car where there would be some privacy. Meanwhile, he'd leave two uniforms guarding the house, especially Finley's room. He'd let his chief make the decision whether to confiscate any docs or hard drives that might contain court materials. That was above his pay grade.

As he walked down the front steps, his phone rang. The screen displayed the number of his partner.

"Hap, you still at tent city?" Glenn asked.

"Yeah, man. You at the victim's house?"

"Just leaving. Since you bummed a ride there, need me to pick you up? I'm ready to head to the station and start the paperwork. First, I'm going to bring the chief in the loop."

Hap Rodriguez laughed. "Rule number one—cover our asses. You know we're going to get steamrolled by the feds."

"You pick up anything new on the homeless guy?"

"Something fishy there. That old lady was right. Good dental work, manicured hands, and a banker's haircut. And a couple of the real homeless men brought credit cards to one of the uniforms. Claim they found them on the ground. Guess who they belong to?"

"Brooke Chaplin."

"You're not bad for an old cop. Now why would someone bring them here, only to discard them?"

"You tell me, hotshot."

"To send the investigation on a wild-goose chase. Easy to blame the homeless."

"Not bad for an almost rookie," Glenn said. "And what does that tell us?"

"That the guy was smart. Planned this out."

"With one exception," Glenn said.

"What's that?"

"I don't think he planned to have his brains splattered all over L Street."

—

Ethel had encouraged Frank to go home and rest, but he'd insisted he wasn't tired, even after seeing his niece unconscious in the ICU for the permitted fifteen-minute visitation. Now, he sat on the waiting room sofa beside Ethel, his head lolled against her shoulder, snoring like a chainsaw.

She turned to look at him. Gray hair that had once been black. Age spots beginning to appear on his hands. Abs transformed to flab. A fifty-five-year-old man moving out of middle age. She remembered him as the twenty-five-year-old police cadet who had rented a room from her. Frank had been one of her favorites. Where others had jockeyed to climb the career ladder, Frank just loved to solve cases. A man after her own heart. Maybe if she'd been a little younger, he could have had her heart.

Above the din of snores, she heard his phone ring in his pocket. At three in the morning, it probably wasn't spam.

She gently pushed him away. "Frank, wake up. You've got a call."

He snorted, blinked his eyes, and momentarily looked around the room, trying to orient himself. "What?"

"Your phone. It's ringing."

He stood and snatched it free. "Mancini."

"It's Glenn Meadows. How's your niece?"

"Stable, but some brain swelling. The next twenty-four hours are critical."

"I apologize if I'm intruding, but I wanted to bring you up to date. Just between us."

"No, man, I appreciate whatever you can share."

"Who's with you?" Glenn asked.

Frank looked at Ethel. "No one."

"Right. If by no one, you mean Ethel, that's okay. Just keep the circle tight, will you?"

"All right," Frank agreed. "Did you learn anything about this guy who had my card?"

"He's what Ethel expected. He doesn't fit the profile of someone who's been on the streets. At least for any length of time. My partner says our John Doe has an expensive haircut in addition to the dental work and manicure. We're running his fingerprints through the national database, including military."

"Anything to tie him to the attack other than my card?"

"Some of the homeless guys turned in your niece's credit cards. They claim they found them on the ground near the tents. The way I figure it, our John Doe was trying to make all of tent city into suspects."

"Sure sounds that way. It was a decent plan, except for the honesty of the homeless."

"And getting shot point-blank," Glenn added.

Ethel waved to get Frank's attention. "Finley's belongings," she mouthed.

"So, I assume you've talked to the roommates. They have any idea why Finley might have been targeted?"

"No, and before you ask, they all agreed Finley should have come home with a backpack. I think that was what the attacker was after. Your niece's bag was just window dressing for a mugging. If the backpack contained court papers, the feds will come in. I've already got my chief contacting the Supreme Court police."

"You've got a jurisdictional stake in both killings," Frank said. "Don't go quietly."

"Oh, I won't."

"One killing caused the second," Ethel whispered.

"Was that Ethel?" Glenn asked.

"Yes. She, uh, just came in the room."

"Right. Put me on speaker. I want to hear what she has to say."

Frank did as the other detective asked and then held his phone out toward Ethel. "All right, Glenn, go ahead."

"Ethel, Frank can brief you on this call later, but what did you just tell him?"

"It's just a possibility, but I think the first killing caused the second. Finley was supposed to be a run-of-the-mill mugging. But he died. The crime far exceeded what it was intended to be. Someone wasn't happy. This wasn't about cleaning up a loose end. This was about eliminating the subject of a murder investigation. A contractor who would have flipped on his employer for the best deal he could get. That was a risk someone wasn't ready to take."

"And the missing backpack?" Glenn asked.

"I'll bet someone in the tent city saw him with it," Ethel said. "He handed it over up on L Street and got a bullet for his troubles. It was a brazen act and tells us one thing."

"What?" Frank and Glenn asked in unison.

"We're swimming in deep waters, gentlemen. Waters that hold secrets worth killing for."

Daniel Ventana heard his mobile ring at a quarter to three in the morning. Although he was lying in bed wide awake, he answered the phone with a hoarse "hello" as if he'd been sleeping. Better to put the caller on the defensive.

"Mr. Ventana, this is Chief Collins with the DC police. I'm sorry to wake you."

He sat up, swinging his bare feet onto the floor. "I'm sure it's important, Chief."

Yolanda Collins dropped the formalities. "It's bad news, Dan. One of your clerks has been murdered and another is in critical condition. She's at MedStar in a coma."

"My God. Who?"

"The fatality was Robert Finley. The severely injured's Brooke Chaplin. Evidently someone attacked them on the threshold of Finley's town house."

"Do you have a suspect? Anyone in custody?" There was no question Ventana was wide awake now.

"Our chief suspect was assassinated a few hours after the attack. Dan, to be honest, we don't know what we've got here. But Finley's backpack is missing and perhaps some court documents as well."

"Finley's a law clerk for Chief Justice Baxter. I saw him with a backpack as he left the building. Is the press on top of this?"

"Not yet," Collins said. "Finley and Chaplin weren't discovered by a roommate till around nine. The suspect was killed several hours later and blocks away. No one's made the connection. Hell, we just made the connection."

Ventana stood up and started pulling clothes from his dresser. "Where are you?"

"I'm home. I just got the news from Glenn Meadows, my lead homicide detective, but I'm heading in as soon as I hang up."

"Then I'll meet you at your office. This is going to cross into my jurisdiction, and I expect full cooperation."

"I called you, didn't I?" Collins snapped.

Ventana reined in his attitude. "Yes. Thank you. But I know how overworked your department is. Maybe some joint task force should be created, low-key of course, so we're all on the same page."

"Maybe," the DC police chief conceded. "But it will probably be more complicated than you and I playing nice with each other. The young woman who's in a coma is the niece of an Arlington homicide detective. Frank Mancini."

"Never heard of him. And he has no official standing in the case. Besides, Brooke Chaplin is one of Justice Parker's clerks. Odds are she was just at the wrong place at the wrong time."

"And she's also staying with Ethel Crestwater. You've heard of her."

"Oh, yeah. But that old lady's out to pasture, isn't she?"

"Don't kid yourself," Collins said. "If she's out to pasture, it's one with no fences. Official standing or not, she'll be all over this. My plan is to let her do her thing while I respectfully evade her departmental inquiries by claiming it's an ongoing investigation."

Ventana wasn't kidding himself. Despite what he told Collins, he knew Ethel had active connections in high places. Collins was the one who was kidding herself if she thought hiding behind the phrase "ongoing investigation" would curtail Ethel's efforts. Better to keep her close than push her away. But he wasn't going to tell Collins that.

"Good plan, Yolanda. I'll do the same. Now I'd better call the chief justice. She might be the only one who knows what Finley was carrying."

He disconnected and immediately thumbed through his phone log until he found the number he wanted. Then, he rethought his next steps. Forget meeting Collins. He didn't want to give the chief justice the news about her clerk over the phone.

He'd see her in person. And that might be a good security move since the only protection Baxter had at home was a German shepherd and a thirty-eight revolver her dad had given her for her eighteenth birthday. She was guarded by his officers while traveling in DC and by the U.S. Marshals outside of DC. But she'd declined overnight protection. He'd tried to convince her otherwise, but she'd insisted she didn't want someone sitting in a car or standing in the elements in the wee hours of the night.

That fact gave Ventana a cold sweat. He'd get there as fast as he could and phone from her gate. As he started his car, he called the number he'd retrieved from his log. At this point, he didn't care who he woke up. He wanted answers.

Chapter 7

Clarissa Baxter felt pressure on her shoulder, and then she heard Max's throaty growl. What she thought was a hand shaking her awake turned out to be the German shepherd's paw. Something wasn't right. The digital clock on the nightstand read 3:54 a.m. She slid open the drawer underneath and grabbed the wooden grip of her thirty-eight revolver. No safety to flip off. Simply pull the trigger.

With the gun in one hand, she stood beside Max, expecting him to move forward toward whatever had set him on edge. But he sat motionless, head cocked as he strained to interpret whether sounds and smells were friends or foes.

"What is it, boy?"

Instead of heading for the bedroom door, the dog circled around her and headed for the window. From the second story, the view took in the expansive front yard and seven-foot-high brick wall that encompassed the property. Clarissa navigated her way through the dark room to the split in the curtains. Barely moving one edge aside, she peered out the small crack in an attempt to see what had alarmed Max.

In the glow of the streetlamp, the yard appeared to be a

nocturnal still life. Japanese maples created a pattern of soft shadows across the lawn and concrete circular driveway. The brick wall that offered a degree of privacy and protection cast the deepest shadow, hiding anything or anyone tucked against its base. The wrought-iron gates at either end of the driveway were closed and locked. Their shadows looked like jail bars keeping her in as much as keeping others out.

Growing up in the wide-open spaces of Wyoming, she rebelled against the concept of gated communities. But the world of Washington DC wasn't a world of wide-open spaces. Declining overnight protection, she'd reluctantly agreed to security cameras and the high wall, even though it meant rambling around in a house that should have sheltered a large family, not a widow and her dog. The only thing missing was a moat. She'd wondered what her husband, Jackson, thought when she'd used his life insurance proceeds to buy the fortress. He must be shaking his haloed head in disbelief.

Max growled again.

A motion caught Clarissa's eye. A shadow by the right gate, and then the silhouette of someone standing behind the bars. She couldn't make out the face, but the build suggested a man of around six feet.

He pulled something from his jacket pocket. If he tried to climb over the gate, she'd call 9-1-1.

She went to her dresser, disconnected her cell phone from the charger, and returned to the window. The man hadn't moved except to raise his hand to the side of his head.

Her phone rang. The screen lit up with the name DANIEL VENTANA.

"Tell me you're at my gate."

"Yes," Ventana said. "Were you already awake?"

"Max woke me. He must have heard your car."

"Sorry to arrive at such an ungodly hour. There have been some developments I didn't want to discuss over the phone."

"Something's happened to one of the justices?" Before he could answer, she said, "No, you said not over the phone. Drive in and I'll meet you at the front door. The keypad code is pound, nine, star, nine." She slipped a white terrycloth robe over her nightgown, patted Max to reassure him all was well, and hurried downstairs to the kitchen to turn on the coffee maker two hours early.

She opened the front door to find Daniel Ventana standing by his black Tahoe as if suddenly reluctant to enter the house. "Come in. We'll talk in the kitchen."

He said nothing, only nodded before following her inside.

As they walked through the living room, Ventana pointed at a pale-blue sofa. "Can we sit there?"

Clarissa saw he'd become more agitated and anxious to get to the reason for his visit. "Certainly." She understood he wanted to sit beside her, and the icy feeling in her stomach intensified.

He took a deep breath. "One of your clerks, Robert Finley, was killed last night."

"What?"

"It appears to be a mugging."

"Appears to be?"

"DC Police Chief Yolanda Collins called me. Finley was struck from behind as he entered his town house. His neck was broken. He was with another clerk, Brooke Chaplin. She was also attacked and is at MedStar in a medically induced coma. The doctors say it's touch and go. Details are sketchy, but evidently the only things taken were Chaplin's handbag and Finley's backpack."

"Wouldn't those be motive enough for a mugging?" Clarissa asked.

"Yes, but Finley was carrying cash that was easily accessible."

Ventana shook his head. "The investigation could be a jurisdictional entanglement. If Supreme Court property was taken, then my team is responsible for its recovery. The DC police think whoever did this might have been killed a few hours later, which creates a conspiracy scenario."

Clarissa raised a palm to silence him. "Has anyone notified Brooke and Robert's next of kin?"

"Next of kin?" Ventana repeated, as if he'd never heard the phrase before. "Maybe the DC police have. I came here as soon as I learned about it. I don't want you blindsided if the press comes calling this morning."

"I don't want their families blindsided," Clarissa said. "And Brooke is Parker's clerk. I'll want to talk to him as well. As for jurisdiction, I hope we can work together with any law enforcement agency that can aid your investigation."

"Of course. Do you know if Robert Finley was carrying any confidential documents with him?"

"He had my notes on one of the cases we've heard, but nothing indicating a vote one way or the other. Certainly nothing I would want the press blowing out of proportion. Let's focus on getting justice for the victims and their families."

"Of course," he said again. "I'm heading to the office now, but I wanted to tell you in person."

Clarissa managed a smile. "I appreciate that. And I have a favor to ask."

"Anything."

"Have a cup of coffee while I get dressed and then give me a ride. I'm going to have one of my secretaries come in. It may be Saturday, but two families need consoling. I want them to know they're not alone."

—

Senator Joseph Mulberry lay in bed, staring at the ceiling, unable to sleep. The phone call from Supreme Court Marshal Daniel Ventana had shaken him. A clerk for the chief justice dead. Justice Parker's clerk severely injured. He knew the woman. Brooke Chaplin from his state of Oregon. He'd written a letter of recommendation for her clerkship. And he'd enlisted her aid in a project he wanted kept secret. A project that could be a political debacle if it came to light too soon.

He considered himself lucky that his wife, Louise, was back in Portland for the birth of their daughter's third child. He would have been hard-pressed to explain why he'd gotten a call in the middle of the night from the head of the Supreme Court police. He wasn't even on the judiciary committee. Better that Louise remained in the dark about Brooke Chaplin. She would only worry that he was jeopardizing his political future.

In a U.S. Congress that leaked like a sieve, Senator Mulberry prided himself on serving two and a half terms without once divulging confidential information. Although he had to admit he wasn't above receiving it, which was why things had suddenly become very complicated.

—

Detective Frank Mancini gave Ethel a bear hug in the middle of her driveway. "Thank you for staying with me."

"You would have done the same." Ethel broke away from his embrace. "You sure you won't come in for a bite of breakfast? I can have eggs and toast in front of you in under five minutes."

"I'd better race the sunrise home and catch what sleep I can. With luck, it won't be much. I'll gladly be awakened by a phone call with news that Brooke's regained consciousness."

"You'll let me know?"

"My first call." His cell vibrated in his pocket. "Cross your fingers." He looked at the screen. "I think it's Detective Meadows." He connected. "Mancini here."

"Frank, it's Glenn. You still at the hospital?"

"I'm at Ethel's but heading home."

"And your niece?"

"No change, but they say that's a good thing because the cranial pressure has stopped increasing."

"Take good news wherever you can. And I have some interesting news myself."

"Can I put you on speaker?" Frank asked.

Glenn grunted. "You mean I'm not already? Yeah, why not?" He paused a few seconds. "Hi, Ethel."

"Hello, Glenn. What's the word?"

"The word describes your homeless man and it's hyphenated. Ex-military. Also ex-mercenary."

Ethel looked at Frank and shook her head. "You sure about the ex part?"

"No, I'm not. Ex only in the context that he used to do contract work for OmniForce Protective Services. They're a smaller version of the old Blackwater paramilitary model. DOD has contracts with them."

"Probably not only the Department of Defense," Ethel said. "The CIA's been known to run some private resource ops. The kind that stay in darkness and off the books."

"I'm not going there," Glenn said. "Not this close to my retirement. Anyway, our man's name is Ronald Drake. Prints got a hit from a bar fight and arrest a few years back. Matt Geyser, the CEO of OmniForce Protective Services, claims they let him go because of it. That's the last anyone's heard of him."

"I'd say he's been freelancing," Frank suggested. "Do you have an address for him?"

"Off a DC driver's license issued last year. An apartment near Dupont Circle. My partner and I are headed there now."

"And the feds?" Ethel asked.

"Chief Collins notified Daniel Ventana. I expect him to show up sometime this morning. If we're lucky, he'll stick to being seen in press conferences and not bog down our investigation."

"Have you worked with Ventana before?" Ethel asked.

"No," Glenn said. "But his role's more of an administrator than an investigator. Not a lot of crimes committed in the Supreme Court. I see more in a day than they probably do in a year."

"Well, thanks for taking the time to call," Frank said.

"And the information about Ronald Drake," Ethel added.

"No problem. Keep me updated on your niece. Use this number. It's my personal mobile. Now get some rest. Both of you." He disconnected.

Frank dropped the phone back to his pocket. "Do you think he's right about the Supreme Court police bogging down the investigation?"

Ethel turned to look at the faint glow where the sun began brightening the eastern sky. "I think they're going to be very cautious, which might have the same effect."

"Cautious? Why?"

She faced him and took a step closer. "Somebody knew Robert Finley brought court documents home with him last night. Somebody knew he was a clerk for Chief Justice Baxter. My understanding is the court hears cases Monday through Thursday, and then conferences Friday to discuss the merits of the arguments and take a preliminary vote on where the justices stand. Debate and persuasion can continue beyond that first conference, supposedly in private. I think someone was interested in yesterday's conference and had made preparations to discover how the court was leaning. Why? I don't know. But the information that put

Ronald Drake outside Finley's town house last night most likely came from inside Ventana's domain. He'll want to make that discovery himself and control the damage. If that's the case, then he'll shut Glenn Meadows out wherever he can."

"And where does that leave us?" Frank asked.

"It leaves you getting some sleep so that you can meet your sister and go to the hospital. Let me worry about Ventana."

Frank smiled. "You're going to call him, aren't you?"

Ethel tried and failed to look innocent. "Ventana?"

"No. Don't be coy with me, lady. You know who I mean. And any jurisdictional squabble will just intensify."

"Well, Frank, that's the point, isn't it?"

Chapter 8

Ethel and Jesse sat side by side on the sofa in her living room. On the coffee table in front of them lay Brooke Chaplin's diary and her legal pad.

Jesse flipped over the top blank sheet of the pad to reveal the two columns of initials. "I've photographed this page and the one underneath it. The rest of the sheets are clean."

"And the diary?"

"I've read through it once but haven't photographed it. There are about sixty pages. It starts when she learns she's received her clerkship and ends with last Thursday night's entry. I guess we'll have to turn it over to Detective Meadows."

"Any correlation between the diary and what's on the legal pad?"

"What do you mean?" Jesse asked. "The initials under REAFFIRM and OVERTURN show the justices are split on some ruling and Baxter's vote is unknown. Brooke doesn't specifically name a case in her diary, but she closes her Thursday entry with the words, 'tomorrow's conference will be very interesting. SM will be anxious to test his theory.'"

"We'll come back to that," Ethel said. "But I meant the

second page with the two lists under 'Parties.' Does that tie into the diary, other than the obvious?"

Jesse stared at the sheet of legal paper. "Obvious? What's so obvious? Why BLM? Black Lives Matter. The diary doesn't mention either the movement or any racial unrest."

Ethel picked up the pad and ran a finger under the three letters. "That's because BLM isn't Black Lives Matter. It's Bureau of Land Management. I think the context of these abbreviations and names is mining. I'm not familiar with what's before the Supreme Court this term, but I'll wager there's a case of mineral rights in the mix. And if her entry referred to the justices' conference yesterday, then they must have heard arguments on the case earlier in the week. Get on your computer and see what you can learn about the court's schedule."

Jesse stood up from the sofa. "And these things of Brooke's?"

"I want to study them closer. And, let's keep their existence between us for now."

"What about Brooke's laptop? I tried to access it, but she's got it password-protected."

Ethel frowned. "I guess hacking past it would be more like breaking and entering than opening an unlocked diary. Leave it be for now. I might have another option for dealing with it." She glanced at the slim watch on her wrist. "Seven thirty. Why don't you grab a few hours of sleep before starting your court research?"

Jesse looked down at Ethel. "How about you? You've got to be exhausted."

"I'll be fine. I can nap after I set a few things in motion." She shooed him away. "Now go on up to bed."

Ethel stayed on the sofa until she heard his door close. Then she gathered the legal pad and diary and carried them to her bedroom. She laid them on the small desk beside her closet and sat on the bed. She was exhausted, but she was also unsettled. She had the feeling she was dealing with an iceberg. Ninety percent of it below the surface. One hundred percent of it dangerous.

—

Rudy Hauser folded the Saturday edition of the *Washington Post* and laid it on the seat beside him. The director of the FBI decided the news could wait. The rising sun brought the promise of a good day, and he wasn't ready to spoil it with whatever bad news awaited in the paper. The only frustration he'd submit to this morning was golf.

He leaned forward in the rear seat of the spacious GMC Yukon XL to get closer to his driver. "Craig, thanks for picking me up so early. I know you must have had other plans."

The FBI agent looked at his boss in the rearview mirror. "No problem. I had no plans, but my wife had a list of chores for me longer than a twenty-foot putt. So, if you need me to stay with you on the course, you'll be doing me a favor."

Rudy laughed. "Well, it was still short notice. When Senator Hathaway called me yesterday evening inviting me to fill out his foursome, I thought why the hell not. It's not every day a senator asks me to the Congressional Country Club. And he is on the Senate Intelligence Committee."

"Senate Intelligence? There's an oxymoron for you."

"Now, now, Craig. We're going to play nice today. I might even let him win. Earn some brownie points for the next time he hauls me in front of a congressional hearing."

"You're a better man than I am, sir."

Rudy leaned back in the leather seat. "Not better. Just older. I've learned where to pick my battles." He felt his phone vibrate in his pants pocket. "Now what?" he muttered.

He glanced at the screen. *Speaking of battles,* he thought. "Craig, I'm going to take this call. If I'm still talking when we arrive, just pull into the parking lot, and then you can drop me and my bag when I'm finished."

He pressed "Accept" and brought the phone to his ear. "Good morning, Ethel. To what do I owe the pleasure?"

"If you have to ask, you're not in the loop."

Rudy Hauser stiffened. Ethel Fiona Crestwater didn't deal in hyperbole. She didn't call to chat. He looked at the newspaper on the seat beside him. Maybe he should have read it. "I'm in a vehicle. Just me and my driver."

"Are you where you can stop and stretch your legs a few minutes?"

"Yes. We're nearing the Congressional Country Club. I can take a little walk there."

"Then just listen until then. Last night two law clerks for Supreme Court justices were attacked at the residence of one of them. One clerk was killed. The other is in a medically induced coma. The investigation started with the DC police and now is crossing over to the Supreme Court police. It looks like court papers were stolen."

"I appreciate the heads-up, Ethel, but I don't see how the Bureau has a play."

"Rudy, I told you to listen until you can ask questions in private. Can't you do that?"

Chagrined, the FBI director murmured, "Yes."

"It's up to you whether the Bureau has a play, but here's what we know. The likely suspect was assassinated a few hours after the attack. A professional hit. Now, if that doesn't smell of conspiracy, I don't know what does. Investigating conspiracies is your métier, which is why I'm bothering you on a Saturday morning." Ethel summarized the attack, the disguise, the missing backpack, and her suspicions that it was tied to something pending before the court. She expressed her concern that neither the DC nor Supreme Court police were capable of handling what could be a very complex case.

Rudy interrupted her. "I'm out of the car, Ethel." He slammed the door shut and walked over to where the pavement met the grass. "No one can hear me."

"You understand why I'm telling you this," Ethel said.

"I guess because we have more resources."

"No, I'm telling you this because the timeline suggests someone had inside information. Yes, the DC police are strapped for resources. As for the court police, Daniel Ventana's got a bigger problem if there's a leak in his own house, especially if the source is one of his officers."

Rudy Hauser did know Ventana's problem. Just a few months ago, Ethel had uncovered a corrupt FBI agent and helped Rudy keep the circumstances out of the media. He knew Ethel was calling in a return favor. He wasn't sure why.

"Well, I'll have to consider what's the best way to get involved," he said. "Mind if I ask what's your interest?"

"The same as yours is going to be. The law clerk who's in a coma is Brooke Chaplin. She's Frank Mancini's niece, and she rooms with me."

"Damn it, Ethel, why didn't you tell me that at the start?"

"Because I wanted you to objectively hear what we know. Not immediately get caught up in the personal connection, although I hope your friendship with Frank will prioritize this case for you."

"Of course. I'll just tell Ventana we're coming in."

"Let me offer another option," Ethel advised. "Brooke's clerking for Justice Parker, and she might know what court documents are involved. She also may not survive. However, her computer is up in her room, and it's password-protected."

"I want it," Rudy exclaimed.

"You can have it provided we come to an agreement on the content of this phone call."

"What kind of agreement?"

"One that has me take the heat from Ventana when he gets his nose out of joint. I'll say that I contacted you because I thought Brooke's laptop might be evidence. And as a former FBI agent, I naturally brought it to your attention."

"Okay," Rudy agreed. "That's the truth."

"Some of it. We'll just leave out the part where you promised to share whatever you discover."

The FBI director couldn't suppress a laugh. "Anybody ever tell you that you're the most conniving woman they've ever known?"

"Conniving? Me? I'm simply negotiating, Rudy. No one's forcing you to take the deal."

"Right. What's a little coercion among friends? So, are you housing one of my agents now?"

"Yes, Lanny Childress. He's been here one month of a six-month assignment compiling background on domestic terrorism."

"Don't know him," Rudy admitted.

"He's good enough," Ethel said. "But still wet behind the ears, at least as far as working a murder case."

"Is he there now?"

"No. He flew to Charlotte for his mother's birthday. He's back tomorrow."

Rudy heard a short beep from the Yukon's horn. He looked across the open parking spaces to see Senator Hathaway and two other men rounding the rear of the SUV. The senator waved him to come on. Rudy raised an index finger, signaling that he'd join them in a minute.

"Senator Hathaway's here. I've got to go. Can your cousin Jesse run the computer to Quantico now? I'll arrange for someone to receive it."

"He was up all night with Frank," Ethel said. "Maybe later this afternoon after a few hours of sleep. Meanwhile, if Ventana or the DC police come to search Brooke's room, I'll just say I've already turned the computer over to you."

"You have turned it over. I consider it mine regardless of the location."

"Good." Ethel hesitated, and then decided to pursue one more question. "Is Senator Hathaway your golf partner?"

"Yes."

"Do you play together often?"

"No. This is the first time."

"Long-standing engagement?"

"No. He just called last night. Why?"

Ethel glanced at the desk where she'd set Brooke's diary and legal pad. "No particular reason. But humor me. Don't bring up last night's attack. If he mentions it, be completely ignorant and ask the questions you normally would."

Rudy looked back at the senator and the other two men. "You think he's involved?"

"You know me," Ethel said. "Right now I think everyone's involved. Text me later who'll be receiving the computer at Quantico. Meanwhile, stay out of the traps, sand or otherwise."

She disconnected, set her phone alarm for two hours, and lay down on the bed. Within five minutes, the only sounds in the house were her soft, rhythmic breathing and Jesse's light snoring. And the click of a Schlage lock being picked by an expert.

Chapter 9

Rudy Hauser slid his phone back in his pocket and hurried to his SUV where the three men waited.

"Sorry to rush you," Senator Stuart Hathaway said. "I was able to book the Blue Course, and we can't miss our tee time."

"My apologies." Rudy shook Hathaway's hand. "Thanks for the invitation."

The senator, a former Marine, was midway through his fourth term. The years of fancy junkets and fine dining had transformed him from fit, slim, and trim into a portly sphere whose belly blocked his view of the golf ball if he stood too close to it.

Rudy turned to the tall, steel-gray-haired man standing beside the senator. For a second, the kaleidoscopic colors of his golfing attire made him unrecognizable. Then Rudy placed the face. Lieutenant General Alan Corbin, recently appointed by the president to be the Director of the Defense Intelligence Agency, the man responsible for all military intelligence that's reported to the Secretary of Defense. Rudy had asked his chief aide to set up a meeting with the general, but that was several weeks out. Rudy wondered if it had been Corbin's idea to have him complete their foursome.

"You know General Corbin, I believe," Hathaway said.

"Yes, and I hope to know him better." Rudy shook the officer's hand. "I look forward to working with you."

"As do I." Corbin held on to Rudy's hand a little longer than necessary. "We've got a lot of challenges to face together."

Hathaway laughed. "The first one will be beating our scratch golfer here. Rudy, let me introduce Roger Diamond with Crane and Weston. He'd hoped to get a little lobbying in with my legislative assistant, but the Chinese sabotaged that."

"The Chinese?" Rudy asked.

"That's what my assistant ate for dinner last night, and it didn't stay down."

Rudy knew Crane and Weston was one of the largest and most influential lobbying firms in DC.

If Diamond was disappointed with Rudy's substitution, he didn't show it. Flashing a smile of perfect teeth, he grabbed Rudy's hand in a firm grip. "An honor to meet you, Director Hauser."

Rudy quickly sized up the man. Probably in his mid-forties, a good ten years younger than the rest of them. Slick, ambitious, and smart, he would be assessing how Rudy could be of use to him and his clients. Rudy would be cordial, but lobbyists and the director of the FBI were like oil and water, not to be mixed.

"Call me Rudy, please. And I'm not a scratch golfer. In fact, Senator, you'd better alert the groundskeepers they're in for heavy-duty divot repair."

Hathaway looked at the agent driving Rudy's SUV. "Sir, before you leave, if you don't mind, would you take the director's bag and shoes to the drop-off?"

Before the man could answer, Rudy said, "I've asked him to stay. Do you mind if he grabs a cart and goes with us?"

"You need protection?" General Corbin asked.

"No. He has a 'Honey Do' list waiting for him at home. I'm aiding and abetting his temporary escape."

Hathaway winked at the driver. "Then consider us co-conspirators. We'll meet you at the first tee."

The senator organized the cart arrangements, assigning Rudy to ride with him. He wasted no time in steering the conversation away from golf.

As they rode along the cart path from the first tee, Hathaway said, "I was half expecting you to cancel this morning."

"Why?"

"Last night's attack on the clerks."

Rudy heeded Ethel's advice to play ignorant, but he also wanted to avoid lying to a U.S. senator. So, he answered with a question. "Clerks?"

Hathaway looked at him sharply. "I assumed that's why you were on the phone. The two law clerks from the Supreme Court who were attacked last night."

"None of my staff has informed me about it. What do you know?"

The senator hesitated. Rudy surmised he was weighing how much to say. If Hathaway knew a lot, then Rudy would want to know his source.

"A member of my staff called me late last night. He has a friend on the DC police force. One of the clerks was killed, and the other is hospitalized with serious injuries. There's speculation court documents might have been stolen."

"Then the Supreme Court police and DC police must be collaborating," Rudy said. "And we'll lend a hand, where appropriate or requested."

Hathaway studied the FBI director a few seconds and then nodded. "And if that request comes this morning, we won't be offended if you have to bail on us."

Rudy thought, *translation—you don't know anything, so we don't need you until you do.* And the senator's call with the golf invitation. It wasn't a coincidence that the timing was so soon after the first police response. Nothing was a coincidence in Washington power politics where information made the difference between winners and losers.

Ethel's interest in Senator Hathaway intrigued Rudy. She must have information herself. He decided to play a few more holes, and then he'd fake receiving a phone call. Let the general and senator wonder about its contents as he offered his regrets and returned to the clubhouse in his driver's cart.

Too bad. The Blue Course and the blue-skied morning were both beautiful. But he needed to talk to Ethel face-to-face. And until he knew more about what was going on, he'd release his driver and take his own car to her house. He'd learned the best way to work with Ethel was off the books.

—

At first, Ethel thought the buzzing came from her phone's alarm, but her inner clock told her she'd not been asleep for two hours. She sat up in bed and shook her head to clear the cobwebs from her mind.

The doorbell rang in short bursts of impatience.

She and Jesse made it to the foyer at the same time. He was barefoot, and his brown hair looked like it had been through a wind tunnel. Ethel patted down her own hair and opened the door.

Rudy Hauser stood on the threshold. His lime green pants, tangerine shirt, and yellow sleeveless sweater-vest made him look like an animated fruit bowl.

"Searching for a lost ball, Rudy?" Ethel looked at his feet. "At least you changed out of your cleats."

"I'm looking for some answers. Are you going to invite me in?"

"Sorry. Jesse and I are both a little groggy." She led him into the living room. "I take it you cut your golf round short."

"After the second hole."

Ethel gestured for him to sit on the sofa and then joined him.

Jesse remained standing. "Can I get you some coffee or tea?"

"No, thank you. Please sit. You might be more communicative." He pointed to the chair opposite him.

Ethel twisted to face the FBI director. "Communicative? Who called whom?"

Rudy waved his hand dismissively. "How did you know Senator Hathaway would pump me for information about the law clerks?"

"He's a man who craves information. He offers you a last-minute invitation so he can go fishing, not just play golf. I didn't know his agenda, only that he had one. And though it wasn't public, the news of the attack on the clerks has to be spreading through Washington at warp speed. How did he explain knowing about it?"

"He said one of his staff told him, supposedly tipped off by someone in the DC police."

Ethel shook her head. "The police didn't learn about it till after ten. Either Hathaway knew about the attack in advance or he had another agenda in mind. I assume you were part of a foursome. Who else was there?"

"The director of the Defense Intelligence Agency, Lieutenant General Alan Corbin, and some lobbyist named Roger Diamond. I think he was disappointed to see me. I was replacing the senator's legislative assistant. Whatever Diamond was peddling, the assistant was probably the conduit to the senator's ear."

"What's Diamond's firm?" Ethel asked.

"Crane and Weston."

"Even I've heard of them. So, you got a last-minute invitation to a golf game with a senator who chairs the Intelligence Committee, the top intelligence officer in the military, and some high-powered lobbyist whom you assume was there to influence legislation. Who organized the foursome?"

Rudy looked confused. "Who organized it? Why, I'm pretty sure the senator did. He bragged about getting us on the Blue Course. That's the tournament course."

"You might want to check into that," Ethel advised. "Now what do you plan to do next?"

Rudy laughed. "Follow your lead. First, I want a look at Brooke's computer. Then I'll approach Ventana and leverage my way into the Supreme Court police investigation, which will include interviewing Chief Justice Baxter."

Jesse leaned forward in his chair, catching Ethel's eye. She gave a slight shake of her head that went unnoticed by Rudy.

The FBI director continued. "And I want to speak to DC homicide's Detective Meadows. You say he's competent. I'll approach him man-to-man and bypass the chain of command that would make him resentful of being ordered to cooperate. It sounds like he's not territorial and is willing to collaborate."

"He's proven that already," Ethel said. "He's looking into a paramilitary connection for the dead suspect Ronald Drake. Ever heard of a company called OmniForce Protective Services?"

"Yeah," Rudy said. "They abbreviate themselves as OPS, like special ops. It's more than just branding bravado. Most of them are ex special ops."

"Maybe Drake was still connected to them, or at least there's a common contact."

"Point taken." Rudy looked from Ethel to Jesse. "Well, if there's nothing else, I'd like to get that laptop to Quantico."

Ethel nodded to Jesse. "Bring it down, please."

Rudy stood before Jesse could rise from his chair. "Oh, no, as long as I'm here, I'd like to see her room."

Ethel got to her feet. "I'd be disappointed otherwise. Come along."

Rudy fell in line between Ethel and Jesse, and they headed for the staircase in the foyer.

As they ascended single file, Ethel said, "Rudy used to have your room, Jesse. You're a lot neater."

She led them down the hallway to the second door on the left. She took a couple of steps into the room and froze. "Jesse, where is it?"

"On her desk."

The two men stepped behind her. All three stared at the desk.

The laptop was gone.

Chapter 10

Ethel, Rudy, and Jesse stood on the porch and examined the back door lock.

"You're sure you threw the dead bolt?" Rudy asked Jesse.

"Yes. I didn't have my keys, so I used the extra one hidden in the outside breaker panel. After I unlocked the door, I returned it and then relocked the door from the inside."

"Well, it's unlocked now." Rudy bent over till his eyes were just a few inches from the Schlage. "Quite a few scratch marks. It's definitely been picked."

"Those are probably Jesse's," Ethel said. "I've had him practicing."

Rudy shook his head. "Of course you have. So, maybe our thief knew about the hidden key."

"Then why bother to put it back?" Ethel asked.

"To make it look like the lock was picked so that we wouldn't suspect someone who's familiar with your key's hiding place."

"You mean one of my roomers, past or present. That includes you, Rudy. You could have let yourself in, taken the laptop, and then rung the doorbell as if you'd just arrived. You won't mind letting me search your car, will you?"

"Search away. But you have to admit someone could have used the spare key."

Ethel grabbed the larger man's arm and steered him off the porch. "Follow me." She walked across the backyard and around the side of the house. She stopped at the breaker box and pointed to a window diagonally above it. "That's my bedroom. I was sleeping fewer than three feet from that window. Now open the panel and get the key."

Rudy curled his fingers under the edge of the lid and pulled. The hinges squealed like a cat whose tail was caught in a food processor. He stopped but the location of the magnetic key holder required the lid to be opened farther. The squeal was even louder.

Ethel stepped close to him. "Now if the front doorbell woke me up, don't you think I would have heard this that's ten times nearer?"

Rudy raised both hands. "Okay. It was just a thought."

"That's fine to have thoughts, Rudy, but not if you're latching onto them prematurely." She slammed the cover shut. "My thought is whoever broke in was very skilled. He or she picked that lock in a few seconds, came up the back stairs, and was in and out of Brooke's room in less than a minute. Since I only have one woman staying here, it wouldn't take long to determine which room was hers."

"They were taking a hell of a chance," Rudy said.

"Yes, they were. Which begs two possibilities. They knew what was on the computer and were afraid, or they didn't know and were afraid. Either way, fear leads to acts of desperation. You might want to have a presence at MedStar Hospital."

"To be there when Brooke regains consciousness?"

Ethel's expression turned grim. "To make sure she has the chance to regain consciousness."

Rudy took a deep breath. "Done. Any other suggestions?"

"Just a request. Can you have a team sweep the house? We might have a bug infestation."

Jesse's eyes widened. "You think whoever stole Brooke's computer planted microphones?"

"Maybe. I'm more concerned that listening devices may have already been in place. Brooke's a person of interest to someone. If we can determine why, then we'll be closer to who."

"If you're right about the bugs," Rudy said, "then they heard our earlier conversation in the living room."

Ethel shrugged. "Only speculation about your golf partners and Senator Hathaway's information sources. The steps you're taking going forward are logical if you're starting an investigation. It's put them on alert, but they should have anticipated your reaction."

"Then I'd better get someone outside Brooke's room immediately."

"I agree," Ethel said. "I'll tell Frank you're on board."

"No. I'll call him from the car." He paused. "You're not holding anything back, are you, Ethel?"

"Rudy, you know me. It's all about solving the case."

He gave her a hint of a smile. "Yeah. I know you. So, good luck with whatever you're up to."

—

"Why didn't you tell Rudy about Brooke's diary and legal pad?" Jesse asked the question as he sat in the front passenger seat of Ethel's black Infiniti.

She was behind the wheel, but they were parked in her driveway where they could talk with reasonable assurance that they weren't being overheard.

"Because I want to more thoroughly understand what they mean. Besides, it's better to let Rudy cast a wider net rather than get too focused on Brooke."

"But you said Brooke is in danger."

"She might be, or with the theft of her laptop, she might no longer be a threat to someone." Ethel swiveled in her seat to face him. "When I heard about Brooke, I knew at least two jurisdictions would be involved—the DC police and the Supreme Court police. I wanted the FBI engaged because that's where I have the most connections and that's who has the most resources. We've made inroads with the DC police through Detective Meadows, but I have no leverage with Daniel Ventana and the Supreme Court police. I need to change that. You see, it works like this. The three investigations will claim to be collaborating, which they will to a certain extent. But they will also be competitive. They each want to receive the lion's share of the credit, which means they'll still be territorial. We're outside all that jurisdictional pettiness. So, if we choose when and with whom we trade information, we stand to gain from all of them."

Jesse smiled. "Cousin Ethel, I knew you were clever, but this time you've outdone yourself."

Ethel shook her head. "Not really. I'm more worried about being undone."

"What do you mean?"

"I didn't anticipate a fourth participant. A shadowy presence that also respects no jurisdictions."

For a moment, Jesse just looked at Ethel, expecting her to explain. Then he realized he was to figure it out himself. "Lieutenant General Corbin."

"Very good," Ethel said with genuine affection. "He and the Defense Intelligence Agency are in this somewhere. I can feel it."

"Why's that bad?"

"Because it means we're involved in something bigger than we might have envisioned. We're playing a game within a game. And with the Defense Intelligence Agency, they may be friend or foe, or what's even worse, both at the same time."

"Does that change what we do next?" Jesse asked.

"Not at this point. I need you to learn as much as you can about what's being heard by the Supreme Court this term. I'll go through Brooke's notes and diary, and then we'll see where we stand."

"Okay. But we shouldn't talk in the house, at least until Rudy sends his sweepers."

"It's a nice fall day. Maybe we'll go for a walk later. And then go shopping."

"Shopping? For what?"

"Burner phones. I wonder if they come in colors."

—

It was mid-Saturday morning, and Senator Joseph Mulberry padded around his Watergate apartment still wearing only blue pajamas and a tartan bathrobe. He'd not been able to go back to sleep since the call from Daniel Ventana. Mulberry had been surprised the head of the Supreme Court police would give him the news in the middle of the night. True, he'd asked Ventana to watch over the young woman as she learned the ropes. Did that mean Ventana thought there was a special relationship between them? Mulberry wondered if Ventana would have to report his call. If so, a "special relationship" would translate in the gossip circles into something unseemly.

He continued to pace through the two-bedroom apartment, debating what to do, if anything. Had their collaboration endangered the young woman? One thing Mulberry did know was that Senator Hathaway from the neighboring state of Nevada would exploit the slightest appearance of impropriety. The odious man wouldn't hesitate to bring down a political rival. Any accusation would only grow stronger the more he denied it.

This wasn't the time to be weakened. He stopped by a window with a spectacular view of the Potomac and pulled his cell phone from the robe's pocket. First, a call to his communications director to work on a statement. Then a shower and a visit to the hospital. Maybe a photo op with the family if they were there. Better yet, a private word with a conscious Brooke Chaplin. He wanted her to recover. He needed her information.

—

Jesse knocked on the jamb of Ethel's open bedroom door. "You feel like taking that walk now? Then maybe grab a late lunch while we're out?"

Ethel turned from her desk. "Sure. Let me grab a coat and my bag. I'll be ready in five minutes." She pointed to Brooke's diary lying open beside the legal pad.

Jesse could see she'd added some notes to one of the blank pages. "Great. Just yell up the stairs when you're ready."

Five minutes later, Ethel locked the front door behind them.

"What if Rudy's debuggers come?" Jesse asked.

"I texted him to use the spare key. And to text me a report when they're done."

"So, where are we going?"

"Zitkála-Šá. If we can grab a bench, we should be able to talk without being overheard."

They headed down North Highland Street toward Zitkála-Šá

Park a few blocks away. When Ethel saw there were no other pedestrians, she asked, "Any luck?"

"I think so. It took only a few minutes to find a website called SCOTUSblog that focuses on the court. What's being heard. What's been decided. Who the principles are and their standings in the suit. Last Tuesday the court heard oral arguments in the case of the *Nevada-Oregon Native American Coalition and Farmers and Ranchers United v. The United States Department of the Interior and the Bureau of Land Management.* Evidently the Department of the Interior rushed through approval of a lease for lithium mining on federal land that extends across the border between Oregon and Nevada. The greatest concentration of mining activity will be on the Nevada side. A suit was filed to contest the lease, and the lower court ruled in favor of the Department of the Interior."

"What kind of mining techniques are we talking about?"

Jesse rapidly spread his hands apart. "Blow up the ground and dig. An open pit going down more than the length of a football field. They extract lithium from the clay through a process that uses and contaminates millions if not billions of gallons of water."

"Sounds nasty," Ethel said. "A dirty operation impacting the environment in the cause of clean energy to protect the environment. So, this case must be about lithium batteries and electric vehicles." Ethel pointed at a Tesla parked at the curb. "Like that one."

"Apparently the president's push to go green is ahead of the resources to make it happen. From the capacity of the electricity grid needed to simultaneously charge millions of vehicles to the raw materials for making the batteries."

"Who was awarded the lease?" Ethel asked.

"A company named Lithium USA. I looked them up. Guess who's the largest shareholder?"

"The Chinese," Ethel said without hesitation.

Jesse stopped in mid-stride. "Wait. How'd you know that?"

"I didn't. I guessed. It's clear to me we're dealing with an issue of global consequences. Once you're in that arena, whom are you most likely to run into?"

"The Chinese," Jesse repeated. He and Ethel started walking again. "More specifically, a Chinese holding company that has a forty percent share of Lithium USA. Other investors include a Canadian company and a plethora of Wall Street investment bankers."

"Can you sum up their argument?"

"A complete role reversal. They claim they're trying to save the planet and that profits are secondary. That they're simply supporting the president's electric vehicle goals while maintaining resource independence."

"What does that mean?" Ethel asked.

"That they don't want to trade dependence on foreign oil for dependence on foreign lithium, cobalt, and nickel, the key elements needed for batteries. The situation's much worse than the oil supply. Currently, we produce only two percent of the world's lithium. So, it's a modern-day gold rush to find and produce more. Geologists say there's lithium in our country that needs to be exploited."

"Save the planet and national security combined. Pretty powerful arguments. What's the counter?"

"That the land leased is sacred to the native tribes. The disposition of the mining rights didn't go through proper hearings. That once again the Indian is being screwed over."

"Is the land on a tribal reservation?"

"No, but they've resurrected a treaty violation of 1863 that they claim illegally seized the land in question. They've been encouraged by what happened in Oklahoma when the court sided with the Indians and recognized the much wider scope of native sovereignty."

"They've got to have stronger arguments than that," Ethel said.

"They do. Environmental impact. Like the farmers and ranchers, the tribes are in a drought-prone region. Where they once fought each other over water rights, everyone understands the impact of the mining harms all of them. Pulling so much water out of the ecosystem will significantly lower surface levels for fishing, farm irrigation, and livestock. Plus, the water that seeps into the ground from the mining site could contaminate an area beyond the leased land, endangering people and animals. There were also several Friends of the Court briefs filed in support of overturning the lower court's ruling. One from an environmental group arguing the operation could dramatically impact several endangered species and another brief by General Motors."

"GM?" This time Ethel stopped mid-strike. "They're publicly opposing the production of the batteries they need?"

"They say there are safer mining techniques that can be used at other sites. GM won't source materials for their vehicles that are obtained through such dirty and destructive methods. They're already implementing that policy with cobalt from the Congo where children are forced to labor in the mines. Blood diamonds have become blood batteries. I also downloaded some stories from the *New York Times* and *Washington Post* that highlight the dilemma."

"It's a dilemma, all right," Ethel agreed. "And Brooke's notes lead us to believe the eight associate justices are split four-four with Chief Justice Baxter holding the deciding opinion."

Jesse's face brightened with understanding. "If the court hears cases Mondays through Thursdays, then yesterday's Friday conference would surely have included discussion of the mining case. They might have reached a decision."

"It's possible," Ethel said. "I think we're zeroing in on why the chief justice's clerk was attacked. But by whom and from which side are yet to be determined."

She stepped off the sidewalk into the public park. A few children were on the playground using the swings, sliding down tunnels, and climbing on the jungle gym.

Ethel spotted an empty bench off to the side. "Let's sit down and go through Brooke's notes again, now that we have the benefit of your research."

When they were settled, Ethel pulled the legal pad from her handbag and flipped the pages to the two-column list under Parties.

"Now Brooke's abbreviations make sense." Ethel pointed to the column starting with BLM. "We know that's Bureau of Land Management, and they have a standing in the case. We can surmise that everyone beneath them supports the government. Apparently, that includes the Department of Defense. And Senator Hathaway is in that column as well."

"That may be why the senator and Lieutenant General Corbin were golfing together," Jesse said.

"Maybe. Both have an interest in how the case will be decided."

"I understand the general's position, national security and all that, but why the senator's? Hathaway might not care about the native people, but I'd think the ranchers and farmers would be a voting bloc he'd want to appease."

Ethel patted him on the knee. "That's not the way Washington works. Behind the scenes, Hathaway is following his self-interest. Who do you think has more money for campaign contributions? Farmers and ranchers or international mining companies?"

"But the individual voters might be more sympathetic when they learn people and animals are being hurt."

"Jesse, money buys media, and I can guarantee you the media will be bombarding Nevada with one four-letter word—jobs. Jobs. Jobs. Jobs. It's all you'll hear. And there will be jobs, but just not as many as Lithium USA will claim. Those numbers are always inflated. This next group on the list, Progressive Mining Coalition, is the new PR face that will craft the message and peddle it through the halls of Congress."

Jesse studied the list again. "I guess NAC in the second column must be the Native American Coalition and F & R United are the farmers and ranchers. But the auto industry and climate and environmental advocates appear in both columns."

"Because each side's argument has merit," Ethel explained. "Senator Mulberry of Oregon must be more answerable to the environmentalists in his state, and from what you learned, Oregon isn't the main site of the mining operation. Fewer jobs, but still the risk of toxic contamination." Ethel pointed to the second column. "Do you know what Brine Extractors means?"

"Not until I read about it an hour ago. It's an alternative lithium source. An example is Salton Sea, a shallow, highly saline lake in California. Lithium can be extracted from the hot, salty depths without the open pit and highly toxic contamination."

"So, if the ruling is reversed and the federal lease is canceled—"

"The Brine Extractors eliminate a competitor," Jesse finished her sentence.

Ethel slid the legal pad back into her bag. "Of course, there's one name on the list that outweighs all the others."

"President Tarleton," Jesse said.

"Yes. He can only be trumped by the Supreme Court. Which makes Chief Justice Baxter's tiebreaking vote crucial for everyone."

"So, either side could have sent someone to Robert Finley's,"

Jesse said. "Why would advance knowledge of the ruling be worth someone's life?"

"To change the ruling before it was issued. The theft of the documents was only phase one."

"And phase two?"

"Pressure or bribe a justice to change his or her opinion."

"And if that doesn't work?"

"Then the old saying 'in for a penny, in for a pound' comes into play."

"I don't get it."

"It means, double-first-cousin-twice-removed, that they've already killed once. Maybe twice, counting the man shot on L Street. They're in too deep to give up now."

"What do we do?"

"It's what *I'll* do."

"And that is?"

"I find a way to talk to the chief justice of the Supreme Court."

"How do you do that?" Jesse asked.

Ethel stood up from the bench and for a moment silently watched the kids playing. Then she turned and looked down at Jesse. "Good question. Right now I haven't a clue."

Chapter 11

Jesse and Ethel left the park to the kids and their parents and headed for home.

"I'll drive us to Whole Foods, and we can eat lunch there," Ethel said. "It's noisy, which is what we want. Drowns out our words."

"We didn't talk about Brooke's diary," Jesse said. "Anything stand out for you?"

"Nothing that's different from what we've seen by living with her. She loves her work, gets along with her colleagues, and admires all the justices. The court seems to be her universe. No mention of a boyfriend." Ethel gave him a sharp elbow in the side. "However, I did like the paragraph where she called you a hottie."

Jesse blushed. "I saw that, although I'll never admit it."

"The only curious thing is how frequently she writes about Senator Mulberry. How he was kind to recommend her for the clerkship. How he was concerned that she find a good place to live. She started using the initials SM. I think that's the senator, and SM appears every week or so, usually referring to a phone conversation. Her words 'nothing to report on his project' concluded some of her entries."

"Then shouldn't we talk to him?" Jesse asked. "If SM stands for Senator Mulberry, then her last entry is about him. I think it read 'tomorrow's conference will be very interesting. SM will be anxious to test his theory.' Whatever Brooke means by theory must be the project she references."

"Yes, but we don't go approaching a U.S. senator without finding out more about the context. We might have one shot to get answers, and I want to know what questions to ask him. Let's see how Brooke progresses. I'd like to talk to her first, rather than reveal to others that we've seen her diary."

Two hours later, Ethel unlocked her front door. Jesse followed her inside carrying a Best Buy bag with two burner phones.

"Start those charging, please," she said. "I'll brew a pot of tea."

"None for me. I'd like to get started on what we talked about." He sat on the sofa and began unboxing the phones.

"Okay," Ethel yelled from the kitchen. "And we can actually talk about what we talked about. Rudy just texted me that the house was clean. No bugs."

"So, no one was trying to eavesdrop on Brooke?"

"Not before, but someone might be very interested in her now that she was found with Robert Finley."

"Did Director Hauser say anything else?"

"Just that he was going into a meeting with Ventana at the court and he'd call later."

Jesse plugged two chargers into the wall outlet and the phones began flashing red. He went to the kitchen. "I'm going up to my room and start the research." He bounded up the back stairs.

"If you change your mind about the tea, I'll bring you a cup," Ethel offered, but Jesse was already out of earshot.

Funny thing about tea, she thought. Must be her British ancestry. In her favorite BBC crime dramas, a cup of tea was always the first response. Marriage break up? "Let me fix you a cuppa." Lose an arm to a chainsaw? "I'll put the kettle on." Ethel turned the flame up on the burner, impatient to hear the whistle.

Her phone sounded first. The screen flashed FRANK MANCINI.

"Any update?" she asked without a hello.

"My sister Susan's flight was on time. We're at the hospital now. She's back with Brooke for her fifteen-minute visitation."

"And Brooke's status?"

"The doctors are more encouraging. If her cranial pressure levels continue to drop, they hope to bring her out of the coma this evening. They don't like to go beyond twenty-four hours."

"Do you need anything?"

"No, I caught a few hours of sleep, changed clothes, and picked up some sandwiches on my way to the airport. We'll stay here at least till a decision is made regarding the coma. And Senator Mulberry was here and gave us a contact number for one of his staff if we need anything."

The kettle whistled and Ethel moved it off the burner. "Mulberry came to the hospital?"

"Yes. He was very concerned. You know he wrote a letter of recommendation for Brooke."

"Did he ask to see her?"

Frank hesitated, picking up a vibe that there was more to Ethel's question than curiosity. "What are you implying?"

"Nothing. Just that it was kind of him to show up, even though he must have known Brooke was unconscious."

"I don't know that he did. I think he just came when he heard. He was already here when we arrived."

Ethel started pacing around the kitchen island, her tea momentarily forgotten. "Frank, did Brooke ever mention working on a project for Senator Mulberry?"

"No. I just know she was appreciative of his help."

"Did he help after she secured her clerkship?"

"He offered to use his connections to find an affordable yet safe apartment. When she told him I was her uncle and that you'd agreed to rent her a room, he said she was in good hands and wished her well. Why the questions about Mulberry?"

"Are you where you can't be overheard?"

"The conference room where we were last night. The senator used his influence to reserve it for Brooke's family and friends. There's no one else with me. I'm to call him when she starts to regain consciousness."

"I've got some information that I haven't shared with anyone. Not Detective Meadows, not Ventana, not even Rudy. I want to learn a little more before turning it over to them. But I'll tell you if you agree to hold it back for now. Of course that means you'll be risking an obstruction of justice charge."

"Damn it, we're talking about my niece. I'll say or not say whatever you want me to."

Ethel stopped at the stove and poured hot water into a cup with a single teabag, electing not to brew a full pot. "Jesse found a diary and a legal pad in Brooke's room. She references some project she was working on for the senator. We have reason to believe it involved some case the court heard last week that probably went into discussion at Friday's conference."

"What case?" Frank asked.

"A lithium mining case involving a lease on federal land." Ethel picked up her cup and headed for the comfort of her living room. "From what I understand, it's both an environmental and national security nightmare. Even normally monolithic interest groups are split." She told him what she and Jesse had learned from Brooke's notes and the internet research on lithium and the controversial impact of its mining.

"So, someone wants advance knowledge on how the justices are likely to decide," Frank said. "And Chief Justice Baxter is the big unknown."

"Which makes her law clerk a possible source of information, or at least the documents they thought he was carrying."

"Not just her law clerk, but her law *clerks* plural. Glenn Meadows called me as we were driving from the airport. He'd just gone through Ronald Drake's apartment. He found photos of all four of Baxter's clerks. From the background, it looks like they were surveillance shots taken outside the court building. Someone was looking for any opportunity that might present itself. That opportunity turned out to be Robert Finley."

"No photos of Brooke then?"

"None. I think she just happened to be in the wrong place at the wrong time."

"Frank, someone broke into my house this morning and stole Brooke's laptop. Whoever did that must think Brooke knows something."

Ethel heard Frank take a sharp breath.

"What's going on, Ethel?"

"I think something went wrong and tracks are being covered. There's a lot we don't know. I've got Jesse working the internet, and Rudy's meeting with Ventana." She paused a second, remembering what she'd forgotten to ask. "Did you see an FBI agent on duty in the ICU?"

"No, but I haven't been back there."

"Find out and let me know. How about Justice Parker? Brooke's his clerk. Have you heard from him?"

"I haven't," Frank said. "But my sister had a call from Chief Justice Baxter expressing her concern and asking if there was anything she could do. Baxter even gave Susan her personal cell phone number. It meant a lot to my sister."

"Very kind." Ethel smiled to herself as she saw the way forward. In a tone allowing for no argument, she made her demand. "Frank, I want that number."

"What are you going to do with it?"

"Play the damn lottery. What the hell do you think I'm going to do with it? I'm going to call the chief justice."

Chapter 12

FBI Director Rudy Hauser had been to the Supreme Court building several times before, always during the week and usually for some meeting involving the FBI, Supreme Court police, and Capitol police. These periodic gatherings grew out of Homeland Security's desire to have its DC law enforcement agencies staying in better touch and sharing information.

The court building was closed on the weekends with only a skeletal staff on duty. Rudy had reached Daniel Ventana by phone and asked to see him in person. If Rudy was going to insist on the FBI's involvement in all aspects of the investigation, then he wanted to do so face-to-face. Ventana had said he would notify the guards and one of them would escort him to his office.

Rudy passed through the security checkpoint and followed a guard to an elevator. The operator had the door open, waiting for him.

"Good to see you again, sir. Sorry it's under such terrible circumstances. I just can't believe what happened."

Rudy gave the man a quick study and saw the metal between

his pant cuff and shoe. An amputee, he recalled. He'd spoken with the man before, but he couldn't remember his name. "Yes," Rudy agreed. "A terrible thing."

"I don't normally work Saturdays, but when I heard the news, I came in. I figured others would be here, and we'd need the elevators running." He stuck out his hand. "I'm Jake Simmons, in case I'd not properly introduced myself before."

Rudy shook his hand firmly, impressed that the man had phrased the remark to take the blame for Rudy not remembering his name.

"Yes, Jake. Of course. I promise we're doing everything we can to catch who did this."

"Thank you, sir."

The guard cleared his throat, a clear signal for Jake and Rudy to move things along so that he could return to his post.

Jake rolled his eyes and abruptly closed the elevator door. "Which floor, Your Honor?" he asked, his tone clearly mocking the guard.

"We're headed to Ventana's office."

As Rudy followed his escort off the elevator, the man called to Jake. "Stay put. I'll be right back."

"Sorry. I've been summoned to the first floor. Try using the stairs. You're looking a little paunchy."

Daniel Ventana stood up from behind his desk as the guard ushered Rudy into his office. "Thank you, Tom. That will be all. You can close the door behind you."

As the man did as instructed, Ventana rounded his desk and gestured for Rudy to join him at a small conference table.

"It's been a while," Ventana said.

The two men shook hands before sitting down.

"Yes," Rudy said. "I think it was the swearing-in ceremony for Justice Wang."

"Am I correct in assuming you asked for this meeting to do more than catch up?"

Rudy smiled. As he'd expected, Ventana cut straight to the point. No chitchat.

"The attack on your clerks," Rudy said. "I think the Bureau has a role to play."

Ventana nodded. "We welcome your support. As our investigation ramps up, I'm sure there will be areas where your resources will be very helpful."

Rudy rested his forearms on the table as he leaned closer to Ventana. In a soft voice, he said, "Our role is going to be leading the investigation."

The other man's jaw tightened, and he held Rudy's gaze. "This is a court issue, and my team won't be sidelined."

"Sidelined? Your team might be the richest source of suspects."

Ventana's face burned as red as a hot coal. "You have a nerve," he growled.

"No, I'm just calmly pointing out that you have a problem, and I'm offering you the chance to mitigate it. I understand Robert Finley was carrying documents from the chief justice. Someone knew that and targeted him. Likely someone on the inside passed along that information. This wasn't a simple street mugging."

"I know. The DC police told me. We're working closely together."

"Yeah, they're not overstretched," Rudy said sarcastically. "Look, Daniel, investigating your own people sets up accusations of a cover-up. I guarantee the attorney general won't want to have that claim circulated. So, you make the announcement that you've asked the FBI to head up the investigation and you eliminate all that. And I'll keep you in the loop."

"Have you railroaded the DC police to back off?"

"No. But I'll be having this conversation with Chief Collins. She should have told me about Ronald Drake and his history with OmniForce Protective Services."

Ventana clearly looked confused. "What are you talking about?"

"The prime suspect for being the actual attacker and his background. I guess maybe the DC police aren't keeping you in the loop as much as you think."

"We'll see," Ventana said. "I have a briefing with Chief Collins at four."

"Perfect. You can invite me. And in exchange, I'll share with you what she hasn't bothered to tell you."

Ventana took a deep breath. "All right. If it gets us to the truth."

"Good. First, I'm confident we're dealing with some sort of conspiracy and it has to do with the pending court case on lithium mining. Here's what I know so far." Without giving up his sources, Rudy outlined what he'd learned from Detective Glenn Meadows and Ethel, emphasizing the assassination of Ronald Drake and the theft of Brooke's computer. He also mentioned Senator Hathaway's interest in the case and that the Director of the Defense Intelligence Agency just happened to be in the morning golf foursome.

"General Corbin?" Ventana asked. "Do you think his hands are in this somehow?"

"Your guess is as good as mine. But that's another reason for the Bureau to take the lead. No offense, but if they're stonewalling something, you don't have the clout to go up against them. It's not that they don't play nice, it's that they don't play at all."

"Point taken," Ventana conceded. "But just because we're not taking the lead on the investigation doesn't mean we won't be following up on our own leads. If a tipoff did come from inside, I don't want to be blindsided. Nine justices with four clerks each, one clerk for each of our two retired justices, plus administrative staff means we're looking at close to fifty individuals with privileged information. I'm going to start talking to them, and you can't stop me from cleaning up my own house."

"No. But we'll be looking from the outside in, and if anyone seems suspicious, then we won't hold back from our own interrogation."

"Fair enough. I assume that includes me?"

Rudy shrugged. "Like I said, anyone who seems suspicious."

Ventana stood up from the table. "Then I guess we're done here. I'll see you at DC police headquarters in an hour." He turned around and reached for his desk phone.

"No need to call an escort," Rudy said. "I know my way out."

Rudy walked down the hallway, thinking the meeting had gone as well as could be expected. If the situation were reversed, he knew he'd be pissed at Ventana. He also knew Ventana's pride would spur him to leave no stone unturned. Unless Ventana himself was under one of them.

As Rudy neared the elevator, the door opened. Jake Simmons smiled at him.

"Heard your footsteps."

"From the ground floor?" Rudy asked.

"Nah. I've been hanging out here. You're the only guest in the building, and you are the director of the FBI."

"I take it you're a wounded veteran."

Jake's expression turned serious. "Yes, sir. Afghanistan. That's where I met a most disagreeable IED. I'm lucky to be alive, although I didn't think so at the time."

Rudy offered his hand. "Well, you have my gratitude."

Jake clutched it with both of his own. "Honored to be your

vertical chauffeur, sir. If you ever need an undercover amputee, I'm your man."

"I'll remember that." Rudy studied the man's earnest face. Perhaps Simmons could be useful. Rudy flipped open his wallet and handed the man his card. "Get in touch if you see or hear something unusual."

"Yes, sir." Jake carefully tucked the card in his shirt pocket.

Rudy stepped away to let Jake close the door. "How well did you know Robert Finley and Brooke Chaplin?"

"Pretty well, I guess. They were supersmart but with a sense of humor. Brooke usually got the best of Robert. At least when I was around them." Jake took a staggered breath. "How's she doing?"

"As far as I know, she's still in a coma."

"I guess I can't visit her."

"No. Not while she's in ICU."

"Will you be talking to her as soon as she regains consciousness?"

"Yes, if the doctors permit it."

"Tell her hello from me. Tell her I'm praying for her."

Rudy met the man's imploring gaze. "I will, soldier. I will."

Chapter 13

Daniel Ventana found himself in a dilemma. He didn't want to appear weak, but he knew if he pushed back against Rudy Hauser and the FBI, then he'd be picking a fight he had little chance of winning. And Rudy was evidently gathering information from sources unavailable to him.

As for Yolanda Collins, she wasn't proving to be a partner who felt any obligation to share discoveries in real time. She must be holding back to try to impress him at their four o'clock meeting.

Ventana considered his options and decided his best course of action was to tell Collins that he'd invited Hauser to join the investigation and that the director would be at the meeting. Ventana would mention that he and Hauser were already checking out the background of one Ronald Drake and any connection he may have had with OmniForce Protective Services. That would knock some wind out of her sails.

He moved from the conference table back to his desk chair and prepared to call the chief justice. He needed to check her schedule and have a car at the ready for when she wanted to leave. He would also advise her that after a one-on-one meeting with Rudy Hauser, the FBI had offered assistance. He'd accepted and was confident that together they'd bring the perpetrators to justice.

After he'd rehearsed this speech for a few minutes, he dialed Baxter's office.

"Office of the Chief Justice."

Ventana recognized Nicole Cramerton's voice and remembered Clarissa was going to request one of her secretaries come in.

"It's Daniel Ventana. May I speak with the chief justice?"

"She's on her cell. Can I take a message?"

"Is she talking to one of the families? Finley's or Chaplin's?"

"I don't know, sir. I'm happy to take a message," she reiterated.

"Thanks, but I'm leaving for a meeting in a few minutes and will check with her later. Nothing urgent." He hung up. Probably just as well that he didn't reach her. He'd drop by her office on his way back from DC police headquarters and see what she needed. And it would give him a chance to give her his version of how the meeting went.

He sent a text to Rudy Hauser giving him the meeting's location. Then he copied Rudy on a brief text to Collins:

> Invited Director Hauser to 4. We're researching a Ronald Drake and possible connections to OPS. Fill you in then.

Satisfied that he'd played his hand the best he could, he focused on his own concern that Rudy Hauser would find whomever had targeted Finley, and that it would be someone with inside information who was working right under his nose.

That meant the FBI snooping through personnel files. Ventana swiveled to his desktop computer on a side credenza. As head of the Supreme Court police, he had clearance to view the records of anyone working in the building.

And he'd start with Chaplin and Finley. Maybe he could finish with them before leaving for his four o'clock meeting, then pick up when he returned.

It was going to be a long weekend.

—

Ethel had given Jesse the assignment of researching the three men who had been at the golf course with Rudy. She also wanted to know all she could about the entities listed on Brooke Chaplin's legal pad—especially the Progressive Mining Coalition and Brine Extractors. But she didn't want Jesse to ignore the other parties whose interests might not be as straightforward. They needed scrutiny as well.

As for her next step, she decided to follow the example set by her father when he was an FBI agent—start at the top. She wanted to open a channel with Chief Justice Clarissa Baxter, not only for what papers might have been stolen, but what Baxter surmised could have been their value, real or perceived.

Ethel opted to use her personal cell phone rather than her burner because the number would appear on the chief justice's log. She didn't want the new phone's existence known by anyone outside her chosen circle. Right then that was limited to Jesse.

Ethel went to what she liked to call her Ruth Bader Ginsburg retreat. She had admired the late justice's spark and spunk. RBG had a spine of steel plus mental acuity coupled with physical agility. At age seventy-five, Ethel wasn't looking for role models. RBG was the exception. Ethel had even equipped her basement to follow Ginsburg's exercise routine. If the workout was good enough for RBG at eighty-seven, then Ethel figured she might last twelve more years herself.

But that routine had been pushed aside by the events of the

previous eighteen hours. Today, her in-house gym became her fortress of solitude. A place where she could think undisturbed.

She sat on the weight bench and unfolded the sheet of paper she'd used to write down the private number of the chief justice. She punched in the ten digits and prepared to leave a compelling message on voicemail.

The line rang once. "This is Clarissa Baxter."

Ethel drew a sharp breath. The woman was actually on the phone. Ethel put as much warmth in her voice as she could. "Chief Justice, my name is Ethel Crestwater. Brooke Chaplin rents a room in my home. Her uncle, Arlington Detective Frank Mancini, shared your number. I apologize for calling out of the blue." Ethel paused, allowing Baxter the opportunity to speak.

"Yes, Brooke told me she was staying with you. I try to get to know all the clerks, not just the ones assigned to me. Are you calling with an update?"

"No, Your Honor, however I did hear from Frank that Brooke's medical team hopes to bring her out of the coma this evening."

"Any word on who might have done this?"

"Not officially."

"Unofficially?"

"Unofficially describes this call," Ethel said. "Brooke might have mentioned that I'm a retired FBI agent."

"No," Baxter replied, clearly surprised. "Are you working as a consultant?"

"You can call me a concerned citizen—concerned because Brooke is part of my household and her uncle is a dear friend, concerned because I have questions about an investigation that's likely to be politicized, and I'm concerned for you, Madame Chief Justice."

"Me?"

"Yes. Your life could be in danger."

"Have you spoken with Supreme Court Marshal Daniel Ventana?"

"No," Ethel said flatly. "He and FBI Director Hauser are already talking. It's you I'd like to talk with. In person, not over the phone. Unofficially."

"I'm at the court. A driver has been assigned to take me home, but we could meet someplace else."

"Would you be comfortable coming to my house? Brooke lives here. You could make some excuse about seeing what you could do for the family. Maybe make the destination change after you're in the car."

"And have my driver wait while we talk?"

"Release him. I'll take you home. Unless you had other plans for Saturday night."

Clarissa had Max and an unopened bottle of Pinot Noir waiting at home. Max had his doggy door to the backyard. He would be fine. Ethel intrigued her. Clarissa suddenly wanted to meet the person behind the voice. "No, no other plans. Give me your address. Would five o'clock be okay?"

"Perfect. I'll have a kettle on." Ethel gave her the North Highland Street address and ended the call.

Ethel glanced at her watch. Ten till four. She knew Rudy was heading into his meeting with DC Chief Collins and Daniel Ventana. Ventana should have already left the court. He wouldn't learn about the chief justice's change of route until later.

But he would learn about it. And wonder about it, which was just fine with Ethel. She climbed the basement stairs. No RBG workout today. Ruth would have understood. Ethel was hosting the chief justice of the U.S. Supreme Court.

—

"The chief justice is coming here?" Jesse reflexively ran his palms down the front of his sweatshirt as if that would flatten the wrinkles.

Ethel sat beside him on the living room sofa. "Yes, but I want you to stay in your room. She might be more comfortable with a one-on-one conversation. I don't know how she'll react to my questions, but the smaller the audience, the less likely she'll withhold information. Now, tell me what you've learned."

Jesse spread a few sheets of scribbled notes on the coffee table in front of them. "I can better organize these, but at this point I just jotted down what struck me as important. I'll start with Senator Hathaway. As you said, he's been pushing job creation as the reason for his support of the Nevada mine. He's received campaign contributions from Lithium USA and the Progressive Mining Coalition. We can also assume these entities have contributed to super PACs that are funneling money to Hathaway. But his position isn't without negative consequences as he's faced angry ranchers at some of his town halls where he plays down the environmental impact."

Ethel nodded slowly. "He'll parrot whatever line the money channels are espousing. Did anything pop up as to why he invited Rudy Hauser to play golf at the last minute?"

"Not directly. But I did learn the name of Hathaway's legislative assistant, the one who supposedly got food poisoning. He has a Twitter account and tweeted, 'my Saturday just freed up. Tomorrow it's beer and college football.'" Jesse smiled. "No mention of being ill."

"Do you have a time?"

Jesse made a checkmark in the air. "Good question, Cousin. Ten-fifteen last night."

"After the call to Rudy," Ethel stated. "The assistant got bumped after Rudy had accepted, not before."

"What's that mean?" Jesse asked.

"What we suspected. Senator Hathaway and maybe the others were anxious for information about the investigation into the attack, an attack that might have been orchestrated to look like a mugging. The director of Defense Intelligence would have had the resources to pull that off."

"And now they're panicked," Jesse said.

"I wouldn't say that. Whoever's behind this might be more dangerous if they're cold and calculating. A panicked person compounds one mistake by making others. Our conspirators could be methodically eliminating potential threats."

"Threats plural?"

"Jesse, we can't assume the assassination of Ronald Drake insulated others involved, just as we can't assume that Senator Hathaway is guilty of the attack. We need evidence. Remember, facts generate a theory, not the other way around. Now, any more on General Corbin?"

Jesse picked up a sheet of paper. "He's fifty-five, a graduate of West Point. Articles I found describe him as a brilliant strategist, especially when it comes to analyzing logistics of moving soldiers and supplies. He applied his system skills in Afghanistan, where he built a network of spies, a number of them even within the Taliban. He used their collected information not only to target key leaders, but to capture them for interrogation. Enhanced interrogation, some detractors have claimed, but nothing that was ever proven."

"Any association with OmniForce Protective Services?"

"Not that I found. But OPS was one of the private contractors on the ground in Afghanistan."

Ethel steepled her fingers under her chin and said nothing for a moment. Whatever she was thinking, Jesse didn't interrupt.

Finally, she asked, "What about the general and lithium? Is he a point person for DOD's appearance on Brooke's list?"

"He's not been that vocal, at least officially. He was asked about it during a *Washington Post* interview six months ago. It was part of a profile the newspaper published when General Corbin was appointed director of Defense Intelligence." Jesse looked at his notes. "Here's the quote that stood out for me: 'If we're going to move to electric vehicles, then we can't do so at the cost of our energy independence, or we'll be facing some lithium equivalent of OPEC. And I acknowledge we need technical advances in clean mining so we're not changing one polluter for another. The balance of benefit to detriment deserves thoughtful analysis.

"'My concern is that the American people understand the complexity of this conversion. As desirable as electric vehicles might be to mitigate climate change, we have to acknowledge one fact: an army doesn't travel on its stomach, it travels on oil. Delivering batteries to a fluid war zone or constructing battlefield recharging stations might prove to be impractical and unsound military policy. If our armed forces are to be the strongest and most effective in the world, then I believe our steady flow of oil must be maintained well into this century.'" Jesse dropped the sheet of paper back on the table. "That's the general's only comment I could find on mining and batteries."

Ethel gave a derisive laugh. "Of course. His position goes counter to the administration's official policy. He's right. The military will probably be the last to abandon oil, but it's his lukewarm endorsement of open-pit mining that probably received the attention, and, shall we say, the displeasure of the president."

Jesse cocked his head and eyed her inquisitively. "So, you're ruling him out?"

"Definitely not. The man has one foot in the world of logistics and the other in the murky, dangerous world of espionage. He's a formidable figure who's not afraid to take action. We'd better not underestimate him." Ethel looked at the one sheet of paper Jesse had yet to pick up. "What about our lobbyist?"

"Roger Diamond. He's a partner in Crane and Weston." Jesse grabbed his page of notes. "He's forty-seven and holds the title of vice president for legislative affairs."

"That's got to be a high-powered position," Ethel said. "The man must have connections on the Hill."

"He was a Republican strategist and campaign manager for some close, high-profile congressional races. His reputation cast him as a street fighter. A very successful one. Crane and Weston wanted his connections, and he joined them five years ago."

"Any public mention of clients in particular?"

Jesse couldn't restrain himself from smiling. "Guess."

"The Progressive Mining Coalition."

"Bingo. When I saw that connection, I remembered what you said about who organized the golf game. Roger Diamond is a member of the Congressional Country Club. He could have booked the tee time and let Senator Hathaway take the credit."

"And had his own agenda," Ethel said.

"Like what?"

"Like scoring some face time with the director of the FBI. I'm sure some of his clients have come under the Bureau's scrutiny before. And he'd certainly be interested in the Supreme Court case. Anything in his background before managing political campaigns?"

"He's a Marine veteran. Two tours of duty in Afghanistan. Then he graduated from Duke law school but opted for politics. He ran a state senator's campaign in his hometown of Richmond, notched a win, and built his reputation from there."

"Anything specific that Diamond's done or doing for the mining coalition?"

"I don't know how directly involved he is, but someone's booking a lot of media interviews for guests touting the urgency of extracting lithium and other rare earth elements. The spin is that those who oppose the federal land leases are unpatriotic."

Ethel sighed. "Say it often enough and people will believe it."

"Well, their message is consistent and disciplined. I'm sure it will be reinforced at next week's conference."

Ethel sat up straighter. "What conference?"

"The Progressive Mining Coalition is having a meeting at the Mandarin Oriental Hotel on Wednesday. It's promoted on their website."

"Is it now? Then book two rooms for Tuesday and Wednesday nights. And I think it's time we bought some shares in Lithium USA, don't you? After all, we don't want to be unpatriotic."

Chapter 14

At precisely five o'clock, Chief Justice Clarissa Baxter rang the bell at Ethel's front door. As it opened, Clarissa looked back at the street and waved to her driver.

"He's hesitant to leave you," Ethel observed.

"Yes. Conscientious to a fault. I feel like I'm living in a fishbowl."

The two women waited for the SUV to pull away from the curb. Ethel began waving as well, demonstrating that she wasn't holding a gun or an axe. The man gave up and slowly drove off.

Ethel stepped back, clearing the doorway. "Welcome, Madame Chief Justice. I appreciate your seeing me." She offered her hand and as the woman shook it, Ethel quickly studied her. What she saw concerned her. Despite the makeup, the justice's face looked drawn and almost haggard. Deep crow's-feet etched the skin at the corners of her brown eyes, aging her beyond her forty-eight years. Ethel suspected her condition was more than the product of last night's lack of sleep and the horrible news about her clerk and Brooke. Ethel knew the woman was recently widowed and thereby adjusting to the pressure cooker of DC on her own.

Ethel closed the door behind them. "I thought we'd sit in the living room. Tea is laid out along with some oatmeal raisin cookies, or, as I prefer to call them, health food."

"You're very kind, Ms. Crestwater."

"Please, it's Ethel."

"And you must call me Clarissa."

Ethel invited Clarissa to sit on the sofa while she fixed the woman a cup of tea.

"How do you like it?" Ethel asked.

"A splash of milk and a half teaspoon of sugar."

"Excellent. I take mine the same way."

When both cups had been prepared, Ethel sat down in the chair opposite her guest.

"Now I'm sure you have questions about why I called and asked us to get together."

"You said you were a former FBI agent and that Brooke lives here. I assume you have questions for me that you don't want to run through the police."

"Something like that. I also believe I can be effective in ways that official law enforcement agencies can't be."

Clarissa's brow furrowed and she lowered the cup from her lips. "I can't be aware of anything illegal. That would be condoning it."

"No, nothing like that. What I bring is a lifetime of investigative experience. These old bones have the FBI permanently embedded in their DNA, and that DNA didn't disappear when I had to take mandatory retirement. You don't have that problem. I suspect you have the law in your DNA, and you have a lifetime appointment to practice that you love. I confess I envy you."

"How long were you with the Bureau?"

"My father was in the Bureau and was close to J. Edgar

Hoover. I was permitted to work after school in the fingerprint department. I was fourteen. Now I'm seventy-five."

"Wow," Clarissa whispered. She stared at the petite, older woman with genuine amazement. "You should write a book."

"No," Ethel said emphatically. "That's the last thing I would do. Agents trust me. For more than fifty years I've been renting them rooms. They're my extended family. I put them in a book and I've sacrificed that bond."

Clarissa smiled. "And I confess I envy you."

The comment surprised Ethel. The chief justice really was lonely.

"So, I have this network that crosses agencies," Ethel said. "I learn things that I'm told from trusted sources. And I draw conclusions that are often outside the traditional because being inside the institutions can create institutionalized thinking."

"The Supreme Court is an institution," Clarissa argued. "That was its strength from the very adoption of the U.S. Constitution."

"But which doesn't prepare it to deal with internal intrigue or corruption."

Clarissa set her teacup on the table, not trusting her hand to stay steady. "You're saying one of the justices is corrupt?"

"No. I'm saying someone knew Robert Finley was carrying court documents, and we need to know if that information came from inside or outside your institution. Supreme Court Marshal Daniel Ventana may be a competent—even an excellent—investigator, but he's still an insider whose natural inclination will be to protect the institution."

"And your investigation—"

"Will not interfere with his," Ethel interrupted.

Clarissa relaxed and reached for her cup. "Okay. Ask your questions."

"Do you know what papers Robert Finley had in his backpack?"

"Not everything. I'd given him some arguments to review for one of our cases. I find it helpful for my clerks to immerse themselves in both legal and consequential aspects of what's being argued before the court."

"Yes," Ethel agreed. "And, of course, we're talking about the case of the Native American Coalition and Farmers and Ranchers United v The United States Department of the Interior and Bureau of Land Management. The one you and your fellow justices discussed in conference yesterday."

Clarissa took a sip of tea to buy time before answering.

She decided there was no reason to deny it. "You're well informed," she admitted. "And we're still in discussions. I find the perspectives of my law clerks to be helpful, and because they're younger, they'll inherit the consequences of our decisions long after I'm gone."

"Especially one as existential and complex as climate change. How much do Native Americans, farmers, and ranchers suffer in the short term to ward off a potentially global disaster? It's not an easy call."

"No, it's not," Clarissa agreed.

"And that's not even counting the money that's at stake. Mining companies, automakers, investors, and jobs. We've got to be talking billions, even trillions. But I'm sure you've heard all that."

Clarissa took a deep breath. "And more."

"Yes. I left out national security."

Clarissa leaned forward, searching Ethel's face as she asked, "So, how do you weigh using public land for a purpose that harms a segment of the public?"

Ethel shook her head slowly. "I don't know." She broke the

solemn mood with a smile. "But I do know these cookies are good. Better have one before I eat them all."

"If it makes you feel better." The chief justice took a cookie from the platter and broke off a piece. "Good," she said as she chewed.

Ethel took a bite of her own and waited a moment for Clarissa to finish. Then she asked, "Who agreed to hear the appeal?"

"You mean the granting of cert where we vote to select which cases to hear?"

"Yes, if I recall correctly it takes four justices to accept an appeal. Were there more than four?"

Clarissa shifted on the sofa, suddenly uncomfortable. "Ordinarily, the vote to grant cert isn't disclosed."

"Ordinarily," Ethel emphasized. "Ordinarily law clerks aren't murdered."

An involuntary shudder passed through Clarissa. "All right. Between us. I was one of the four votes to grant cert."

"Should I read into that any indication of your opinion on the case?"

"Most definitely not. I felt we needed clarity on the legal principles at play. Did the lower court properly address the protection of citizens from the consequences on their lives and livelihoods by the action of the federal government? It's not the same as eminent domain. That's a proven right of the government to expropriate private property for public use as long as the owners are fairly compensated for it. Here the government is leasing public land that will impact private property without compensation, not to mention the destructive nature of open-pit mining that will lay waste to that public land."

Ethel paused to take a second cookie. Clarissa did the same.

After swallowing a bite, Ethel asked, "You're from Wyoming, right?"

"Yes. What does that have to do with anything?"

"Just that from the outside looking in, I envision you as being sympathetic to the ranchers and farmers. The independent spirit of the West."

"You're wrong. I'll make my decision on facts applied against the law and the U.S. Constitution."

"But can't you see how others might think otherwise? I doubt if it's a secret that you voted to review the case. And I have information that the associate justices are split four to four."

Clarissa's eyes flashed. "Who told you that? Brooke?"

Ethel let the chief justice's moment of anger pass before answering. "Brooke has told me nothing. But from your reaction, you've told me it's true."

"We have not taken a vote," Clarissa insisted.

"But someone wants to know whether you have, or, if not, then how you're leaning. Let's face it. You are the maker of the majority. Both sides know that."

Clarissa's jaw tensed. "I can't argue about something that hasn't happened yet. If you won't take my word for it, then we have nothing further to talk about." She started to rise from the sofa.

Ethel raised her palm as a signal to stay seated. "Are Brooke Chaplin and Senator Joseph Mulberry having an affair?"

Clarissa fell back against the cushion. "What?"

"Are they in a romantic relationship?"

The chief justice looked offended by the idea. "I have no reason to think so, not even the slightest indication that anything is going on between them. Frankly, I'm stunned by the question. Brooke lives here. You're the one in the position to monitor her personal life, not me."

"And I've seen no indication either. But I needed the question out in the open because I've discovered references she made to some project she was working on with Senator Mulberry. Do you know what that would be?"

"No. Have you asked the senator?"

"Not without first talking to Brooke."

Clarissa nodded her approval. "It might be something as simple as a project for their home state of Oregon. School visits. That kind of thing."

Ethel refilled their cups from the bone china teapot. "I'm sure you're right. You understand why I had to ask, especially since she was with Finley. Although it's highly unlikely, there's the possibility she was the target, not him. But there's no apparent motive."

"Like covering up an affair with a powerful senator," Clarissa said.

Ethel managed a smile. "A bit melodramatic, right?"

"Not in this town." Clarissa accepted that she couldn't help but like the woman seated across from her.

"Then let me push the melodrama a little further," Ethel said. "What happens to the Lithium USA case if something happens to you?"

"The eight associate justices would vote and a ruling would be issued."

"And in case of a tie?"

"The lower court ruling would stand."

"Exactly," Ethel said, and took a sip of tea.

—

Daniel Ventana emerged from the multiagency meeting with little more information than when he'd entered. DC Detective Glenn Meadows had shared they were pressing OmniForce Protective Services CEO Matt Geyser for information on fired employee

Ronald Drake, but didn't expect significant cooperation until the office opened on Monday. FBI Director Rudy Hauser said he would lean on OPS through the Defense Department to make sure they cooperated. Detective Meadows shared the update on Brooke Chaplin's medical condition, and Hauser said he had assigned an agent to the ICU. Ventana told them Brooke and Finley had been colleagues and nothing more. He passed along Chief Justice Baxter's desire for full cooperation among the agencies. She claimed Finley had planned to review some of her notes on the lithium mining case that came before the court earlier in the week. Ventana said the notes weren't conclusions but factual data.

DC Police Chief Yolanda Collins expressed her confidence in Detective Meadows and promised to provide him whatever manpower and resources he needed for his part in the investigation.

All in all, Ventana had to admit the meeting had been cordial in tone but short on substance. They just didn't have productive leads. Ventana had learned nothing that changed his priority of looking for potential suspects within the court. It was back to the personnel files.

As soon as he was out of DC Police Headquarters, he checked his cell phone. The damn thing had vibrated throughout the meeting. He read the first text:

> CJ doesn't want to go home. Insists on visiting home of Brooke Chaplin. Waved me off saying she has a ride from there. Ran cross-check on address. House owned by an Ethel Fiona Crestwater.

"Crestwater," Ventana muttered to himself. Just who he didn't need sticking her nose into things. As if he didn't have enough trouble.

The aide knocked on the office door of Lieutenant General Alan Corbin. The director of the Defense Intelligence Agency had just returned to headquarters at Joint Base Anacostia-Bolling in DC to catch up on work he should have done that morning instead of enduring eighteen holes with the pompous senator. *Go along to get along,* he thought.

"This came from the computer lab, sir." The aide handed Corbin a manila envelope.

The general waited until the man left before checking the contents. The written report was short. A few documents had been found with vague references to Project Insider but nothing more. The hard drive had been wiped and the laptop destroyed.

Everything would be fine if Brooke Chaplin kept her mouth shut.

Chapter 15

"I'd like you to stay for dinner." Ethel set her empty teacup on the tray and folded her linen napkin beside it.

"Oh, I couldn't impose," Clarissa said. "Besides, I have a loyal German shepherd waiting at home."

Ethel stood, lifting the tray. "I'm not talking about an imposition. I'm talking about a sandwich and a bowl of chicken noodle soup that will take me all of fifteen minutes to prepare. Then we can take you home."

"We?"

"Jesse Cooper. My double-first-cousin-twice-removed. He's up in his room."

Clarissa laughed. "Double-first-cousin? You're putting me on."

"No, but I'll only explain over dinner. Now, when's the last time you had a grilled pimento cheese sandwich?"

"I'll have to say never."

Ethel started for the kitchen. "Then that oversight stops tonight. Follow me. What say we trade in these teacups for two glasses of chardonnay? If it pleases the court, that is."

New energy flowed through the chief justice as she got up

from the sofa. The vitality of the older woman was contagious. "The court would be very pleased," Clarissa said. "So ordered."

Good, Ethel thought. Nothing more conducive to gaining a person's confidence than sharing wine around a kitchen table. And she liked Clarissa. For all her accomplishments, the chief justice was down to earth. A welcome change from the arrogance that ran through so much of government. The Supreme Court was not immune, but Ethel sensed Clarissa could be a breath of fresh air. If someone didn't kill her first.

—

Frank Mancini stood up and stretched. His neck and arms felt stiff from sitting slumped in the patient conference room chair for hours. He bent over to touch his toes and failed. They might as well have been in the next room.

He looked at his sleeping sister curled up on the sofa. Frank had laid his coat over her as a blanket and been struck by the gray that now streaked through her auburn hair. Eight years his junior, Susan had always been under her big brother's watchful eye. They had been there for one another during times of grief. The loss of their parents, and then spouses. Frank's wife had died first, and Susan had been there on a red-eye flight. Then her husband three years ago, and Frank had flown standby to Oregon when he couldn't book a seat soon enough. He and Susan had no other siblings. Brooke was the only family of the next generation. He knew losing her would destroy his sister.

He checked his watch. Ten after seven. He could go back to the ICU for a few minutes. Someone should be making a decision on whether to begin bringing Brooke out of the coma this evening.

He stopped at the secure door of the ICU, used the

intercom to give a nurse his name, and was buzzed through. As he approached Brooke's room, he saw the posted FBI agent get up from the chair placed just outside her glass door. Frank would have to thank Rudy for delivering the protection he'd promised.

"Has a doctor been in to see her?" Frank asked the agent.

"About ten minutes ago."

"Any update?"

"They're going to bring her out of the coma. That's what I overheard the doctor tell the senator."

"What senator?" Frank nearly shouted the question.

The agent frowned. "Senator Mulberry. He said he was a family friend. The hospital's chief medical officer even accompanied him." The agent saw Frank was clearly upset. "But I had eyes on them at all times. No one touched her other than the supervising physician. The senator only bent close to her ear and whispered something."

"What?"

"I couldn't hear. I assumed it was a word of encouragement. But the doctor said she wouldn't be responsive until morning."

Frank forced down his anger. "Okay. It's just that our understanding was that visitations should be limited to family only. But you did the right thing. No harm done."

Despite what he said, Frank wanted to confront the chief medical officer and Senator Mulberry, but his cop instincts told him to leave things alone. Find out more about the senator's interest in Brooke and, most importantly, don't make a move without consulting Ethel.

—

Daniel Ventana prioritized his search of Supreme Court personnel records to those persons likely to have come in contact with Robert Finley or Brooke Chaplin the previous afternoon. That meant focusing on the law clerks, all thirty-six of them, not counting Robert and Brooke. He tagged them for financial background checks and tried to recall if he'd witnessed any over-the-top competitiveness. He found most of the clerks to be smart with triple type-A personalities fueling grand ambitions. But would one of them collude with an outsider?

He'd assign a team of his officers to begin the reviews first thing in the morning. Then he remembered the next day was Sunday, which would possibly limit access to people with information. But he'd do what he could to stay ahead of the DC police and FBI. Ventana recognized he could be as over-the-top competitive as anyone.

He rechecked the previous day's duty roster for his own officers, knowing he had to be impartial in his scrutiny. And there was the administrative staff. He remembered one of Chief Justice Baxter's two secretaries had been in the office when Robert Finley dropped by with the full backpack. Nicole Cramerton. She'd been hired a little over two years ago. Ventana knew she'd previously worked on Capitol Hill as a stenographer, primarily on the senate floor and in committee hearings. Ventana wondered if any of the chief justice's stolen documents had been typed by her. She could have easily heard Clarissa, Finley, and himself talking in the hallway outside her door. Finley had even said he was going to the Dubliner. Had Nicole Cramerton tipped someone off? Ventana reviewed the electronic copy of her résumé. She'd received recommendations from several senators including Senator Hathaway and Senator Mulberry. *That was a first,* Ventana thought. *Those two couldn't agree on the time of day.*

It would be awkward if he had to bring up Cramerton's name to the chief justice, but no one was above suspicion.

The secretary was ideally positioned to handle confidential information.

He looked at his watch. Six fifteen. He felt like he was spinning his wheels. What did he know for sure? That the chief justice had gone to see Ethel Crestwater and released her driver. That bothered him. Something was going on. And he was determined to discover what exactly the old lady was up to.

—

After clearing the dishes, Jesse brought two cups of coffee to the dining room table. Both Ethel and the chief justice had offered to help, but Jesse insisted that since Ethel had fixed the meal and Clarissa was a guest, the least he could do was clean up.

When they'd carried their empty cups to the kitchen, Ethel said, "I'll just grab my handbag, Jesse, and be ready to go. Bring the car around front. Clarissa, would you like to use the bathroom?"

"No, I'm just out River Road across the Maryland line. In fact, why don't I just order a cab and save you the trouble?"

"We're going to see you to your front door," Ethel insisted. "No argument. No appeal. I'll join you in the foyer in a moment." Ethel headed back to her bedroom.

Clarissa looked at Jesse and shook her head. "You don't say no to Ethel, do you?"

"No, Your Honor. So this is me going for the car." He left by the back door.

Clarissa smiled, feeling the most relaxed she'd been in weeks. *No, you don't say no to Ethel,* she thought, *because the woman was probably always right.*

Ethel grabbed a lightweight parka from her closet to counter the November chill. She noticed the cold more now that she neared her seventy-sixth birthday. Thinner blood or just thinner skin? She'd also acquired a pacemaker a few months ago, a reminder of her mortality. Well, she wouldn't go quietly. Old age wasn't for sissies.

She went to her nightstand, opened the drawer, and picked up her thirty-eight revolver. The G-men of her father's era would have called it packing heat. She called it a sensible precaution. She slung her handbag over her shoulder, locked the back door, and met Clarissa in the foyer.

"Take the front seat with Jesse," she told the chief justice. "He can drive, and you can give him directions."

As they pulled away from the curb, Ethel twisted in her seat to look out the rear window. Half a block down, headlights flashed on. Ethel patted her pocket and felt the reassuring outline of her loaded pistol.

"Take the GW Parkway," Clarissa said. "Traffic will be light this time of night."

Which will make us easier to follow, Ethel thought. Again, she looked back to confirm that the headlights were trailing them. As the other vehicle passed beneath a streetlamp, she saw the dark shape of an SUV, the vehicle of choice for half of Washington.

Jesse and Clarissa kept the conversation going. He talked about his computer science studies at American University and how he'd developed an interest in the movement of money across the internet, particularly using cryptocurrencies.

"Would you like to work for the FBI?" Clarissa asked. "Maybe take after your double-first-cousin-twice-removed?"

"Six months ago, I would have said no."

"What changed your mind?"

"Uh..." Jesse fumbled for an answer, realizing he'd said too much.

"I changed his mind," Ethel said. "If I could make it in the FBI, he surely could."

Jesse forced a laugh. "Right. My cousin's a legend. I've got a lot to learn from her." *Like watching what I say,* he thought. He knew there was a pending lecture on the horizon. He and Ethel sat on $20 million of Bitcoin they'd uncovered, but had no way to make its existence public without hurting innocent people. That investigation had changed Jesse's mind. And he and Ethel had vowed only to use the funds in a search for justice. He sensed such a time had come. Justice for Robert Finley. Justice for Brooke Chaplin. Maybe even justice for the chief justice of the U.S. Supreme Court.

After they crossed into Maryland, Clarissa directed them to turn off River Road and after a few blocks, the houses looked more like mini-estates.

"My driveway is the next right. Pull up to the keypad, Jesse, and I'll give you the code. Then you can park in front and come in for a nightcap." Jesse waited for Ethel's response, expecting her to say they needed to get back to Arlington.

"If it's no trouble," Ethel said. "And I'd like to meet Max. Maybe get on his good side."

Jesse lowered his window.

"The code's pound, 9, star, 9," Clarissa said.

While Jesse entered the sequence, Ethel took note of a sedan parked on the apron of a driveway half a block away. The house behind the gate was dark except for spotlights under the corner eaves. The SUV that had followed them passed by at normal speed.

Double surveillance, Ethel thought. FBI? Supreme Court police? Or maybe the surveillance wasn't coordinated at all. At least not with any government agency.

The gate opened, and Jesse drove through.

—

Daniel Ventana found a parking spot about thirty yards down the street from the house belonging to Ethel Crestwater. He didn't know if the chief justice was still inside, or if she'd already been driven home. He decided to wait thirty minutes and if she didn't appear, he'd call her cell and make sure she was in for the night. He'd save the speech about not ditching marshal protection for when they next saw each other face-to-face.

Ten minutes into his stakeout, a black Infiniti backed down her driveway and parked in front of the house. Two women emerged from the front door, and one of them paused to lock it. He assumed she was Ethel Crestwater. When the front passenger door opened, the courtesy light confirmed the other woman was Clarissa Baxter. Ventana started his engine. He would protect the chief justice, whether she wanted it or not. Then he'd have a little chat with Miss Crestwater.

He had no trouble keeping the Infiniti in sight. The route they traveled was consistent with the way to Clarissa's house. Ventana turned his thoughts back to the personnel records. He might need warrants for searching into certain aspects of their lives. Maybe consult with Clarissa. You can't get an opinion higher than the chief justice's.

The Infiniti turned onto Clarissa's street. Ventana dropped back, knowing they would stop at the gate's keypad. As they turned into the driveway, Ventana noticed a reflective flash come from inside a car parked by a neighbor's gate across the street and a few houses up. Ventana flipped his beams on high and caught the motion of someone ducking down. He couldn't tell if it was a man or a woman, but he could see the light reflecting off the glass of a camera lens.

Ventana drove on, keeping his eyes straight ahead as if he'd not seen the figure. The street curved enough so that the bend soon hid him from view. He parked on the shoulder and considered his options. He could make a U-turn and pass the sedan again, but that might spook the driver. He could walk back on foot and stay unseen in the shadows until he had a better idea of what was going on. But if the person drove off, he wouldn't be able to follow. The third option was simply to confront whoever was there. Drive back and angle his large SUV to pin the sedan against the neighbor's closed gate. He expected the occupant to be an FBI agent. It would be just like Rudy Hauser to take on surveillance without coordinating with him.

Ventana whipped his vehicle around and sped back, braking hard to pull across the driveway. Leaving the engine idling, he got out and walked around the front of his SUV. The headlights of the sedan came on, catching him in the face. He squinted enough to see the door with the tinted window swing open.

He couldn't see the face. Or the gun.

Chapter 16

Clarissa inserted her house key into the dead bolt. "Now Max will greet me at the door. Both of you stand behind me and I'll say, 'Friends.' Then he'll come to you. You can pet him. In fact, he'll expect it. From that point on, he'll associate you with the word friend."

"And if we weren't friends?" Ethel asked.

"He'd react to anything he thought was aggressive or if I called you 'Foes.'"

"React?" Jesse said nervously.

"Well, my husband, Jackson, wanted to keep things simple for Max. Friend or foe. We've never had to use the foe label, but Jackson trained him to growl menacingly unless he saw a weapon. Then Max would immediately attack, going for the hand with the gun or knife."

"And if Jesse or I entered without you?" Ethel asked.

"He would growl and try to force you back. He's very protective of his territory. If you'd like to see, go in first."

"We'll take your word for it," Ethel said.

Clarissa turned the lock, opened the door, and switched on an overhead light. "Friends, Max, friends." The German shepherd sat on his haunches in the foyer, his tail swishing across the hardwood floor. Clarissa stepped forward and scratched the black and tan animal behind his pointed ears. "Friends, Max. Go say hello."

The dog went first to Jesse, sniffed his legs and shoes, and then moved on to Ethel. She crouched down with her arms away from her side, ready for a hug. "You're a beauty, Max. You know that?"

The shepherd cocked his head and his tail thumped as if he were saying, "Of course I know that."

Ethel gently stroked his sides for a moment. "You're just a big teddy bear, aren't you, Max?"

"Looks like you're his new BFF. Come in. Let me take your coats."

Ethel stood and turned to close the door behind her.

The gunshot broke the stillness of the night.

Ethel slammed the door shut. She pulled the revolver from her pocket. Max growled and the fur on his neck bristled.

"Friend, Max," Clarissa shouted. "Friend." The dog ran past Ethel and scratched at the door.

"Don't let him out," Ethel ordered. "Keep him with you. Do you have a gun?"

"A thirty-eight in my bedroom."

"Get it. Then you and Jesse stay inside. For God's sake, no lights and keep clear of the windows. If you're not comfortable using the pistol, give it to Jesse. I've been giving him lessons, and he's a good shot."

"I can handle it," Clarissa said. "What about you?"

"I'm going to see what happened. How do I open the gate?"

"There's a keypad on the inside. Same code. But shouldn't we call the police?"

Ethel turned to Jesse. "If you don't hear from me in ten minutes, call 9-1-1."

"You're going out there alone? Let me come with you."

Ethel shook her head. "Here's what's going to happen. Clarissa, hold on to Max. As soon as I leave, get that revolver and pack an overnight bag. We'll get you and Max to a safe place. Jesse, I'm thinking Curt Foster's."

"But the marshals," Clarissa said. "Shouldn't they be notified?"

"We'll sort this out with them later." Ethel glanced at Max. "When we know who's friend or foe."

Clarissa grabbed the dog by the collar. "Be careful, Ethel."

"Always. Now kill the overhead light and stand clear of the door."

When the room was dark, Ethel slipped outside and headed for the deep shadow of the brick fence. She followed it along to the keypad by the gate, entered the code, and squeezed through as soon as the opening grew wide enough. She crouched down and looked up the road. A second vehicle had parked across the neighbor's driveway. This SUV could have been the one following them. It blocked a sedan that was trying to maneuver around it. Both vehicles had their headlights on and engines running. No one was visible within either interior. The car moved forward and backward trying to clear a way around the SUV.

With revolver in hand, Ethel edged along the road's shoulder, careful to avoid the beams. Before she could get close enough to identify the sedan's model or license plate, the car managed to swing off the concrete driveway, then bounce across the road's grassy shoulder and speed away in the opposite direction.

Dropping all attempts at concealment, Ethel ran to the remaining vehicle.

She found what she feared. Blocked from view from the road by the SUV, a man lay faceup on the concrete. Blood flowed from beneath him. His white dress shirt was stained crimson.

There's an entry and an exit wound, Ethel thought. High caliber to have torn through the body like that. She understood that was what sprawled before her. A body. Eyes open. Seeing nothing.

Although she'd never met the man before, she recognized him from newspaper photographs. Supreme Court Marshal Daniel Ventana. She needed to work fast. Careful to stay on the concrete and avoid the imprints the fleeing sedan made on the nearby ground, Ethel went to the open driver's door. Wrapping her hand in a tissue, she turned off the headlights and engine, and then closed the door to kill the courtesy lights. Fortunately, the streetlamps were spaced far enough apart that the murder scene fell within a dark zone between them.

Ethel traded her pistol for her cell phone. Jesse answered immediately.

"You okay?" he asked.

"Yes. Now listen. You have my car keys. Take Clarissa and Max to Curt's immediately. I'll let him know you're coming."

"What about you?"

"Supreme Court Marshal Daniel Ventana has been shot and killed. I want Clarissa clear of the scene. Tell her no argument. This is fifty-five years of FBI experience talking. Once she's safely away, we can assess the situation. At this point, we don't know friend from foe. I don't want to have to worry about her whereabouts."

"And if she won't leave?"

"Then tell her she's undermining what Daniel Ventana gave his life trying to do—keep her safe."

"Got it."

"One more thing. Tell her to leave her phone. Someone might have a tracer on it."

"Should I turn it off? Remove the battery?"

"No. We want people to think she's still here. Now go."

Ethel disconnected and immediately called Rudy Hauser's private cell.

"What is it, Ethel?" he gruffly answered.

"Ventana's been shot and killed outside the chief justice's house. I'm with his body. You're the first call. He's a federal officer, your jurisdiction, so I suggest you get forensics and agents to secure the scene. He's out of sight from the road, but we're on somebody else's driveway, and I don't know whether they're home or not."

"Jesus! When did this happen?"

"Less than fifteen minutes ago."

"Why are you there?"

"Me? It's not about me. Come on, Rudy, you need to lock down the Supreme Court building, especially Ventana's office, and get your men out here to take control of the crime scene. I'll leave it to you how you want to handle it with the Montgomery County police."

"You're sure he's dead?"

"I wish I were mistaken."

"What's the status of the chief justice?"

Ethel saw the gate slide open and her Infiniti exit. "She's safely off the premises. No one will find her."

"Okay. I'm on my way. I'll set things in motion from the car."

"We'll be waiting." Ethel ended the call and looked down at Ventana's body. "You knew your killer, didn't you, Mr. Ventana? That's why you had to die."

—

Leaving her home, Clarissa Baxter had lain across the back seat while Max obeyed her command to stay down on the floorboard. Jesse drove until they neared the beltway before telling her to sit up.

"I've been checking behind us and even doubled back on some side streets. We're not being followed, but I'm going to continue a circuitous route, even if it takes us longer to get there."

Clarissa slid over behind the front passenger seat where she could see the side of Jesse's face in the glow of the dashboard lights. Max turned around and rested his head on her feet. She buckled her seat belt. "Who is Curt Foster?"

"A retired Air Force colonel. A Vietnam vet. He has a horse farm near Manassas. He also has a private grassy airstrip. It's for UFOs."

"UFOs? What is he, some kind of nut?"

Jesse suppressed a laugh. "UFO is a flying club. United Flying Octogenarians. Pilots in their eighties. Ethel's too young, so they made her an honorary member."

"Ethel's a pilot?"

"Oh, yeah. She owns a share of a Cessna 172. That's probably why she's sending us to Curt's. If we need to move on, we can do so by air. We'd really be hard to follow then."

"But I can't just stay hidden. Not after what happened to Daniel. People will be expecting me to say something."

"I'm sure Ethel and Rudy Hauser will work something out," Jesse said. "They're just buying time to assess the situation. I expect we'll hear from them soon."

They rode in silence for a few minutes. Then Clarissa said, "The last thing Daniel gave me was his plan to protect the court from an attack on the building. It looks like the attack is coming away from the building, and no one is safe."

No one is safe, Jesse thought. Would Ethel's plan put them in the crosshairs as well?

—

Senator Stuart Hathaway poured himself three fingers of Maker's Mark. He knew the liquor would trigger his acid reflux, but that was the least of his worries. He'd be up all night anyway. The call from Roger Diamond had been short and devastating. Daniel Ventana had been shot and killed outside the home of Chief Justice Baxter. No suspects.

Hathaway wondered how the lobbyist had managed to build such a deep network of contacts. In DC, information was power, and the information Diamond collected put him at the top of Washington's influence peddlers. He not only knew people, he knew things about people. Things that they wanted kept hidden.

Hathaway understood Diamond's game and made an effort to be guarded around the man. He downed the bourbon. It wasn't fair. He'd done nothing to create the mess at the Supreme Court. Since he didn't trust Diamond, he'd build other allies. He checked his watch. Ten forty-five. Probably not too late to call General Corbin with the news about Ventana's death. He'd also reach out to Rudy Hauser in the morning. They'd keep him in the loop. After all, he was chairman of the damn Senate Intelligence Committee.

And Nicole Cramerton, the chief justice's secretary. He'd call her with concern for how she was doing. She'd be grateful. And he could use a grateful person sitting next to the office of the chief justice.

Information was power.

Chapter 17

Ethel sat quietly in Rudy Hauser's Tahoe. Outside, the crime scene bustled with activity. A forensics team in white bunny suits crawled over Ventana's SUV and the surrounding area. The body had been tented off from view. FBI vehicles with blue flashing lights closed the road a hundred yards in either direction. Curious neighbors were ordered to remain in their homes and were told only that a man had died under suspicious circumstances.

Ethel had given her story twice—once for Rudy and then over Rudy's speakerphone for U.S. Attorney General Louis Vandiver. At first, the AG made no secret of his disapproval that Ethel had sent the chief justice into hiding without an FBI or U.S. Marshal escort. To his credit, Rudy had declared that under the circumstances there was no one better than Ethel to take smart, decisive action. If the AG had any doubt, he could ask Cory Bradshaw, the director of the Secret Service, because Bradshaw also knew Ethel's capabilities firsthand. That seemed to mollify the AG, and he, Rudy, and Ethel were in agreement that Ethel's role and name wouldn't be made public.

Now she sat listening to Rudy as he finished the conversation.

"Yes, sir. I'll have our communications people coordinate

with yours. Also, the communications team at the Supreme Court should be brought in so we're unified in our messaging. And I'll work with Baxter on a statement we'll run by you before releasing. When this breaks, the public will want to hear from you. Maybe even from the president."

Then, as Rudy listened to the AG's response, Ethel saw him visibly relax. That meant Rudy was being cleared to run the investigation without jurisdictional conflicts with the U.S. Marshals or Supreme Court Police.

After several minutes of silence, Rudy said, "I'll tell her, sir. And I'll update you every hour if not sooner." He lowered the cell phone from his ear and ended the call.

"Are we good?" Ethel asked.

"Yeah. For the time being. AG Vandiver will support me as long as he thinks we're making progress. He'll be getting pressure from the president and God only knows how many conspiracy nuts spouting ludicrous theories."

"Hard to counter since we know we are dealing with a conspiracy."

Rudy shot her a sideways glance. "No need to remind me."

"So, what next?"

"We exhaust the scene here. I've deployed agents to the Supreme Court building to begin looking through Ventana's files. I've also got two agents posted with each of the other eight justices. And I want to look at any threats made against the court. There are always letters, emails, and phone calls demanding that cases be decided a certain way."

"We won't find a lead through threats," Ethel argued. "This was meant to be a surreptitious operation. I think it blew up with Finley's death."

Rudy started the Tahoe. "And tonight's killing?" He flashed his high beams to the agent left in charge, signaling his departure.

"Someone was staking out Clarissa's house," Ethel said. "I'm sure I saw a long camera lens."

"Why?"

"To see who brought her home. The marshal who drove Clarissa to my house didn't like being dismissed. I'm sure he texted Ventana and probably covered himself by telling some of the other officers. Someone was curious but didn't bank on Ventana showing up after us."

"Which supports why Ventana got out of his vehicle without drawing his weapon. He recognized the person. Didn't see him as a danger."

"Or didn't see her as a danger," Ethel added. "Even more reason to let his guard down."

"So, we talk to the driver."

"And anyone else who might have known or heard that the chief justice had a spur-of-the-moment destination change. I'd get a list of everyone in the building from late afternoon to early evening. And I'd check their phone logs, both cell and landline."

"Are you telling me how to do my job?" Rudy teased.

"No, I'm telling you how I would do your job," Ethel said. "How you do it is your own business. But, can I ask where we're going?"

"The AG wants me to have eyes on Clarissa. We're going to Curt Foster's. You okay with that?"

"As long as you make sure we're not followed."

"Thank you. I never would have thought of that."

Ethel laughed. "Got to keep you on your toes. You won't always have me around."

"I can only dream."

They rode in silence for a few minutes. Then Ethel asked, "What are you supposed to tell Clarissa?"

"What do you mean?"

"The end of your phone call. You said 'I'll tell her, sir.'"

Rudy took his eyes off the road for a quick glance at Ethel. "Tell me the day and time because the great Ethel Crestwater just made a false assumption. The 'her' wasn't Clarissa. The 'her' was you. AG Vandiver wanted you to know how much he appreciates your fast action, unorthodox as it was. I think you've made the AG the latest recruit in Ethel's army."

"I don't want an army, Rudy. I just want space to operate with minimal restraints, which means there might be things you don't want to know."

Rudy reached over and gently patted her shoulder. After all these years, she was still his mentor. "I'll go with you as far as I can."

"Then let me make two requests. Frank called me and said Brooke is being brought out of the coma. She might be able to talk sometime in the morning. I'd like someone you trust, maybe your agent on guard, to bug her hospital room."

"Why? If we or DC Detective Meadows interview her, we can openly record."

"That's not the conversation I'm interested in. Senator Joseph Mulberry has been very anxious about Brooke. That's admirable and understandable, but Frank told me the senator bypassed protocols to try and speak with her alone. That strikes me as significant. I think he'll try again, and I want to know what he says."

"But I can't bug a U.S. senator without a warrant and probable cause."

"Who says you're bugging him? It's a monitoring device that's part of your protective due diligence. You just do it without telling Frank because he'll worry Brooke might be mixed up in something she shouldn't be."

"What's that?"

"That's the point, Rudy. What indeed?"

"And your second request?"

"Your agent that's boarding with me. Lanny Childress. I'd like you to assign him to the case. He knows Brooke. They're friends. And he's a way for me to get information to you. You know, if I hypothetically learn something through methods that might not be kosher in your world."

"Assign him how?"

"Some way that I can have easy access to him. I promise I won't have him directly involved in anything that would compromise him as far as FBI rules and regs."

"Why don't I just assign him to you?"

"Neither you nor I want me to have twenty-four/seven FBI contact. I'd just have to elude it. Better if Lanny's given some flexible assignment which allows us to be in touch several times a day, or more often at my request. Think about it as a way for you to keep an eye on me."

"You may want me to keep an eye on you, Ethel." Rudy's voice was devoid of any teasing. "You think you saw a camera lens tonight. If so, then someone has pictures of you and Jesse with Clarissa. Possibly pictures of you looking at the camera. You may have moved from person of interest to loose end. And we know what these people do to loose ends."

Ethel said nothing.

—

Lieutenant General Alan Corbin pushed aside a briefing report on Russian tank deployments and rubbed his eyes. It had been a long day. First, the golf game with Hathaway, then work in his office at headquarters, and finally three hours of reading in his office at home. His wife had bid him good night an hour earlier.

He could tell from her voice she resented that he'd spent no time with her. She was used to his long hours, but this new posting had proven to be all-consuming. Encrypted phone calls and travels to the Defense Intelligence headquarters or Pentagon on a moment's notice happened day and night. He and his wife hadn't gotten away once in the six months since he'd taken on the role of director.

He'd find a way to make it up to her as soon as he could get a handle on this Supreme Court issue. Maybe he'd open a back channel to the FBI director and try to learn what Hauser might know. His instincts told him things were escalating. He slid the briefing documents into a folder. Satellite pictures could show Russian tanks. They couldn't show what was going on in a person's head.

His cell phone vibrated. He recognized the number. Senator Hathaway. The man was like a leech he couldn't shake off, and here he was calling at nearly eleven o'clock on Saturday night.

The general sighed and answered, "Corbin here."

"General, sorry to bother you."

The senator sounded out of breath. Corbin knew it wouldn't have been from running.

"What is it?"

"I've just learned Supreme Court Marshal Daniel Ventana was killed a few hours ago. Shot outside the chief justice's house."

"What?" Corbin was on his feet, his fatigue instantly swept away. He started pacing around the room. "And the chief justice?"

"Unharmed, as far as I know."

"Where'd you get your information?"

Hathaway hesitated a few seconds.

"Stuart, I can't act upon information I can't source."

"Diamond. Roger Diamond. He got the word from a Montgomery County deputy."

"Suspects?"

"No. And they don't know what happened. Just that Ventana was found shot by his vehicle. He might have been personally guarding the house, given what happened with the clerks."

"Did his source say if the FBI was on the scene?"

"No, but I'm sure they must be."

And the FBI would have sealed information tighter than a drum, he thought. He'd definitely check in with Director Hauser, now that they'd been golfing buddies for all of two holes.

"You there?" Hathaway asked.

"Yes." Corbin realized his thinking had left the senator dangling in silence, something a politician couldn't bear. "Thank you for letting me know."

"What do you think we should do?"

The general could hear a trace of panic in Hathaway's voice. And to think the man had been a Marine.

"Well, Senator, I suggest we let Director Hauser do his job."

Corbin disconnected and immediately dialed another number.

"Hello?" came the sleepy voice.

"It's Alan. What's the status of Brooke Chaplin?"

"Supposed to be coming out of the coma and able to talk sometime tomorrow."

"I feel like we're close. I don't want to stumble at the finish line."

"I'll find a way to get to her."

"Good. Sorry to have woken you, Senator."

Chapter 18

"There should be a mailbox with the name Foster somewhere along here." Jesse slowed down, keeping one eye on the country road ahead and the other on the left shoulder.

"I see it." Clarissa had moved behind Jesse on the back seat and pressed her face against the side window. "At the end of the fence."

Jesse turned onto the single lane. The white slat fence continued on either side.

"The horses are pastured on the left," he explained. "They're in the stables now. The right pasture has shorter grass for the runway and oversized barns that house a few planes, one of which Ethel flies. The road and separate fencing keep the horses clear of the airstrip."

The shadowy shapes of stables and barns appeared on either side illustrating Jesse's description. Directly ahead, they saw a large two-story farmhouse with a wraparound porch. In contrast to the unlit outbuildings, every window of the first floor glowed. Spotlights blazed from under the eaves.

"Looks like we're expected." Jesse parked near the porch and turned off the engine.

Before they could get out of the car, the front door opened and a tall, lanky man stepped outside. He wore a red flannel shirt, weathered jeans, and square-toed brown boots. His tanned face was topped with a full head of snow-white hair.

He gave a wave and walked to the edge of the porch. "Welcome!"

Max hopped up on the back seat and growled.

Clarissa stroked his side. "Friend, Max. Friend."

Jesse grabbed Clarissa's overnight bag from the front passenger seat and then opened the door for the chief justice. The dog jumped out of the car first and waited. As soon as Clarissa stepped to the ground, Max edged protectively beside her.

"Thank you for taking us in, Colonel Foster," she said.

"Please, it's Curt. And it's our privilege to have you here, Chief Justice."

"Clarissa," she said.

"Clarissa," Curt repeated. "I understand this is Max."

The German shepherd cocked his head at the sound of his name.

"Go ahead, Max," Clarissa said. "Say hello."

The dog went through his sniffing routine and then let Curt pet his neck.

"Well, come in, and I'll get you settled. Connie and I ramble around in this old farmhouse, so we've got plenty of extra bedrooms. She's upstairs. The doctor tries to keep her on a strict sleep schedule." He looked at Clarissa. "In case Jesse didn't tell you, Connie has Parkinson's."

"I'm sorry to hear that," Clarissa whispered. "We certainly don't want to interfere with her care."

Curt led them into the house. "You stay as long as necessary. Connie will be thrilled to wake up and find the chief justice under her roof. And no need to whisper. She's a little hard of hearing." He looked at the dog. "Does Max need to go out? I can walk him."

"He's good for now," Clarissa said. "Do you know what the plan is?"

"Yes. We sit tight until Ethel and Director Hauser arrive. They should be here a little before midnight." Curt smiled. "Then Ethel will tell all of us the plan."

The Tahoe pulled in behind Ethel's Infiniti at eleven forty. Curt had prepared coffee and herbal tea. No one took coffee. No one needed caffeine. Everyone was wide awake.

They sat in the den. Curt had built a small fire in the stone fireplace to combat the November chill. The rustic furniture, wide-plank floor, and large braided oval wool rug created a scene that could have been from a hundred years ago.

Jesse and Rudy sat in chairs; Ethel and Clarissa shared a sofa; and Max lay in front of the hearth.

Curt stood at one end of the mantel. "If you need me to leave because of any confidential information, just say the word. Need-to-know isn't a foreign concept to me."

Rudy waved him to an empty chair. "Thank you, but as long as we're in your house, you're part of this discussion."

Curt nodded and took the chair beside the director.

"Now, we know very little," Rudy began. "We suspect Daniel Ventana's death and the attack on Finley and Chaplin are connected, but we don't have conclusive proof. We also suspect that Ventana might have known his killer." He turned to Clarissa. "I've been authorized by the attorney general to supplant any internal investigation Ventana was conducting with one by my team. The Supreme Court police will continue with their security operations, but the investigation is to be handled by the Bureau. Do I have your cooperation, Chief Justice?"

"Yes, provided any records of court deliberations remain

confidential unless their public disclosure clearly ties into any charges that you may file."

"Of course," Rudy agreed. "And that extends to any correspondence or testimony as well. I understand you're not hearing oral arguments next week."

"That's correct."

"Good, because we'll be conducting staff interviews over the next few days."

"Everyone?"

"We'll start with everyone who was in the building this afternoon. We think the fact that your driver didn't take you home made someone curious about where you did go. They staked out your house. Ethel thought she saw a camera in a car across the street. Someone was taking photographs. Daniel Ventana must have followed you and also seen the car. From the crime scene, we think he might have known his killer. Unfortunately, we have no license plate or description other than what Ethel could make out."

"A gray or silver sedan," Ethel said. "The body style that every manufacturer offers."

"So, the stakes have risen," Rudy said. "From an attack on clerks that might have gone wrong to the cold-blooded killing of the head of one of our federal law enforcement agencies." The FBI director's eyes narrowed. "This murder will not stand, will not go unsolved."

"But the court has to carry on its constitutional responsibilities," Clarissa argued. "We can't just shut down."

"I'm getting extra protection in place for you and all the justices. But I'd like you to steer clear of public appearances for a few days, including the court building. We hope to be able to talk to Brooke Chaplin as soon as she regains consciousness. And we may have some other leads."

Rudy looked at Ethel, but she shook her head indicating that she had nothing more to add.

"And what am I supposed to do in the meantime?" Clarissa asked.

"Ethel and I discussed the benefits of your making a short video," Rudy said. "Reassurance that you and the other justices are safe. You should say something about Daniel Ventana's life of public service and your confidence that whoever did this will be brought to justice. Whatever you feel appropriate. Then the Bureau will put out a statement that you're being moved to a secure location for a few days. You and your fellow justices can work remotely like you did during the height of the COVID pandemic."

"Can that secure location be my home?"

Rudy frowned. "I don't think that's wise just yet. Ventana's death will create a steady stream of curiosity seekers driving by the house. Before last night, your residence was relatively unknown. Once the story breaks, the exterior will be shown every few minutes on cable news."

Clarissa swept her eyes across all of them. "Where then? Some safe house where Max and I can't go outside?"

Curt Foster cleared his throat. "You got horses back on your ranch in Wyoming?"

"Yes, four. I love to ride."

"I've got horses that need to be exercised. You're welcome to stay. No one knows you're here, do they?"

"Only the people in this room," Ethel said.

"I don't want to put you and your wife in danger," Clarissa said.

Curt waved her concern aside. "Nonsense. Director Hauser could discreetly bring in a couple of agents and some high-tech electronic gear for encrypted communications, including virtual conferences with the other justices. No one will be the wiser. And like Director Hauser said, it's only for a couple of days."

Ethel gave the chief justice a nod of encouragement. "The government vehicles could be hidden behind the stables and hangars," Ethel said. "If we needed a fast evacuation, we could be in the air in five minutes, or a helicopter could come in."

Clarissa said nothing, which told Ethel she had no immediate objection.

"Exactly," Curt agreed. "And you and my wife Connie are about the same size, if you don't mind wearing ranch clothes. Or maybe we could rig you up a black robe."

That comment drew a laugh and released some of the tension in the room.

"Do you need anything from your house?" Ethel turned to Rudy. "You could have an agent bring it, right?"

Clarissa reached over and petted Max. "Dog food. I can give you the brand if someone could buy it."

"Sure," Rudy said. "No problem."

"We lost our shepherd Quinn a year ago," Curt said. "I still have his food and water bowls. And Max is welcome to sleep in your room or anywhere he wants."

"So that settles it," Ethel said, trying to close the deal before the chief justice could object.

"But what about this video you want me to record? Won't that risk giving away this location?"

"No," Rudy said. "I'll film you on my phone with a neutral background and then send the video to our Quantico lab. They can alter the image to place you anywhere, even on the moon."

Clarissa gave a wistful smile. "I'd just be happy to be back in Wyoming."

Chapter 19

With Clarissa Baxter safely in the hands of Rudy and Curt, and with FBI agents on their way, Ethel and Jesse returned to Arlington. In the wee hours of the morning, traffic was practically nonexistent. Yet, even making good time, it was nearly three a.m. when Jesse pulled into Ethel's driveway.

She unsnapped her seatbelt before the car stopped. "Watch the front door from the corner of the house. I'm going in the back. If I flush someone out, don't try to intercept them."

Jesse felt his heart race as he saw Ethel pull her revolver from her handbag. "You think someone's waiting for us?"

"Someone broke in once already. We can't be surprised if we're prepared."

Jesse eased out from behind the steering wheel and followed Ethel's example of closing his door as quietly as possible. He crouched behind a boxwood growing at the front corner of the house. The thought struck him that he might be mistaken for a burglar for the second night in a row.

After a few minutes, his legs began to cramp from his awkward position. He heard no sound from inside the house and no light appeared through any window. Ethel must be going floor to floor and room to room in the dark. Finally, after what felt like an interminable length of time but, in fact, was only ten minutes, Jesse heard the front door unlatch.

"All clear," Ethel called.

Jesse stood and hurried into the house. "Any sign that someone's been here?"

"No. I think Ventana learned our address from Clarissa's driver and only came here to make sure she made it home safely. He didn't set up any other surveillance or put a search in motion."

"What do we do now?"

Ethel pointed to the front staircase. "You get some sleep. This town's going to go crazy when it wakes up in a few hours and learns the news. Hopefully, we won't be part of the story. Rudy agreed to keep us out of it."

"What are you going to do?"

"Go to bed and set my alarm for seven thirty so that I can catch Frank early. He'll have lots of questions about Ventana's death, and I want to brief him. He doesn't know it but he has his role to play." She hugged Jesse. "And so do you, double-first-cousin-twice-removed."

Ethel managed four hours of sleep before the alarm snapped her awake. Not wanting to disturb Jesse, she brewed a pot of black coffee and with her cup in one hand and cell phone in the other, descended the stairs to her RBG workout room. She bypassed the weight bench and sat at a small writing desk she kept in the far corner. With pen and paper handy in case she needed to jot down notes, she called Frank.

"Good morning, Ethel." The detective's voice sounded husky and tired.

"Are you at the hospital?"

"Yes."

"How's Brooke?"

"Conscious but too drugged to really engage in any coherent conversation. We hope by noon to be able to talk to her. I've let Detective Meadows know."

"Good. How about Senator Mulberry?"

"Mulberry? Did I tell you he showed up in her room?"

Ethel ignored the question. "He's obviously worried about her."

"Fine," Frank said dismissively. "Very admirable of him, but right now Brooke needs rest, not visitors. It'll be exhausting enough being questioned by Glenn Meadows."

"Now listen, Frank. I need you to trust me. Let the senator visit with her. Alone."

"What?"

"It will probably just be for a few minutes, but it could be important to him."

"Is there anything..." Frank struggled for the right word. "... anything improper about their relationship?"

"No. I'm sure there's not. But I need the senator's cooperation, and your doing this for him will help get it." Ethel didn't like keeping Frank in the dark, but she also wanted to keep her word to Rudy not to expose his bugging of the hospital room.

"Well, he did ask me to call him when Brooke regained consciousness."

"Perfect. See if he can come a few minutes before Glenn Meadows so that you can honestly tell him your niece hasn't spoken to the police."

"Okay. Whatever you say." He paused and then said, "I saw the news about Ventana. Is his murder tied into this?"

"I think so. And I'm doing my best to untie it."

Frank sighed. "Thanks for whatever you're doing that you're not telling me."

"Just call me after the senator's gone. I'm glad Brooke's doing better. I really am."

Ethel heard the catch in Frank's voice. "Me too, Ethel. Me too."

—

Nicole Cramerton cinched her powder-blue robe over her nightgown and put on pink fuzzy slippers. Living alone, she could dress for comfort, not fashion. She walked into the kitchen of her small one-bedroom apartment and flipped the switch to start her coffee maker. She dropped an English muffin in the toaster and retrieved a jar of fig jam and a carton of orange juice from the refrigerator. The light breakfast would carry her through until the customary after-church lunch with her brother and his family.

While she waited for the coffee to brew, she turned on CNN like she did every morning. The image on the screen showed the perpetual "BREAKING NEWS" banner. The images beneath it took her breath away. There were photos of Chief Justice Baxter and Daniel Ventana. The text crawling at the bottom read, "Supreme Court Marshal Murdered…Justices Under Heightened Security."

The toaster popped up and the coffee maker gurgled its final drops. Both were forgotten as Nicole stared at the screen. She stood frozen, not bothering to sit down. The reporter said no motive was apparent and that the crime had been committed on a public road in close proximity to the chief justice's house. She was safe and under the protection of the FBI. There was an FBI news briefing scheduled for eleven.

Nicole heard her cell phone ringing in the kitchen. *My brother,* she thought. *He knows there'll be no church or lunch for me today.* She snatched it up but didn't recognize the number. She hoped it wasn't a reporter.

"Hello?" she answered tentatively.

"Miss Cramerton, it's Stuart Hathaway."

"Yes, Senator?"

"I'm calling to make sure you heard the news."

"Yes, sir. It's awful. I just saw Mr. Ventana yesterday. First the two clerks and now this."

"You went into work yesterday?"

"Yes. The chief justice asked me to come in. She wanted to speak to the clerks' families, and I pulled up the personnel records."

"Do you know where she is now?"

"No, just what the TV news says. At a secure location. I'm thinking I should go in today in case the chief justice wants something from her office or the FBI needs help."

"That's a good idea," the senator said. "And you might want to note whatever documents if any that the agents take. I'm not sure if an interim head of the Supreme Court police has been named or is up to speed. I understand the AG has entrusted the investigation to Director Hauser. I'm confident he'll appreciate any aid you could provide."

"I'll do that, sir."

"And if I can help in any way, call this number. It's my private cell. I'd appreciate your keeping me informed."

"Yes, sir."

"Nicole, we miss you in the halls of the Senate. I miss you. Maybe when this is cleared up, you'd consider returning to the Hill. I'd love to have you on my staff."

"That's very kind. I'll certainly keep it in mind. And thank you for your concern."

"You're welcome, dear. Take care now." He disconnected.

Nicole's dismay over Daniel Ventana's death eased a little. She was flattered by the attention of a powerful senator. Then she wondered how he'd gotten her private number. The thought quickly faded. He was the chair of the Senate Intelligence Committee.

—

Ethel heard the patter of footsteps overhead. Jesse was probably getting coffee and maybe scrounging around for breakfast. She picked up the sheet of paper with the list she'd compiled and hurried up the stairs. They would discuss his assignment over scrambled eggs and sausages.

She found him standing in front of the television, a mug of coffee halfway to his lips.

"What's the press saying?" Ethel asked.

"That Ventana might have stopped someone suspicious and been shot. They don't know whether it was a specific attack on the chief justice or Ventana interrupted a break-in at the neighboring house. The family was out of town for the weekend."

"What are they reporting about Clarissa?"

"That she was never in any immediate danger, but as a precaution, all nine justices will be issued extra protection until the investigation can determine the nature of the attack. The justices will be working through teleconferencing until the FBI is satisfied it's safe for public appearances."

The TV showed footage of the exterior of Clarissa's house in Maryland. A group of curious onlookers stood behind sawhorse barricades that had been erected by law enforcement. The red "BREAKING NEWS" banner swirled across the screen and the excited reporter announced a video of Chief Justice Baxter had just been released by the FBI. Then Clarissa appeared.

Ethel had watched Rudy record the message last night, but she was surprised at how the image had been cleverly doctored. Instead of a wall in the Fosters' den, a bay window appeared behind the chief justice. Through it could be seen a landscape more appropriate to Wyoming than Virginia. The crests of the distant ridges of a mountain range were highlighted with the golden light from the rising sun. Ethel appreciated the created impression that Clarissa was safely in her native state where dawn was arriving two hours later than Eastern Time.

Clarissa spoke strongly and boldly. She emphasized that she and the other justices were safe and that they were following the precautions recommended by the FBI. She went on to praise Daniel Ventana and condemn those who had murdered him. She then closed with the forceful words, "If anyone thinks they can impede or influence the workings of this court, they are mistaken. We are sworn to defend our great Constitution and nothing will prevent us from fulfilling our role to administer justice fairly and impartially on behalf of the American people." Her steely resolve came through the screen and left no doubt she was a woman who would not be intimidated.

The network returned to the news studio where pundits had been hastily gathered to pontificate between commercials.

"Turn it off," Ethel said. "We've nothing to learn from them. I'll fix us eggs and sausages, and then we'll lay out our battle plan."

Twenty minutes later, the two of them huddled together on the sofa with notes and legal pads lying on the coffee table in front of them.

Ethel picked up the list she'd made in the workout room. "Where are we on funds to buy Lithium USA stock?"

"I've prepared an order to route cash from the offshore account into U.S. banks. I'll keep the transactions under ten thousand each, capping our total investment at fifty thousand."

"That's spread across how many accounts?"

"Six. The ones I set up several months ago when we decided to keep the Bitcoin stash we uncovered."

"Our do-gooder money," Ethel said. "Lord help us if that little indiscretion becomes public. Not even Rudy could protect us then."

"I've shielded the source as deeply as I can, and no one's going to be looking for something that they don't know exists."

"And the actual stock transactions?" Ethel asked.

"I've opened a trading account for you. I'll make the buys tomorrow when the market opens."

"And when I show up at the Progressive Mining Coalition conference on Wednesday?"

"You'll have an electronic receipt and a printout of your Lithium USA shareholdings as physical evidence of ownership. But I don't know if that will get you admitted into the conference. I just hope they don't give you any trouble."

Ethel waved his concern aside. "Do you think a prestigious lobbying firm like Crane and Weston wants to be seen throwing a little old lady out of the Mandarin Oriental Hotel? A little old lady with a cane and a limp?"

Jesse smiled. "I'd like to see them try."

Chapter 20

Roger Diamond parked his Mercedes sedan in his coveted reserved space in the small lot behind Crane and Weston's K Street office building. His was the only vehicle, and he doubted anyone else would be coming in on a Sunday morning.

Daniel Ventana's death made it look to the world as if someone was launching an assault against the Supreme Court. However, his concern was more self-serving. With the Progressive Mining Coalition conference only three days away, he didn't want to deal with the uncertainty of when a ruling might be made on the Lithium USA case. The justices had heard the oral arguments last week, and they should have taken at least a preliminary vote Friday. The administration had petitioned for an expedited ruling, but now with the FBI controlling the murder investigation, everything would be pushed back, which meant the internal squabbling within the mining coalition could become more public. There was no love lost between the brine extractors and the open-pit contingent who were trying to protect their federal leases. Diamond wondered if the schism was irreparable and whether the coalition he'd worked so carefully to create was on the verge of disintegrating—not because he gave a damn about climate change and electric vehicles but because the trade organization poured money into Crane and Weston and therefore into his seven-figure bonus.

His plan for the morning was to review the conference's agenda and rewrite his own welcoming remarks and speaker introductions to avoid getting caught up in debating the Supreme Court case. He'd have to acknowledge it and ask the members to project their unified support for the authority of the Department of the Interior and Bureau of Land Management to lease public lands. He hoped his appeal would rein in those companies using less toxic mining methods that might look for an opportunity to take a holier-than-thou posture. They had to understand federal leases were in everyone's interest—except maybe the ranchers' and the Indians'.

And Diamond thought he had a way to lessen their opposition. He was working behind the scenes to get his member companies to commit to substantial financial payouts to the native tribes, hoping to split them from the ranchers' interests. Then he'd lobby for rancher relief from the federal government so that all the burden didn't fall on the mining coalition. Subsidies historically silenced objections. He had Senator Hathaway in his back pocket to put forth a bill that would address that component.

But all his strategy and tactics would go for naught if the Supreme Court ruled against the government. That's why he needed the ear of Lieutenant General Alan Corbin.

It was true, he thought. *Sometimes the best offense is a good defense.*

Ethel nodded her approval. "You've done a good job setting up the transactions, Jesse. We'll dump the stock as soon as we can and send the money back offshore."

"What now?"

"Did you book two rooms for Tuesday and Wednesday nights at the Mandarin Oriental?"

"Yes. Actually, two suites, since you're supposed to be a wealthy shareholder."

"Excellent. Tomorrow, I'll want to scope out the hotel and look for entrances and exits that exist in addition to the front lobby. That whole section of the wharf around Maine Avenue has changed dramatically since my father and I used to buy fish right off the boats. I need to get my bearings."

"Can I go with you?"

"Maybe to drive me to the hotel. You can come back here or go to class. I'll probably be a couple hours."

"Surely I can do something," he argued.

"You can." Ethel reached for the legal pad Jesse discovered in Brooke's room. "I need you to find out who heads the coalitions for the Native Americans and the ranchers and farmers. I want not only names but ways to contact them today." She gathered up the rest of her papers. "Show me how good your computer skills are."

Jesse's face brightened. "Challenge accepted. Can Tracy help? She's an even better hacker than I am. We're supposed to Skype at ten our time."

Ethel knew Jesse's girlfriend, Tracy Lorton, was a grad student at the London School of Economics. Her field of study was cryptocurrency and its impact on global economies, particularly crypto-accounts used to hide money obtained through criminal activities. Although Ethel had only met Tracy virtually, she didn't doubt the young woman's brilliance and suspected her research meant she had the ability to navigate the dark web.

"All right," Ethel agreed. "Bring her up to speed and warn her to be careful. I don't want you or her to hit any trip wires that could lead back to us." Ethel paused as a thought struck her. "Can you or Tracy set up our own trip wires in case someone starts to investigate us?"

"I think so. Tracy's probably the best one to create those safeguards."

"Then try to reach her before ten. I need those contact names and numbers ASAP."

"What are you going to tell them?"

"That the Mandarin Oriental is certainly worth seeing."

"Especially on Wednesdays," Jesse added with a devilish grin.

Ethel stood up. "Thank Tracy for me. Now I'm going to work out, shower, and be ready to go to the hospital as soon as Frank calls."

She changed into sweats and went down to the exercise room. It was nearly nine, late enough to call Rudy wherever he was.

The FBI director answered on the first ring. "Ethel, I can't talk long. We're getting ready for a press conference."

"Any progress?"

"Not really. Our team in the Supreme Court building is going through Ventana's office. Tech people are reviewing his computer entries for any leads."

"Excellent job with Clarissa's video," Ethel said.

"Thanks. I hope it creates the impression that she's been flown to Wyoming."

"How's she holding up?"

"She was sleeping when I left, which is a good sign. I'm inclined to keep her at the farm rather than move her to an interim location. I've also spoken with your FBI boarder, Lanny Childress. He's now on special assignment for me."

"Which means what?"

"Continuing to work on domestic terrorism, only remotely from your home. Is that okay?"

"Yes," Ethel said. "Domestic terrorism might be what we're dealing with."

"Childress should be there this afternoon. Now if that's it, I've really got to go."

"Just one more thing, Rudy."

He sighed. "Let me guess. A certain medical monitoring device."

"Yes. I'm coming to the hospital in a few hours. I think it will have served its usefulness by then."

"Do I want to know the contents?"

"I think plausible deniability is your phrase of the day. Is your agent at the door aware of the situation?"

"Only where the micro-recorder is located. He was told we were using the voice-activated device in case Brooke said something while coming out of the coma that she couldn't recall later."

"That's almost believable, Rudy. I'm impressed. Will he give it to me or did you have another plan?"

"Actually, when you say the word, I'll have Childress pick it up and bring it to your house. He knows you and that you're retired FBI. And he lives there. The only handoff at the hospital will be agent to agent."

"Excellent. You're wasted behind a desk. You should be back in the field."

"Where the hell do you think I've been the last thirty-six hours?"

"Doing your job and doing it very well. A heads-up. When I call you back, it won't be from this phone. I've got a burner, as they say."

"A burner? Geez, Ethel. Why can't you take up knitting?"

—

Jesse used WhatsApp to send a short, encrypted note to Tracy in London:

–Skype ASAP. The game's afoot.

He knew the Sherlock Holmes quote would elicit a rapid response. When they'd met as undergrads at Berkeley, they quickly discovered their computer science major wasn't the only thing they had in common. A mutual love of the great detective had sealed the deal.

In less than two minutes, Jesse's laptop chimed with an incoming call. He connected, and Tracy's face filled the screen. Her blond hair was tucked under a Washington Nationals ball cap and her pale skin had the sheen of perspiration.

She flashed a warm smile. "Hey, cutie. If the game's afoot, can I lend a hand?"

Jesse paused a beat before speaking, and Tracy read the seriousness of his expression.

"What?" she asked, immediately losing the smile.

"I guess it hasn't made the news there, but last night the head of the Supreme Court police was shot and killed outside the home of the chief justice."

"That's terrible. I haven't seen any news today, and I just got back from a run. Has someone been arrested?"

"No. And this is where you and I come in. Ethel's on the case."

Tracy's eyes widened. "Why?"

"Because we were at Chief Justice Baxter's house when it happened. I had to drive her to a secure location. But that's only half of it. A Supreme Court law clerk was killed the night before last. He was with Brooke Chaplin, the woman who rents a room here. She's been in a coma, and Ethel is taking matters into her own hands."

"And our hands as well," Tracy said. "You'd better give me the whole story since I'm going to be part of it."

Jesse recounted everything from the Friday night lock-picking fiasco to the assignments Ethel had given him that morning.

Tracy listened without interrupting. When Jesse had finished, she said, "I'll work on setting up Ethel's trip wires and maybe expand them to include you and Detective Mancini. I suggest you let me take control of your and Ethel's computers to strengthen their firewalls."

"Maybe you should monitor for anyone seeking data on you," Jesse said. "We don't know how deep this conspiracy goes."

"I will." Tracy pointed her finger at Jesse. "Your priority is to get the contact numbers Ethel wants. Let me take a deep dive on the others. We have to assume they have their own trip wires, and I am, shall we say, more subtle in my approach."

"You're saying I'm more like the bull in the china shop?"

"More like the bull who gets skewered by the matador. Jesse, the last time you helped Ethel, you were nearly killed. Please don't make me fly back for your funeral."

Chapter 21

Senator Joseph Mulberry entered the small hospital conference room where Detective Frank Mancini and his sister, Susan, were waiting. He wore his obligatory congressional uniform: blue pinstripe suit, white shirt, red tie, and U.S. flag lapel pin.

Susan and Frank stood up to shake the senator's proffered hand. *He may have come from church,* Frank thought. *Or he might sleep in those clothes.*

"Thank you for calling me," Mulberry said. "So glad to hear Brooke's regained consciousness."

"You're kind to be concerned," Susan said.

"Has she said anything about what happened?"

Frank shook his head. "She's disoriented. The doctors say that's normal after a traumatic head injury. Detective Glenn Meadows of the DC Police is coming by later this afternoon. We thought if you wanted to see her briefly, it would be better to come early so that she can rest before the police interview."

"Yes," the senator agreed. "I promise I won't stay but a minute or two." He paused, uncertain what else to say.

Frank didn't know why Ethel wanted Mulberry to talk to Brooke alone, but his cop radar picked up the senator's discomfort. He decided he'd establish his own channel with the man. "Detective Meadows has extended the courtesy of allowing me to sit in," Frank said. "If we learn anything, I'll share what I can."

"Thank you." Mulberry stepped closer to them as if buttonholing one of his colleagues. He lowered his voice, even though they were alone. "This business with the murder of the Supreme Court marshal is very disturbing, especially in light of the attack on Brooke."

"You think they're connected?" Frank asked.

"You tell me. You're the detective."

Frank gave the senator a hard stare. "I think we don't know what we don't know."

Mulberry nodded. "Aptly put. We're missing something, and it might take a Congressional hearing to determine what."

With that comment, the senator left.

"He seems nice," Susan said.

"Yeah, he seems nice." Frank pulled out his cell phone and texted:

> Mulberry talking to Brooke now. Alone.

He pressed send and waited for Ethel's response. What did she know that the rest of them didn't?

Ethel was drying her hair after her shower when the single chime alerted her that a text had arrived on her smartphone. She read Frank's message and wrote the one-word reply:

> Received.

Then she dialed Rudy on her burner. The call went to voicemail. She left a message. "I guess you're still in your press conference. When you can, instruct Lanny Childress to pick up that item I need and bring it to Jesse."

She dressed and then sat on the edge of her bed, thinking about her next move. More money may need to be wired but only as a last resort. She'd know more after her phone calls. She glanced at her watch. Close to noon. She hoped Jesse was making progress. She hated waiting, but there was nothing she could do at the moment. Correction. She could pack and have Jesse do the same. They might need to leave on a moment's notice. At some point, someone was going to be very unhappy with her.

—

"Henry Birdsong seems to be the name that occurs most frequently in the Native American Coalition's social media posts." Jesse handed Ethel a printout of screen captures supporting his claim.

The two sat at the kitchen table going over Jesse's findings while eating a lunch of tuna salad sandwiches and chips.

"And that gave you his cell number?"

"That got me to public records that included the tribal enrollments of the Fort McDermit Paiute and Shoshone Indian Reservation. It spans the Nevada-Oregon border and will be directly impacted by the open-pit mine. Once I had Birdsong's name and residence I just kept digging until I found a document containing his mobile number. It's a Nevada area code."

Ethel nodded her approval and picked up another sheet of paper. "And Bud Carson? Did you find him the same way?"

"Basically. His ranch borders the federal land. He was outspoken in his Facebook postings and organized several protests blocking the roads going into the mine. He also showed up at

Senator Hathaway's town halls. The same town halls where Birdsong and other Indians voiced their concerns. It's logical to assume they know each other."

"And can coordinate their efforts," Ethel said. "Good work. I'll start with the two of them." She set the papers aside.

"What do I do next?" Jesse asked.

"Finish your lunch. Then wait for Lanny to bring you the recording that I hope captured Senator Mulberry. Don't tell Lanny what it is or allow him to listen to it. I'm anxious for Frank to tell me what Brooke says and see if there are inconsistencies in her story. Then, when she's feeling a little stronger, I'll ask her about the diary. I'm not going to tell her you read it. She'll be embarrassed enough talking to me. And I can use it as leverage. Promise to keep it just between the two of us if I think she's telling the truth."

"And if you think she's hiding something?"

"Then it goes to Rudy and Detective Meadows."

"Who do you think stole her laptop?" Jesse asked.

"Maybe the same person who photographed us entering Clarissa's gate and killed Ventana. Maybe someone completely different. Right now I think we're facing multiple agendas. We need to sort out who's who, and we'll do that by shaking the tree and seeing what tumbles out."

Agent Lanny Childress flashed his FBI credentials as he intercepted a nurse about to tap her badge against the entry pad to the locked ICU.

"Excuse me, ma'am. I need to speak with my colleague guarding Brooke Chaplin. Could you escort me there?"

The nurse looked up at the tall, freckle-faced man. He

appeared more like an Iowa farm boy with his carrot-colored hair, husky build, and winsome smile. He couldn't be out of the training academy more than a few months, she thought. And the way he said, "ma'am." His politeness had the effect of making the thirty-five-year-old RN feel like a grandmother.

"Certainly, sir." She pressed her badge against the pad and the automatic doors swung open. "Follow me."

Lanny didn't recognize the agent sitting outside Brooke's room, so he showed his shield and introduced himself.

"I'm Childress. Director Hauser said you have something for me."

The other agent stood, reached inside his suit coat pocket, and pulled out a small blank envelope. There was no name or address.

Lanny frowned. "Is this it?"

"My instructions are to give you the card, not the device. It's a microSD." The agent looked back into the room. "Who is she? Surely not just a law clerk."

Lanny took his first look at Brooke and felt sick to his stomach. She lay on her back with an IV drip in each arm and a half-full bag of urine hanging from a side rail. The only sound was the steady beep of a monitor.

A bandage encircled her head down to her eyebrows. Her face was swollen and discolored. Director Hauser had told him she'd been struck from behind, but she must have fallen forward and hit either the floor or a piece of furniture. Her eyes were closed, and he hoped she was sleeping. He was glad she couldn't see him. See how upset he was. He liked her. Liked her a lot.

"I mean even a U.S. senator came to see her. Is she some star witness?"

Lanny realized he'd zoned out. "Maybe," he said. "You know

as much as I do. Like my dad always tells me, 'Don't worry that the mule's blind, just load the wagon.'"

The other agent stared at him. "Huh?"

—

Ethel took her regular cell phone, the new burner, and Jesse's research printout down to her desk in the RBG workout room. She sat for a few moments weighing the best approach. Both men would be getting her call out of the blue. Her name would mean nothing to them, but mentioning the court case should pique their curiosity. Ethel was confident that all she needed was a chance to pitch her idea. They would either see the value or they wouldn't. And there was always the old trick of telling each of them that the other was on board whether it was true or not.

She decided since she was giving them her real name, she should use her regular smartphone. Most likely her call would go to voicemail anyway and she'd have to wait on a return call.

Henry Birdsong's number went straight to voicemail. *The two-hour time difference,* Ethel thought. *Maybe he was in church with his phone off.*

"You've reached Henry Birdsong. Leave a message." The short statement was over tweeting birds. Cute. Ethel waited for the beep.

"Mr. Birdsong. My name is Ethel Crestwater. I'm calling from Washington DC about the Lithium USA case. It's urgent that I speak with you." She left her number and reiterated the request to return her call as soon as he could.

Bud Carson's phone rang longer but eventually went to voicemail as well. No birds. No cows mooing. Just the succinct words, "It's Bud. If I don't owe you money, I'll call you back." Funny, and probably true. Ethel changed her pitch. "Mr. Carson. My name is Ethel Crestwater. I'm concerned about the Lithium USA open-pit mine. You don't owe me money, but I may have some for you if it will help your cause. But we have to act quickly." Again, she left her cell number and the request for an immediate response.

The lure of money netted the first reply. Bud Carson must have been screening his calls because Ethel saw his number flash on her screen after barely the length of time it would have taken him to listen to her message.

"Mr. Carson, thanks for calling back. I know I sounded like some sort of scam, and I won't assure you I'm not because that's the first thing a scam artist would do."

Ethel heard a deep throaty laugh, and then Carson said, "Well, darlin', at least you're up front about it. So, what's this about?"

"I'm in Washington, DC. Actually Arlington, to be exact. I've followed your case because I have ties to a law clerk at the Supreme Court. She's above reproach, and I have no inside information on how your ruling might go. I do think your arguments have merit, and I'd like to arrange a more, shall we say, high-profile opportunity to get those arguments in front of the public."

"Are you with some nonprofit activist group?"

"No. I'm a seventy-five-year-old woman unafraid to shake things up if I feel a mind to."

He laughed again. "Then tell me what's on that mind of yours."

Ethel felt her cell phone vibrate with a second incoming call. She checked the screen. "Can you hang on? Henry Birdsong's calling, and I'll tie him in."

"Birdsong? Well, if he's involved, then you've got my attention."

Thirty minutes later, Ethel concluded the impromptu

conference call with the promise to send both men funds to accomplish their roles. She left the logistical arrangements to them, and they agreed to keep her name out of it. The finer details would be solidified after she gathered more information.

She returned to the kitchen and put on the kettle for an early afternoon cup of tea. While the water heated, she updated her list of tasks, including the need for Jesse to pull more funds from the offshore account. Henry Birdsong and Bud Carson needed to see the promised money hit their bank accounts first thing in the morning if she wanted them to have confidence in her plan. Confidence. She was the one taking a shot in the dark with no guarantee that anything would come of it.

And even worse, she had no confidence that she could predict where that shot might ricochet.

Chapter 22

Clarissa Baxter watched as Curt Foster brought two saddled mares out of the stable and into the paddock. The magnificent animals pawed the ground, anxious to stretch their powerful legs.

"Come take your pick," Curt said. "Crystal here is a little more spirited." He patted the dapple-gray horse on the neck. "Suzy Q is a homebody and will take it on her own to head to the barn." The roan horse whinnied and shook her head. Curt laughed. "She knows I'm talking about her."

Clarissa looked at the FBI agent standing beside her. "What do you think, Ed? You're the one in the suit." She pointed at her own outfit of jeans and windbreaker she'd borrowed from Curt's wife.

"I'm good with Crystal. The Bureau didn't train me to ride a horse for nothing."

When Curt had offered Clarissa a chance to ride, Ed Tucker, one of the two agents guarding the chief justice, announced that when he'd had a posting to Nevada, he'd been issued a horse instead of a car. Since Clarissa couldn't be without FBI protection, Ed was the logical choice.

"Sorry I'm a foot taller," Curt said. "If you wore my jeans, you'd have to roll them up to your knees."

Clarissa swung easily into the saddle. Max gave a bark of encouragement and ran to the gate. Neither horse shied at his antics.

"Max looks like he's been around horses before," Curt said.

"Oh, yeah. My late husband and Max would be out on the range for hours. I hope Max doesn't make the horses skittish."

"They don't spook easily," Curt assured her. "If you want to give them their heads, I suggest the main pasture."

"Staying out of sight of the road," Ed Tucker insisted.

"Right." Curt pointed to the tree line behind the farmhouse. "There's also a half-mile trail that loops through the woods. Connie preferred riding through the forest in the early morning. She really misses it."

"The trail works for me," Clarissa said. "If that's all right with you, Ed."

"Lead on, Your Honor." He looked down at his fellow agent leaning against a fencepost. "I'm leaving you in charge, Logan. Don't let anybody sneak up behind us."

"Not to worry. If they do manage to get by me, they'll still be confused as to which is your ass and which is the horse's. The chief justice and Suzy Q can easily make their escape."

"Gentlemen," Clarissa said with mocking rebuke. "Such language in front of our host."

"Yes, I'm appalled," Curt said. "Me, a sheltered Air Force veteran having to hear such talk."

"Sorry, sir," Logan said. "If I'd known you were Air Force, I'd have cleaned up my vocabulary. And also used simpler words."

Clarissa laughed and gave Suzy Q a gentle kick in the ribs. "Come on, girl. Let's go before the manure gets spread any deeper."

—

Ethel unzipped the hanging bag in her bedroom closet. The pantsuit inside still had the dry cleaner's ticket attached. She couldn't remember the last time she'd worn it, but she was glad she'd had it cleaned and pressed. It was her last dark blue pinstripe that she'd worn as an active agent. She'd gained no weight so she was confident it would fit, and it was appropriate attire for the Mandarin Oriental Hotel.

She zipped the bag closed, started to shut the closet door, and then paused. She looked up to the top shelf and decided to take a few moments with her memories. Unfolding a small stepladder, she climbed three steps to reach the brown leather-bound scrapbook lying on its side. She sat on the bed and opened it in her lap. It was the kind with protective plastic sleeves and a binder that allowed pages to be added. Over the years, she'd added many.

Black-and-white pictures filled the first page. The oldest showed her and her father. He wore a double-breasted pinstripe suit. She was in a frilly dress and bonnet that her aunt had picked out. The date penciled in the photo's white border read, "Easter—1949." She was two. The motherless child of the family. They'd gone out to the cemetery after church. Although she didn't remember that specific trip, she remembered the other times. The headstone had been scary. Her mother's name was her name. Her mother's death date was her birth date. She and her father always celebrated her birthday one day early.

Ethel turned pages that turned the years. Her favorite picture showed her and her father standing in front of the little single-wing Cessna 195, vintage 1951, but fourteen years old at the time. She was eighteen and had just flown solo. The broad smiles of both father and daughter summed up the joy of the moment.

Ethel flipped through the decades of faces of those who had roomed in her house. She stopped at Frank Mancini and smiled to see his waist thinner and his hair thicker. Next to him was a photo of Rudy Hauser, a young man whose ambition would carry him all the way to the top of the FBI but never break the bond between Ethel and him. The last page had only one photo slid underneath the clear plastic cover. Jesse proudly showing off the lockpicks she'd given him. Some families pass down china or silver. Not Ethel. She made a mental note to add a photograph of Brooke. Maybe Brooke and her uncle Frank together.

She returned to the photo of her with her father and the old Cessna. Two years later, he would be murdered, betrayed by a fellow agent. Ethel would track him down. She would kill him. In self-defense. Or so J. Edgar Hoover would write in the file.

She ran her fingers over the photo. Her father's death was as real to her as the book in her hand. So was the code he lived by. He'd drilled it into her. Integrity, fairness, justice. They were not just words to him. They were not just words to Ethel. And she knew they were not just words to Chief Justice Clarissa Baxter and the U.S. Supreme Court.

But now someone had assaulted that code and undermined the principles upholding it. The attack wasn't just on Brooke, and the tragic murders of Robert Finley and Daniel Ventana weren't isolated to them. The threat went to the very foundations of the country's ideals. Her father wouldn't have stood for it. Ruth Bader Ginsberg wouldn't have stood for it. And, by God, neither would Ethel Fiona Crestwater, even if it meant breaking a few laws to protect the law.

Her cell phone vibrated. Frank. She set the scrapbook and the memories aside.

"What's the word?" she asked.

"Amnesia. Specifically localized amnesia."

"Did Detective Meadows question her?"

"Yes. But I was there as a familiar, calming face. Glenn was gentle with her. Brooke remembers playing basketball with Finley. Then she woke up in the hospital. Evidently, Senator Mulberry had broken the news of Finley's death. She took it hard."

"Did she say anything about what was in Finley's backpack?"

"No. Then the doctor came in and told us to let her rest. She's being moved into a regular room later this afternoon where visitation restrictions will be looser. Glenn's left it with me for any follow-up questioning. He'll come back if she remembers something of significance."

Ethel stood up, thinking better on her feet. "And the doctor's prognosis on the amnesia?"

"He said it's not uncommon in victims of physical trauma. The loss is localized to the window of time around the event. He expects her memory will clear up in a few days, although the moments of the actual assault might stay forgotten."

"That could be a blessing, Frank. And I think we have a good idea what happened. Our fake homeless man, Ronald Drake, attacked them from behind. I'm more interested in what transpired between Brooke and Finley during the time between when they left the Supreme Court to when they entered Finley's front door."

"Well, we'll just have to wait," Frank said.

"I'd like to see her, if that's all right with you and your sister."

"I'm sure Susan won't mind."

"Maybe this evening?" Ethel pressed. "Let you and Susan take a dinner break."

"So, you can talk to her alone," Frank said.

"Brooke and I have a good relationship. Maybe there are some things she'll tell me that she wouldn't share with her mom or her uncle. I don't know what those things would be, Frank, but I'm just asking for the chance to engage her in a conversation and see if it leads anywhere."

Ethel heard only silence for a few seconds. She added, "And if she has nothing to say, then I promise I won't turn it into an interrogation."

"Okay." Frank agreed. "I guess it can't hurt. Why don't you come around six? I'll tell Susan I asked you to visit while we take a break for dinner in the cafeteria."

"Thank you. I'm anxious to see her."

"She looks up to you, Ethel. Remember that." He disconnected.

Ethel replaced the scrapbook on the upper shelf and folded up the stepladder. She heard footsteps from the front of the house and then Jesse's voice.

"Did you get to see her?"

"Just through glass windows in the ICU."

Ethel found them in the living room and Lanny Childress turned to face her.

"She looked pretty beat up," he told Ethel. "But she's out of danger."

"I just spoke with Frank Mancini," Ethel said. "Brooke has no memory of the attack. The doctors say that's not unusual. Like you said, the good news is she's out of danger."

Ethel saw Lanny's eyes moisten. She knew the young agent had a crush on Brooke.

"Any suspects?" he asked.

"One who was killed shortly after the attack." She gestured to a chair. "Sit down. I'll bring you up to date."

Ethel carefully limited her information to what the DC police and FBI had said publicly. She didn't mention Brooke's diary, her stolen computer, or the location of Chief Justice Baxter. She offered no speculation about the motive for either the attack on

Brooke and Finley or the murder of Ventana. She ended by telling Lanny and Jesse she planned to see Brooke that evening and perhaps learn something helpful to the investigation.

During her summation, Lanny sat quietly without interrupting. When she'd finished, he leaned forward in his chair and spoke barely above a whisper. "Director Hauser has asked me to work remotely from here on my current assignment. He said he wants a direct link so that you can share information." The agent frowned. "But I'm not to be involved in whatever you might be doing on your own. He said I was need-to-know only."

Ethel gave him a reassuring smile. "Director Hauser doesn't forget loyalty. And he doesn't compromise his agents. You can trust him to have your back."

Lanny nodded. "I know. He said the same thing about you." He reached into his pocket and pulled out the blank envelope from the hospital. "I was instructed to give you this." He leaned across the coffee table and handed it to Ethel.

"Thank you." She passed it to Jesse. "You know what to do."

Chapter 23

When it became obvious that Ethel and Jesse weren't going to comment on whatever was in the envelope, Lanny said he needed to set up his secure FBI laptop in his room.

Jesse waited until he heard the large man's footsteps overhead before saying anything. "I'm glad he's at the opposite end of the hall from me. Still, I should probably listen through earbuds."

Ethel pointed to the envelope. "Let's see what we have first."

Jesse tore open the sealed flap and dumped a single microSD card into his palm. "Good. I have an adapter and a card reader that will work." He held it up for a closer look. "Surely they wouldn't have encrypted the data or recorded it with some special software. I'll know when I view the file structure."

Ethel stood up. "Bring your laptop down to the workout room. We'll check it together."

As Jesse carried his laptop down the stairs, Ethel moved the straight-backed chair from the small desk and placed it facing the weight bench. "Put your computer in the seat, and we'll share the bench."

They sat side by side and Jesse pushed the card reader into a USB port. Almost immediately, the data card's icon appeared on the computer's desktop. Jesse double-clicked to open it. A string of files populated the screen.

"MP3 files," Jesse said. "They should open with a simple audio program. They're not very big, but there are a lot of them."

"Voice-activated. I'm sure today's technology meant the actual device was minuscule but we had voice-activated recordings back in my day. Saves data storage and battery life. Check the larger files first when it was probably more than a nurse checking on Brooke."

Jesse scrolled through the list and stopped at one that was several megabytes larger than the others. He opened it and heard the first word slightly clipped. "Honey, it's Mom. I don't know whether you can hear me—"

"That's enough," Ethel interjected. "Senator Mulberry wouldn't have been in the room with a family member. Try another one."

It took four more attempts as they skipped through the voices of Frank, a nurse supervisor at shift change, and a doctor softly calling Brooke's name. A faint response sounded.

"She's out of the coma," Ethel said. "Keep it playing."

The doctor started asking her some simple questions—name, age, birthday, any pains. Although Brooke's voice was weak, the doctor seemed pleased with her answers. Her strongest statement was a question. "How's Robert?"

The doctor hesitated a beat. Then he said, "He's not under my care. I'll have someone else update you. For right now, you need to rest." The clip ended.

The next audio file started with a gravelly whisper. "Brooke, can you hear me? It's Senator Mulberry."

"Turn it up," Ethel ordered. "This is it."

"Brooke, I'm so sorry."

"Senator? What happened?"

"Someone attacked you at Robert Finley's house. Don't you remember?"

"We were playing basketball. Where's Robert?"

Like the doctor before him, Mulberry hesitated, although he had no way to evade her question. "I'm afraid he didn't make it, dear."

For the next few minutes, all Jesse and Ethel heard were muffled sobs so low that it was a wonder the recording device didn't shut off. Finally, Brooke said, "We were playing basketball. That's all I remember."

"Nothing he might have said about the chief justice's position?"

"No. I planned to ask him after the game. And then tell you if there was any news. Is the general upset?"

"The general," Ethel muttered to herself. "Corbin?"

"He's upset you were hurt," Mulberry said. "He's upset with me for getting you involved. But he's determined to press forward. So, I need to ask you not to say anything about our project to anyone. I don't think the police have reason to look beyond your being in the wrong place at the wrong time."

"Is that what it was?" Brooke asked.

"I sure hope so. Now you rest and don't worry. You have a new assignment."

"What's that?"

"Get better."

For another moment, the only sound was the beep of a monitor and then the clip ended.

Jesse moved the cursor over the next file. "More?"

"Yes," Ethel said. "Just to check there wasn't a break in the recording."

The next clip started with the voice of a nurse. "She's

sleeping." A second nurse spoke. "Then we'll change the head dressing when she wakes up again."

"So, that's it," Jesse said. "The last file. Someone must have removed the device after that."

"What do you think?"

Jesse closed the laptop. "It sounds like Senator Mulberry was getting inside information on the court deliberations. And a general who could be Corbin is involved somehow. Did I miss something else?"

"Maybe you missed what was missing," Ethel said.

"What do you mean?"

"Senator Mulberry didn't tell Brooke about Daniel Ventana's murder. Either Mulberry was trying to spare her more grief, or Ventana wasn't part of whatever the senator's up to."

"Which is it?"

"I don't know," Ethel said. "It could be both." She pointed to the card reader still plugged into the computer. "Back that file up and hide it somewhere separate. We can tie Mulberry's statements with the entries in Brooke's diary. I'm going to the hospital tonight. It's time for a little Sunday night come-to-Jesus."

Jesse stood up and took a step back. "She's barely out of surgery."

"And Daniel Ventana's dead and Clarissa Baxter's in hiding. But I won't be browbeating her. Give me credit for a little compassion."

Jesse reddened. "Sorry. What can I do?"

Ethel looked up to the ceiling. "Take Lanny out and treat him to pizza and beer. He's hurting and he's been helpful. When I get back, we'll finalize our plans for tomorrow."

—

When Ethel checked in at the hospital reception desk, she discovered Frank had given her name as the patient's aunt. Since Brooke was no longer in ICU, Ethel was cleared to go straight to the room. She stopped at the nurses' station, introduced herself, and was told that Brooke was resting comfortably. Ethel was welcome to sit by the patient's bedside, but to be aware Brooke might be asleep for several hours.

A man sat in a chair just outside the room. His blue suit shouted FBI as much as a white coat shouted doctor. He studied her as she walked closer.

"Special Agent. I'm Ethel Crestwater here to see Miss Chaplin."

He quickly got to his feet. The way his wide eyes moved over her told Ethel he'd heard the stories. Here was the woman who tracked down and killed her father's murderer. The woman who solved a crime that J. Edgar Hoover and his top G-men couldn't. There were benefits to being a legend.

"Yes, ma'am. I'm Randall Pressley. Director Hauser said you might be stopping by. Everything's been quiet since she was moved."

Ethel started to step by him to open the door.

He extended his arm, blocking her entry. "I'm sorry, ma'am. I need to see a photo ID."

"Yes, you certainly do, Agent Pressley. Thank you for your diligence." She pulled her wallet out of her handbag and handed him her driver's license. "You should also check the contents of my bag."

The man didn't argue and practically turned the lining inside out.

When he was satisfied, he returned her handbag and opened the door. "Go ahead, Miss Crestwater. I'll be right here if you need me."

Ethel thanked him, stepped over the threshold, and closed the door behind her. She scanned the room before entering any farther.

The head of the bed was elevated about thirty degrees so that the young woman wasn't lying flat on her back. As the nurse had said, Brooke seemed to be resting peacefully. Her breathing was steady and the monitor measuring her vital signs beeped its soft tone with reassuring regularity. A single IV drip was inserted into the back of her hand, and Ethel didn't know if the bag hanging from the adjacent stand was a simple saline solution or a concoction of nutrients or antibiotics. Whatever the medical treatment, Ethel was heartened to see a little color in Brooke's cheeks.

There were two chairs in the room. The larger one could be adjusted for sleeping. The other was identical to the chair used by Agent Pressley, a chrome metal frame with padded seat and back. Ethel pulled it to the side of the bed opposite the IV and monitor. For a moment, she sat and studied the young woman's relaxed face. A bandaged angel. Or had Ethel misjudged her? Was Brooke an opportunist whose duplicity violated court confidentiality? Or was she an innocent pawn naively caught up in a conspiracy created by others? Others like Senator Mulberry and Lieutenant General Corbin?

Ethel stared at the monitor and the green waves that rhythmically crossed its screen. How close had Brooke come to dying? To having those waves flatline? Despite the assault, despite the hospital surroundings, and despite her promises to Frank and Jesse, Ethel couldn't be too easy on Brooke, not if she wanted to get to the truth. Brooke held the key to at least part of that truth, and Ethel was determined to extract it from the young woman. But her methods could alienate Brooke from her forever. Worse, they could alienate Frank.

"Ethel?" The whispered name snapped Ethel out of her brooding thoughts.

She looked at Brooke's upturned face. The blue eyes brimmed with tears.

"They killed my friend, Ethel. He didn't know anything, but they killed him anyway."

Ethel gently patted Brooke's arm. "I know, honey. That's why we've got to talk. Just you and me. A serious talk."

"About what?"

"Senator Mulberry's project."

Brooke turned her head away. Ethel saw the woman's hands grip the sheet.

"What project?"

"The one Senator Mulberry came to see you about this morning. The one you wrote about in your diary."

Brooke took in a sharp breath. "You read my diary?"

"Yes. Just me," Ethel lied. "I was searching for a motive as to why you might have been attacked. I wanted to be ahead of the DC police. They've not seen it."

Brooke said nothing.

"Dear, I can't help you if you don't tell me what's going on."

"Nothing's going on."

"You told the senator this morning that you'd hoped to get him information about the chief justice's position. I have the recording of your conversation."

Brooke turned to face the older woman. "I don't remember talking to him. Like I told the police, the last thing I recall was playing basketball."

Ethel thought the memory gaps were probably real, but the diary entries and the recording clearly demonstrated that Brooke was involved in something with the senator. Something that predated the attack. She decided to press harder.

"Was Supreme Court Marshal Daniel Ventana part of this project?"

"No. Why would you think that?"

"Because he was murdered last night."

What little color had been in Brooke's cheeks immediately drained away. "Mr. Ventana's dead?"

"Yes. Shot outside Chief Justice Baxter's home. She's in hiding and all the justices are working remotely under protective custody. Now I know you can shed some light as to what the hell's going on." Ethel got out of her chair and leaned over the bed, her face inches from Brooke's. "Forget Senator Mulberry. I want to know why you're worried about Lieutenant General Alan Corbin, the director of defense intelligence."

Tears flowed from the corners of Brooke's eyes. Her voice broke as she tried to speak. "I can't tell you. I promised. National security. Please don't say anything, Ethel. None of this was supposed to happen." She turned her face away again and made no attempt to stifle her sobs.

Ethel decided she'd pushed the injured woman far enough. Getting confirmation of Corbin's hand in the matter meant there were forces at work that maybe even Rudy and the FBI couldn't penetrate. She would tread carefully so as not to trigger any unintended consequences. Until she learned more, that meant keeping Brooke's role off the radar.

"All right, dear," Ethel said. "This stays between us for now. But we'll talk again."

Brooke wiped the tears from her eyes and nodded that she understood.

Ethel kissed her on the forehead and left.

Chapter 24

When Ethel returned from the hospital Sunday evening, she soon grew impatient waiting on an update from Rudy Hauser. She decided it was time to use her burner phone to call his private cell. It would keep her name from being tied to an official FBI investigation and give him a way to contact her outside her more traceable personal number.

He answered with a one-word question. "Yes?"

"It's me. I told you I'd be using a burner."

"Right. What's up?"

"Brooke has localized amnesia like Frank reported, but she might have been lying when she told me she didn't remember Senator Mulberry visiting her earlier."

"You got the recording?"

"Yes. When she talked to Mulberry, she was groggy but not incoherent. He told her about Finley's death, which upset her. He then pressed her not to say anything about 'our project,' as he phrased it. Brooke agreed." Ethel withheld Brooke's mention of the general, deciding she needed reciprocity of any information Rudy might have before disclosing everything she'd learned.

"Our project," the FBI director repeated. "Did either of them say who else might be part of the 'our'?"

"I found it interesting that Mulberry didn't tell Brooke about Ventana's death," Ethel said. "Maybe he didn't want to upset her further. Maybe Ventana played no part in their project."

"Did you tell her?"

"Yes. She was shocked. Nothing in her reaction indicated Ventana was involved in whatever she and Mulberry were up to."

"And just what were they up to?"

"She refused to say. Only that it was national security."

"Then I think Miss Chaplin and I need to have a little heart-to-heart talk."

"I'd advise against that, Rudy. You'll just shut her down. Senator Mulberry will deny everything, and we'll probably hit a dead end."

"Then what do you suggest?"

"We approach things from the angle of Ventana's murder. That's something that no one can deny happened. Ease off Brooke and Mulberry for the time being."

"That's easy for you to say. Attorney General Vandiver's not breathing down your neck."

"You'll have an irate senator breathing down both your necks if you confront Mulberry prematurely. Give me a few days, Rudy. I might find some more pieces to the puzzle."

After several seconds of silence, Rudy said, "All right. A few days."

"What have you learned about Ventana's death? Any luck with tire tracks?"

"No usable impressions on the grassy shoulder. No one saw the sedan better than you did."

"And Ventana's own investigation into the attack on Brooke and Finley? Where did that stand?"

"Our tech guys found he'd been reviewing personnel files in an effort to ascertain if anyone inside the court raised a red flag."

"All personnel?"

"He'd prioritized the clerks who were there Friday afternoon when Finley would have left with his backpack."

"How do you know that?" Ethel asked.

"We took the list of names Ventana tagged to the security detail that monitors comings and goings. Ventana had also flagged some support staff who were the last to see Brooke and Finley."

"Like whom?"

"Like one of the chief justice's secretaries, Nicole Cramerton."

"Any irregularities pop up?"

"We're just getting started, Ethel. We'll have more in-depth interviews tomorrow morning. The justices will be working remotely, but the clerks and staff will be here. We'll determine who saw Finley when."

Ethel thought for a moment. Rudy didn't interrupt the silence.

"You might want to work from the outside in," she said.

"What do you mean?"

"I mean who outside of the court has a connection to inside the court? I'm thinking of your last-minute golf game yesterday morning. Like Senator Mulberry has a connection to Brooke. Does Senator Hathaway, General Corbin, or Roger Diamond each have their own similar source?"

"I'll have to tread lightly, especially with the senator and the general."

"Rudy, there's a time for subtlety and a time for a sledgehammer. You've been around Washington long enough to master when to use what."

The FBI director laughed. "Got an extra sledgehammer?"

"No. But I'm trying to get you one."

—

The night-duty nurse came into Brooke's room as soon as Frank Mancini and his sister left for the evening.

"Can I get you anything, dear? I need to turn down the lights so you can get some rest."

"Is there a phone I can use? My uncle's going to get mine back from the police tomorrow, but I want to call a friend who I know is worried about me."

"Not handy."

"Oh. Then nothing."

The young woman sounded so sad that the nurse took pity on her. "Wait a second, hon." She left the room.

Wait a second, thought Brooke. *Where does she think I'm going?*

The nurse returned a minute later. "You can use my cell. But keep it short or we'll both be in trouble." She handed Brooke an iPhone. "It's unlocked but will lock up again if there's no activity for fifteen minutes."

"Thank you," Brooke whispered. The simple kindness caused her eyes to tear up, and she conceded she was an emotional wreck. "I promise I won't talk long."

"Then I'll let you have some privacy." She patted her patient's shoulder and left.

With trembling fingers, Brooke punched in the ten-digit number, preparing herself to be sent to voicemail, where she'd have to leave an innocuous message. She hoped the sound of her voice would be enough to spur a return call.

The phone rang six times before Senator Mulberry answered. "Who is calling, please?"

"It's Brooke. I've borrowed a phone."

"From whom?"

"A nurse. She's not in the room, but I can only talk a few minutes."

"What's so urgent?" His question carried an urgency all its own.

"My landlady, Ethel, came to see me earlier. She knows about our project."

"What? How?"

"She read about it in my diary."

"Your diary?" Alarm turned to anger. "You wrote about it in your diary?"

"I just said we were working on a project together. She said she knew you came to see me. That you'd told me not to talk about it."

Mulberry quickly recalculated. He'd obviously blundered by so persistently trying to see Brooke. Had that, coupled with the diary entries, raised the old lady's suspicions? He knew her reputation and wouldn't put it passed her to have somehow bugged the room.

"Does she know exactly what's going on?"

"No. But I had to tell her something since she knew you'd told me to keep quiet. So, I said I'd been sworn to secrecy for national security reasons."

Damn, Mulberry thought. *Gasoline poured on a fire.* He was surprised Ethel hadn't confronted him already. Which gave him pause. Why hadn't she? Because she was cunning enough not to overplay her hand when she wasn't sure what was going on. Just like he wasn't sure what was going on. Maybe the best strategy was to do nothing. Let things play out a little more. If anyone pressed Brooke about an alleged project, she should have them speak to him.

"I'm sorry if I've screwed everything up," Brooke said. "I wasn't thinking clearly."

"Do you remember anything more about the attack?"

"No. Just playing ball with Robert. It's like the time between then and waking up in the hospital was only a second apart."

"Okay. Now listen. If anyone else asks about our project, you tell them you're interested in foreign affairs, and I was willing to share nonclassified perspectives on current issues. You are interested in international law, aren't you?"

"Yes, sir."

"And we kept it a secret because I don't have the time to offer that for everyone. And you are my constituent after all."

"I understand." Her voice brightened. "I can do that."

"And if Ethel Crestwater questions you again, you tell her to speak to me."

"Yes, sir. She said we were to keep our conversation just between us."

"Good. But thank you for telling me."

"You won't say anything to her about this call, will you?"

"No," the senator assured her. "Let's keep it just between us."

"Thank you, sir. I'm sorry to have bothered you."

"Not a bother in the least." He paused. "One last thing. The phone you borrowed. Are you familiar with it?"

"It's an iPhone like mine."

"Then delete this call from the log. No sense raising anybody else's curiosity."

The senator disconnected, scrolled through his own phone log for another number and dialed it.

"It's Mulberry. We've got a problem."

—

It was after dark when the black satellite van and small motor home parked behind Curt Foster's stables. The drivers, two FBI communication experts, had been careful to make sure they weren't followed during the trip from Quantico, separating their departure by fifteen minutes and each taking a slightly different route.

Agents Ed Tucker and Paul Logan met the technical team and introduced them to Curt.

"There's power inside the stable." Curt pointed to a multi-outlet box visible on an interior post. "If you want to run a drop cord, I think the amperage will be sufficient." He looked at the motor home. "Will the chief justice hold her teleconference from the RV?"

The driver of the satellite van shook his head. "It's bunks for us, but if there's a problem being in the house, we can make it work for her teleconference."

Curt looked back at the farmhouse. "No, you can set her up wherever you like. I assume you won't want Connie or me over-hearing the justices' discussion."

"Chief Justice Baxter will be on a headset, so you'll be fine if you're in another room. We're scheduled for ten tomorrow morning, and I understand the meeting shouldn't last more than an hour. Mainly the justices are getting together for the first time since the deaths of Finley and Ventana. They want to issue a public statement about the tragedies that can be signed by all nine of them. Then the chief justice will be working remotely by linking to the court's network. Director Hauser is prepared to get her whatever she physically may need from her office."

Curt shifted his gaze from agent to agent. "So how many people in the Bureau know she's here?"

"No more than absolutely necessary, sir," Agent Tucker replied. "That's why we brought in the sleeper van. We'll work in shifts with a small number of agents rotating in and out. We'll be here as long as we're assigned and as long as we're welcome."

"Oh, you're welcome all right." He looked up at a second-story window. "I don't want anything happening to that woman."

Clarissa Baxter stood silhouetted behind the panes, watching her guardians below. Max stood by her side, his head just able to clear the sill. The German shepherd growled softly.

"Friends, Max. They're friends." She closed the drapes and sat on the edge of the bed. Suddenly, she felt exhausted. She would turn in early so that she could help Curt with the horses in the morning. Maybe Agent Tucker would accompany her on a short ride. That would be something to look forward to. Something she could dream about instead of the haunting faces of Robert Finley and Daniel Ventana, the faces of the dead.

Chapter 25

The Monday edition of the *Washington Post* carried the story of Daniel Ventana's murder on the front page below the fold. The facts of his death offered no motive nor any connection to the Friday night attack on Robert Finley and Brooke. The prominent placement of the story was driven by the unprecedented video recorded by the chief justice and the extra protection assigned to the other justices.

A spokesperson for the FBI said their actions were precautionary but that they had no evidence of a concerted assault against the court. A spokesperson for the Supreme Court assured the public that the work of the court would not be impeded by the temporarily heightened security measures.

Ethel slid the morning paper to Lanny Childress, who sat nursing a cup of coffee across the kitchen island from her.

"It looks like Rudy was able to contain wild speculation," Ethel said.

"But Director Hauser knows there has to be a connection between the two events." The young agent was uncomfortable calling his boss Rudy.

"Of course there's a connection, but keeping the press

focused on Ventana's murder allows him to pursue the investigation of Friday's attack out of the media spotlight, the investigation Ventana was beginning."

"The one you're advising," Lanny said.

More than advising, Ethel thought. But perhaps that's the way Rudy had presented her role. "I'll help any way I can."

Lanny refilled his cup and offered more coffee to Ethel.

She waved it off. "No, thanks. I've got to go out this morning and need to get ready."

"Is Jesse sleeping in?"

"No, he was up earlier preparing for his afternoon class. I've asked him to run me into the city for a few errands so I don't have to park."

"I could take you."

Lanny's eagerness to be involved in what he suspected was more than errands was palpable.

"Thank you, but I wouldn't want to have to tell Director Hauser that I'd pulled you away from your domestic terrorism research."

She excused herself and went to her room. She pulled her blue pinstripe from the hanging bag, changed, and then checked herself out in the full-length mirror on the back of the closet door. Aside from the gray hair and encroaching wrinkles on her face, Ethel felt transformed into the agent of twenty years ago. Maybe she looked a little too confident. Better to have a balance between being self-assured and needing assistance. She reached back in her closet and selected one of the canes she kept as props. A woman with a cane could come across as regal or she could appear unsteady, it all depended upon the way she walked. The ebony one with the silver hooked handle could serve either pretense.

A few minutes after nine, Ethel and Jesse headed for the

Mandarin Oriental Hotel. They'd only traveled a block when Ethel asked, "How did you do?"

"The money transfer is set to post when the banks open. We'll get acknowledgments from Henry Birdsong and Bud Carson. They've assured me the funds are sufficient to cover transportation expenses."

"And the stocks?"

"I'll finalize those trades from the university."

"I've been thinking," Ethel said. "Can you pull more money from the offshore account?"

"Sure. Why?"

"I'd like to up the stock purchases and include the Brine Extractors as well as Lithium USA. Having a presence in both camps might be useful. Any update from your girlfriend?"

"Tracy texted that she's set up an ongoing search for anyone seeking information on you or me with a back loop to immediately tag their identity. Now she's going after whatever she can find in a deeper web dive into Senators Hathaway and Mulberry, as well as the lobbyist Roger Diamond."

"I trust you told her to be careful, especially regarding Senator Hathaway."

"Yes. And I didn't ask her to research General Corbin. Military intelligence is much more formidable than a senator sitting on a committee."

"And we should remember that ourselves," Ethel warned.

They joined the creeping pace of traffic on I-395 North into DC, took the exit for Maine Avenue, and pulled to a stop on Maryland Avenue in front of the luxurious Mandarin Oriental.

"You sure you don't want me to wait for you?" Jesse asked.

"No. You go on to campus and take care of what you've got to do. I'll text you when I'm done, and if it's not convenient for you to pick me up, I'll Uber home." She grabbed her cane and a leather portfolio. "How do I look?"

Jesse gave a thumbs-up. "Like a lawyer about to argue in front of the Supreme Court."

Ethel laughed. "I'll settle for the role of site chair for AARP's Annual National Conference of Gerontologists."

"Is there such a thing?"

"If not, there will be for the next few hours."

With her portfolio tucked under her right arm and her cane in her left hand, she strode purposely to the front entrance, nodded a greeting to the doorman, and entered the spacious lobby.

The first thing that struck her eye was a magnificent Christmas tree towering at least twenty feet in the center of the dark marble floor. Elegant decorations of white lights, multicolored satin balls, and magenta bows adorned every limb. Perfectly wrapped gifts surrounded the tree's base. A life-sized nutcracker soldier stood to one side. On the other side, an easel held a placard announcing that Santa would be arriving on Thanksgiving and staying till Christmas Eve. Parents were urged to make reservations for their children to meet Santa in his on-site cottage before all the time slots were filled.

Ten days till Thanksgiving, thought Ethel, and Santa's already booking appointments. Who got preferential treatment, Democrats or Republicans? In today's atmosphere in Washington, Santa would probably be hauled before a congressional hearing investigating whether he was showing partisanship in who was on his naughty list and who was declared nice.

To the right arced a long registration and concierge desk. A few people were checking out, but the desk was well staffed, and she only waited a few minutes before a woman who looked more Nordic than Asian waved her forward with a "Welcome to the Mandarin Oriental DC. How may I be of service?"

Ethel leaned over the desk as if she was imparting classified information. "My organization is considering holding a conference here, and I'd like to speak with someone about that possibility."

"Wonderful," enthused the woman as if she'd won the lottery. "Do you have an appointment?"

"No. I'm in town for the day from New York and found some unexpected free time. Your hotel is beautiful, and I'd like to put it on our short list of possible sites."

"No problem. Let me contact someone in our business services office who can assist you. May I have your name?" Ethel glanced at the woman's nameplate on the lapel of her blazer. "Certainly, Eva. I'm Ethel Crestwater. I'm chair of our conference site selection committee."

Eva picked up a phone, asked for a manager, and relayed the request. She smiled as she disconnected. "Helen Hopkins, our senior event manager, will be right out."

"Thank you, Eva," Ethel said. "I'll step aside so that you can help others." She moved farther along the desk and studied the room more closely.

Beyond the Christmas tree, the floor dropped down a few steps into another large area where tables provided seating for dining. At midmorning, very few patrons were eating. Scattered throughout the space, isolated guests lingered over coffee and newspapers. Ethel considered having an early lunch as a reason to hang around beyond whatever time she'd spend with Helen Hopkins.

"Ms. Crestwater?"

Ethel turned around to greet a smiling woman who carried her own portfolio. "Yes. Ms. Hopkins?"

"It's Helen." She proffered her hand. "A pleasure to meet you."

The senior events manager appeared to be in her early forties, a distant thirty-plus years from Ethel's senior status. Ethel gripped the woman's hand firmly but didn't offer to be on a first-name basis.

Helen Hopkins gestured to a group of cushioned chairs on the edge of the lobby tier. "Why don't we sit down and you can tell me what you're looking for."

"That will be fine." Ethel let the woman lead the way.

When they were seated, Ethel said, "Are you familiar with the National Conference of Gerontologists?"

"No. I must confess I'm not."

"It's an annual conference supporting the research and clinical work of doctors specializing in medical care of seniors. Our sponsor since the beginning has been AARP."

"I've heard of them."

Ethel smiled. "Just wait until you turn fifty, and then you'll definitely hear from them." She shook her finger playfully. "Don't tell them I said that."

"No, I wouldn't."

Ethel made a show of looking at the surroundings. "Everything AARP does is first class. I can tell that's the philosophy of the Mandarin Oriental."

"Oh, yes. I've worked for some of the other major hotels, and Mandarin Oriental is in a league of its own. How many attendees would you be expecting?"

Ethel glanced up at the high ceiling as if the answer was suspended there. "Oh, four hundred, maybe even five hundred." She again looked at the woman. "That segment of medicine is growing as our population ages. We need more gerontologists, and we certainly want to keep the ones we have. Our conference is half educational and half celebratory, making sure our doctors enjoy themselves."

"Well, we can provide tour guide packets, arrange excursions, just about anything you'd like. What time frame are we looking at?"

"The conference lasts two and a half days. We're booking four years out."

Helen Hopkins relaxed, relieved there would be no scheduling conflict. "Then we should be able to accommodate any days you prefer."

"I'd like to see your meeting rooms. We often have breakout groups in addition to the main gathering. Schematics and floor plans would also be helpful for me to share with the site committee."

"No problem. Why don't we do a walkthrough, and then I'll give you some materials to take with you."

For the next thirty minutes, Ethel followed as her guide pointed out various attributes that would make the luxury hotel the conference's ideal venue. Ethel asked few questions until they came to the Grand Ballroom.

"This would accommodate everyone attending a conference twice your size," Helen said.

"Impressive. I love the high ceilings. Can this be subdivided?"

"Yes. Both the Grand Ballroom and the slightly smaller Oriental Ballroom can be divided into thirds. Depending upon your needs, you can have a banquet setting up in one section while conducting a meeting in another. The soundproofing is phenomenal."

"Is nothing going on today?" Ethel asked.

"No. We had three weddings this weekend, the largest with over five hundred guests. Staff is clearing out the Oriental Ballroom and resetting for a smaller event that will need only a third of the space. Frankly, they could have used one of our smaller rooms, but they liked the ballroom decor and spaciousness."

"May I see it?"

"Of course, it's our next stop."

They found the staff breaking down banquet tables but leaving the chairs.

"Very nice," Ethel complimented. "So, the next setup will be chairs and a dais?"

"Yes, and the space allows us to spread the audience a little for everyone's comfort."

"What is the conference?" Ethel asked off-handedly.

"The Progressive Mining Coalition."

"I've never heard of them."

"Me either. But everything's been booked through the PR division of Crane and Weston. We deal with them all the time. In fact, I'm the manager for this event, so I'm glad you came by today before I have to transform into my operational, all-hands-on-deck mode."

"I am too, Helen. You've been most helpful. And I won't keep you any longer. If you could just provide me with those floor plans and your business card, I'll be most grateful."

"No problem. Let's drop by my office and I'll give you a comprehensive information packet. Several, if you need more for your committee."

"Maybe include some extra copies of the floor plans I can share. I'll be recommending we come back to you for a request for a proposal."

Ethel left a smiling Helen Hopkins standing by the Christmas tree. The woman had been helpful. Ethel felt guilty that the senior event manager would soon find herself swallowed up in the middle of a PR storm.

Chapter 26

The temperature was unseasonably warm for mid-November, and Ethel took advantage of the mild weather to walk along the wharf and marvel at the variety of shops and restaurants that had transformed the area from an off-the-boat fish market into a high-end tourist destination. She also used her stroll to check out other access points to the hotel, including loading docks and service entrances. Ethel believed she could never be too familiar with an operational site. You could plan for everything but the unexpected, which was why it was called the unexpected. Sometimes the smallest detail of knowledge meant the difference between success and failure when the unexpected happened.

When she was satisfied that she'd learned all she could, she decided to return to the Mandarin Oriental for an early lunch. She hoped to avoid running into Helen Hopkins again, but if that happened, she'd simply claim she was doing due diligence on their food service and didn't want special treatment. And eating at a table with a view of the lobby enabled her to observe the movement of the staff with an eye for discreet security.

While waiting for her Caesar salad, Ethel opened the

marketing packet and reviewed the floor plans. Once she was home, she'd email them to Henry Birdsong and Bud Carson and suggest a quick conference call. Minimal risk with maximum impact would be the strategy.

Her salad arrived. Before eating, Ethel texted Jesse:

Pick me up in 30?

He replied almost immediately:

Confirmed.

—

"Straight home?" Jesse asked as Ethel got in the car.

"You can take a longer route so we can talk without risk of Lanny overhearing. Maybe over Roosevelt Bridge."

"Success then?"

"Somewhat. But first I want to hear your report."

"Congratulations," he said. "You're the proud owner of twenty-five thousand dollars' worth of Lithium USA stock and twenty-five thousand dollars' worth of Brine Extractors stock. I have ten thousand of each. The e-broker is issuing receipts electronically. I'll print them out if we need shareholder proof on Wednesday."

"And Birdsong and Carson?"

"They're all on an early flight tomorrow."

"Not tonight?"

"No. They both said there was organizational stuff they could more easily do there. Each has support here that they're coordinating."

"Just as well," Ethel conceded. "We have things to go over

today, and we can't do that if they're on a plane. Did they say anything about the money?"

"Just that it had come in and should cover everything."

"They're going to need to stay at the Mandarin Oriental tomorrow and Wednesday. Have them book rooms in their own names."

"All of them?"

"Just those coming from Nevada. I'll cover any additional expense. When we get home, set up a conference call for four o'clock, two their time."

"Anything else?"

"Yes. When they book their rooms, they should ask for ones on the lowest level available."

"To avoid elevators?" Jesse asked.

Ethel turned toward him in her seat. "You know, Cousin, you might have the makings of an FBI agent after all."

"No. You're just contagious. I should report you to the CDC. A one-woman pandemic."

"Be quiet and drive," she teased. "I'm going to call Frank." She used her regular phone.

"Hello, Ethel."

"Any update on Brooke this afternoon?"

"I'm at the hospital now. Detective Meadows is coming by to interview her again."

"Is she remembering anything more?"

"A little. She recalls inviting Finley to the Dubliner. She said he had a lot of work to do for the chief justice over the weekend. She doesn't remember walking to his house, or anything about the attack."

"Ask her who might have seen them after their basketball game or at the Dubliner."

"Gee, really? Thanks, I never would have thought of that."

Ethel ignored his sarcasm, knowing he was emotionally stretched to the limit. She waited for him to calm down.

"I'm sorry," he said. "Didn't mean to snap at you."

"Snap all you want. You're right. This isn't your first dance. But Rudy told me that Ventana was reviewing personnel files. Brooke's memory might narrow the focus. Get any names to me, and I'll pass them along."

"All right. Did you learn anything from Brooke yesterday? About Senator Mulberry?"

"No," Ethel lied. "I think he's just worried about her."

"That's what she told me. But something's bothering her. She's not herself."

"Frank, her friend was killed and she was severely injured. She's bound to be unsettled. Have they said when she might be released?"

"Wednesday or Thursday if she continues to improve. She's coming to my house with her mom. We'll need to get a few things from her room—clothes, toiletries, stuff like that. Her mom will know what she wants."

Like her diary, Ethel thought. *And her missing computer.* Ethel doubted anyone had told Brooke about that theft. "Tell Susan to come whenever. I'll make sure Lanny is here."

"Where are you and Jesse going?" Frank asked.

"Call it a little infiltration."

"Sounds like bail money might be involved."

"Frank, you know me too well."

She disconnected.

"Is he okay?" Jesse asked.

"Not really. He's conflicted. He's worried about Brooke, and he's frustrated that he's not on the case. But he knows his priority is his niece."

Jesse looked at Ethel. "Bail money?"

"Brake!" Ethel stiff-armed the dashboard.

Jesse saw the SUV in front had suddenly stopped. He slammed on the brakes and the Infiniti skidded before coming to a halt only inches from the rear bumper of the other vehicle.

Ethel let out a sigh of relief. "And to think I could have taken an Uber."

Jesse relaxed his grip on the steering wheel. "Or you could get out and hail a cab with your cane. It's not too late. But remember, I did drive the chief justice safely to Curt's."

"The chief justice. Too late," Ethel repeated to herself. "Damn it. I hope it's not too late."

"Too late for what?"

"Shush." Ethel scrolled through the log on her personal cell, found the number she wanted, and called.

The chief justice answered. "Ethel?"

"Yes. I hope I'm not interrupting."

"Not at all. I should have called to thank you. The Fosters are wonderful and nothing lifts my spirits more than riding a horse. I'm afraid they're going to have to run me off."

"I'm glad it's working out." Ethel paused as she shifted the direction of the conversation. "Listen, I know I'm sticking my nose where it doesn't belong, but did they get the secure comms in place down there?"

"Yes. In fact, the other justices and I had a video conference this morning. Everything worked like a charm."

Ethel felt her stomach knot. "Without disclosing the result, did you discuss the lithium mining case?"

"Briefly. I said Robert Finley had been rereading the arguments for both sides and I wanted to review the merits of each. His tragic death has delayed that plan."

"Then I have a favor to ask."

"What is it?" Clarissa asked cautiously.

"Don't tell anyone—clerks, justices, secretaries—if you come to a decision on that case."

"Why?"

"I think the investigation can benefit from having that still be up in the air. I don't know how exactly, but if your position is the swing vote, I think you should keep it under wraps."

"For how long?"

"A week. Two at the most."

"All right," Clarissa agreed. "I can postpone deliberations for a while. Tell me what's going to change in a week or two?"

"That's a very good question, Your Honor. I wish I knew the answer."

—

Jesse gently knocked on Ethel's bedroom door. He hated to wake her but with the Nevada call to Henry Birdsong and Bud Carson less than thirty minutes away, he wanted to share what he'd discovered.

He'd noticed Ethel had started taking an afternoon nap more frequently. Perhaps that resulted from her recent acquisition of a pacemaker. Or maybe at her age, she was more easily fatigued. Either way, when she was awake, no one was sharper.

"Come in." Her voice gave no indication she'd been sleeping.

Jesse found her sitting at her computer. "What are you working on?"

"Some notes for our call. I want to get everything straight today since they won't be flying in until tomorrow afternoon." She stood up. "Is Lanny in his room?"

"No. I suggested that Brooke might like a visitor who wasn't there to interview her about the attack. Lanny was gone in ten minutes."

Ethel smiled. "Devious of you. Then let's put on the kettle and we can talk over tea."

Jesse followed her into the kitchen. "Tracy found an agenda for the Wednesday conference posted on the website of the Progressive Mining Coalition." He waved a sheet of paper.

Ethel held the kettle under the running faucet. "Kind of late getting the word out."

"It was in a password-protected 'members only' section that Tracy hacked. It has the subheading of 'final' displayed on the document's heading."

"Interesting. Somebody wants to control who sees what."

"And who registers," Jesse said. "Tracy took the liberty of adding our names to the list of attendees."

Ethel set the kettle on the stovetop and turned on the burner. "Did she now? You'd better hold on to her, Cousin. She's a real catch."

"She has you down as a Brine Extractors shareholder and me as Lithium USA."

"Can she look at the other attendees?"

"She can and already has to some degree. Other companies are represented, like operations in Arkansas, Tennessee, and North Carolina."

"So, what's the meeting agenda?"

Jesse read from the paper. "Welcoming remarks at nine by the executive director of the coalition. At nine thirty, Roger Diamond speaks on the status of government and media relations."

"That will probably include the Supreme Court case," Ethel said. "I'm sure he'd hoped to have an expedited ruling and not have to wait till the end of the court's term."

"Diamond's slated for forty-five minutes including questions. Then there's a fifteen-minute midmorning break."

"That will last twenty. All those old men and their enlarged prostates camping out at the urinals."

Jesse tried to chase that image from his mind. "The next agenda item is a panel of auto executives discussing where they see the E/V market and the demand for rare elements. They can make up time there because they won't want to delay their keynote speaker who's scheduled for eleven thirty."

The kettle started a soft whistle.

Ethel smiled. "Let me guess. Senator Stuart Hathaway."

"One and the same. There at the invitation of his good golfing buddy, Roger Diamond. At noon, they break for lunch. Then the program is a series of afternoon panels with selected attendees discussing environmental issues, technical advances, and global resources. The conference concludes with a five o'clock cocktail hour."

"They'll be ready for it," Ethel said.

Jesse handed her the agenda. "So, what do you think? During the environmental session?"

"And have the senator miss out on all the fun?"

The kettle whistle built to a high shrill.

"Divide and conquer, my boy. Divide and conquer."

Chapter 27

Ethel and Jesse checked into the Mandarin Oriental on Tuesday at three thirty. They registered together, confirming they had adjacent suites. As soon as she was settled, Ethel texted Henry Birdsong and Bud Carson, asking if they could meet at four in her room. Just the two men as she didn't want to draw attention by having a crowd converging upon her door.

Jesse joined her and they laid out printed copies of the conference agenda and the meeting room floor plans on the coffee table.

The knock came at precisely four. Jesse opened the door.

Two men entered. Both wore dark suits that made them indistinguishable from any other businessmen staying at the hotel. Although they both had the weathered, leathered look of outdoorsmen, their physical resemblance ended there. One couldn't have been more than five-foot-six. He was wire-thin with jet black hair pulled back into a discreet ponytail. The other man was an inch or two over six feet and broad-shouldered with a square head and receding red hair.

"Welcome, gentlemen," Ethel said, stepping toward them with an outstretched hand. "Jesse and I thank you for coming."

"Thank you for making this possible," said the smaller man. "I'm Henry."

"I guess that makes me Bud," quipped the other man. "Henry and Bud sounds like a vaudeville act."

"It's more believable than cowboys and Indians fighting on the same side," Henry said.

"Both of you getting good numbers?" Ethel asked.

"Yes. Some drove all night and are still on the road," Henry said. "Good representation from the East Coast tribes. They're anxious to show solidarity and are awaiting instructions."

"We've got environmentalists committed," Bud said. "They'll be arriving this evening. Shows you how much we've both got at stake."

Ethel gestured for them to be seated. "Well, let's talk about how we can make people understand exactly what's at stake. Jesse and I have a few suggestions."

—

The Progressive Mining Coalition had a long check-in table set up outside the doors to the Oriental Ballroom where attendees could pick up their name badges. Although the meeting didn't begin until nine, the doors opened at eight thirty to avoid a last-minute crush.

Ethel and Jesse approached the four women manning the table just as they finished laying out the badges in alphabetized sections—A to F, G to L, M to R, and S to Z.

"Cooper and Crestwater," Ethel told the woman behind the A to F section.

"Cooper and Crestwater," the woman repeated, as she flipped through the Cs. She frowned. "I don't seem to find either name. Give me a second to go through them again."

"Is there a problem?"

Ethel and Jesse turned around to see who had asked the question. Roger Diamond smiled but no warmth reached his eyes.

Jesse looked to Ethel to respond. She leaned over her cane and cocked her head as if presenting Diamond with her better ear. "This young lady hasn't been able to find our names. I know we registered. We're both shareholders in Lithium USA and Brine Extractors."

"But this isn't an open shareholders meeting. Those who were invited represent managers and directors of our member companies."

Ethel lifted and then tapped her cane close to Diamond's foot. "Then explain to me why I was notified and made the journey here only to be turned away?"

Diamond became aware that others around him were now watching. The last image he wanted to project was a man throwing out somebody's grandma. Maybe a very rich grandma.

"Mr. Diamond." The woman at the table held up an iPad.

He stepped around Ethel. "Yes?"

"I checked the list of confirmed attendees on the conference website. There's an Ethel Crestwater and Jesse Cooper registered."

"That us," Ethel said. "We registered at the same time. Jesse's my double-first-cousin-twice-removed. A lot of people don't know—"

"I apologize for the error, Ms. Crestwater," Diamond interrupted, not wanting Ethel to bend his ear any longer. He turned to the woman at the table. "Sharon, make them official name tags so that there will be no more confusion." He offered his hand first to Ethel and then Jesse. "Roger Diamond. If you need anything further, feel free to see me. I'm glad you're here."

"Apology accepted," Ethel said. "Glitches happen. Computers will be the death of us all."

As the check-in woman manually created the two name tags, Ethel watched Diamond walk down the hall and speak to a man in a dark suit standing near the entrance doors. He might as well have had the word *Security* tattooed on his forehead. The man quickly cut his eyes to her and gave a nod to whatever Diamond was saying.

Not hotel security, Ethel thought. She'd watched them yesterday. This man's demeanor was more Secret Service, efficiently scanning the scene without lingering over any particular person too long. Ethel kept him in her peripheral vision as she appeared to be studying the conference agenda posted behind the check-in table.

It was clear to her that Roger Diamond had augmented the hotel's team with men of his own. From the cut of the observer's suit coat, she suspected he wore a shoulder holster. The danger of escalation became a real possibility. She took her name tag and retreated to the opposite end of the hallway. She texted Birdsong and Carson that timing now became critical. They would need to move fast.

At nine o'clock, Roger Diamond stepped up on the dais and asked everyone to please take a seat. Ethel and Jesse sat on the back row close to the door. She noted the man Diamond had spoken with took up a position just inside. Three clones were also posted around the room from where they could survey both the front and rear of the ballroom. Ethel looked for a communication earpiece, but saw none. With today's technology, it could have been minuscule.

Diamond welcomed everyone on behalf of his company, Crane and Weston, then made a few housekeeping announcements and introduced the executive director, Charles Eagleton.

Eagleton jumped up on the stage like the floor was on fire.

His exuberance belied his white hair and creased face. Fifty-something with the energy of a fifteen-year-old.

"Look around you! Look around you!" he exhorted. "You're seeing the future."

Ethel leaned over to Jesse. "If I'm the future then we're all in big trouble."

"Better you than hyper-man. This is more pep rally than meeting."

"Each of you is building the future for this great country," Eagleton continued. "Don't let anyone tell you any different, whether that's some tree-hugging extremist or the chief justice of the Supreme Court."

The mention of Chief Justice Baxter drew a few boos, and the executive director gave a suppressing motion with his hands. "Now, now, we don't know how the court will rule. Rest assured, either way, they will not have the last word. We will prevail."

That proclamation elicited cheers. If they'd been wearing hats, they'd have tossed them into the air.

Eagleton settled down and went into a monologue of all the good things the Progressive Mining Coalition was doing to further their interests. He acknowledged they had some internal differences regarding mining methodology, but urged his members to remain unified in their support of unencumbered federal leases.

That led into Roger Diamond's report on government relations and support on Capitol Hill. Senator Hathaway was named as one of their key allies and a champion of pushing a bill granting more subsidies for rare mineral exploration and technical innovation. Diamond kept to his time limit and the midmorning break occurred on schedule.

Ethel watched the executives stream out of the ballroom to return phone calls and use the restroom. Probably simultaneously, she regrettably envisioned. She and Jesse remained seated.

Ethel pulled her phone from her pocket. "I'm going to text Birdsong and Carson that I'll meet them right outside these doors. Diamond has his own security team, and I want to make sure we have access to the room. You've got the networks' numbers?"

"Yes."

"Tip them thirty minutes ahead. We'll alert everyone else when Senator Hathaway arrives. They'll have fifteen minutes to get in place."

"Got it."

Ethel dropped her voice to a stern whisper. "Do not confront any of Diamond's team. Understand?"

"Yes. And Ethel?"

"What?"

"Heed your own advice."

After the break came a panel discussion moderated by Executive Director Eagleton that featured participants representing the big three American automakers—Ford, GM, and Chrysler. They offered optimistic sales projections that could be hampered by the critical shortage of lithium and other rare earth elements. They all agreed that lithium was the new oil and unless exploration and production were increased, the nation would find itself once again severely dependent upon the resources of potentially hostile countries.

At eleven twenty, when the discussion had moved into Q and A, the door behind Ethel opened, and Roger Diamond escorted Senator Stuart Hathaway into the room. Diamond's men brought two chairs and placed them against the back wall. The senator and Diamond sat and turned their attention to the panel.

"Congratulations," Ethel heard Hathaway say. "Nice turnout."

"I'll make sure you get a list of names," Diamond promised. "All of them can afford substantial campaign contributions."

"Even better," the senator said.

Ethel leaned closer to Jesse. "You texted our network friends?"

"Yes. And our own crew."

Ethel opened her message app and typed:

senator here.

"No turning back now," she said.

The auto executives finished, and Charles Eagleton called upon Roger Diamond to introduce the keynote speaker. Leaving Hathaway, Diamond went to the dais and extolled the senator as a great champion of mining and a true patriot.

Ending the lavish praise with his arms outstretched, Diamond practically shouted, "Please give a rousing welcome to your friend and mine, United States Senator Stuart Hathaway."

The senator stood and the volume of applause rose with him. He took a slow walk the length of the room, clearly milking the adulation.

When he reached the dais, he gave Diamond a photo-op handshake and then stepped to the microphone.

"Thank you. Thank you. Please be seated."

"Everyone is seated," Ethel told Jesse. "The egomaniac's fantasizing a standing ovation." She looked at her watch. "Eleven thirty-five."

Hathaway started his remarks asserting that he would do everything he could on Capitol Hill to ensure restrictions and regulations didn't strangle their efforts to make our great country energy-independent. More specifically, he said, "I know there's a court case you're worried about. Well, worry no more. If the Supreme Court makes a foolish ruling, President Tarleton and I have a plan that will accomplish our goals and save the hundreds of good paying jobs you're creating."

The room erupted in applause.

"It's got to be the Defense Production Act," Ethel stated. "The president's planning to invoke the act to support increased mining. How that's supported may or may not undercut a Supreme Court ruling."

"National security?"

"Which could circle back to Director of Defense Intelligence Corbin." Ethel looked at her watch. "Which doesn't change our strategy at all." She stood up. "Showtime."

As she walked toward the door, the security man who had spoken with Roger Diamond moved to intercept her.

"Ma'am, can I help you?"

"Nature calls, young man. At my age, I always answer. I'll be back soon."

Up on the street level, two passenger vans stopped in the cul-de-sac in front of the hotel and the entrance to the adjacent wharf. Ten people emerged from each. They began walking in a circle carrying placards and posters with block-lettered messages—SENATOR HATHAWAY DON'T KILL OUR CHILDREN. OPEN PIT = 300 YEARS TOXICITY. WE SUPPORT BRINE EXTRACTION. COWBOYS AND INDIANS FOR BRINE EXTRACTION.

Some of the Native Americans wore traditional braids and headbands. Some of the ranchers sported bandannas, boots, and hats more likely to be seen at a rodeo than in DC. The protesters marched in silence, careful not to block traffic or stray onto hotel property. Soon an assembly of tourists and hotel guests started posting photos and videos on social media.

Helen Hopkins, senior event manager, got the word from

the front desk. Why did this have to happen today? With Roger Diamond, her biggest client? She made it to the front entrance just as a news van pulled up. A second followed. Helen looked for her security personnel and saw two of her men in the crowd.

She grabbed one of them by the arm. "Get rid of those people," she demanded.

The man yanked his arm free. "They're not on our property. We don't have jurisdiction."

"Well, find somebody who does!"

She spun around and hurried just short of running to the ballroom. If Roger Diamond could keep his attendees out of the lobby, maybe his event wouldn't be disrupted. The senator was to speak until noon. If the ruckus out front hadn't been dispersed by then, she would slip Hathaway out a service exit.

Outside the ballroom, Ethel met Henry Birdsong and Bud Carson. The men no longer wore their business suits. Henry had on a leather tunic, moccasins, wheat jeans, and a featherless headband. Bud wore a fringed buckskin jacket, pointed snakeskin cowboy boots, a red shirt with string tie, and ten-gallon hat.

Each man's wife stood beside him in jeans and western shirts. All wore COVID masks and held posters with the blank side facing out.

Ethel gave a thumbs-up. "You ready?"

The four nodded.

"Stand along the back wall. The senator can't help but see you. I'll go in first."

She opened the door and entered. Diamond's security man was standing just inside.

"Sir, I feel a little dizzy. Could you lend me your arm until I get to my seat?"

"Yes, ma'am."

As he turned away from the door, Bud, Henry, and their wives noiselessly slipped inside and lined up along the rear wall. They lifted their placards and turned them around. The signs spelled out a four-word sentence—SENATOR, SAVE OUR CHILDREN!

The movement caught Senator Hathaway's eye, especially seeing the word *Senator*. He halted his speech and looked down at Diamond seated on the first row.

The lobbyist turned around and saw the protesters. He stood up. "This is a private meeting." His action only caused everyone to turn around as well.

With a captive audience, Bud bellowed, "Senator, save our children. No open pit. Brine extraction only."

A few boos sounded, but none came from the brine extraction companies.

"We're your constituents," Bud continued. "Make a commitment now. No open pit." He shifted his poster to free up a hand. "Or face the consequences." He reached his hand inside his jacket.

The security man beside Ethel let go of her arm and snatched his pistol from the shoulder holster.

Ethel cracked her cane across the man's wrist so fast and so hard that it pushed the gun toward the floor with his finger caught in the trigger guard.

The gunshot sounded like a cannon. The man yelled. As he raised the pistol, Ethel dropped the cane, twisted his wrist, and accelerated the upward motion until she wrenched his arm high behind his back. She stepped forward, driving his face into the floor. The pistol dropped from his hand.

Chaos erupted as people fled toward the exits.

"Quick," Ethel ordered the four demonstrators. "Keep your masks on until you get back to your rooms. Then change your clothes and go out to lunch. You don't know what happened."

"I was just reaching for my phone," Bud said.

"Don't worry. He's the one in trouble unless you don't go now."

They left without argument.

Jesse had his phone out filming the mayhem. Ethel gave him the cut sign and bent over the wounded man.

"What was that move you put on him?" Jesse asked.

"An improvisation of something I learned during my jujutsu training. Finally got some benefit from my black belt."

Jesse stared at her in disbelief.

"Come on. Let's get this poor joker away from the door before he's trampled. Can you believe it? He literally shot himself in the foot."

She and Jesse slid the man out of the aisle. People hardly looked at them as they scrambled for safety. Ethel took out her cell phone.

"Who are you calling?" Jesse asked.

"An ambulance. I don't want this guy limping away. Then I'm calling Detective Glenn Meadows. The District frowns upon people discharging firearms."

Helen Hopkins had just stepped off the elevator when she heard the gunshot. *Not the senator,* she thought. *Not killed at my event.*

A swarm of people streamed out of the ballroom. She saw Diamond and Hathaway running toward her.

"Roger!"

"Not now, Helen." They ran past her before she could say another word.

If the senator wasn't shot, who was? And what about all the food prepared for the luncheon?

Ethel knelt beside the wounded man. "I've called an ambulance and the police. We'll stay with you until they arrive." She looked down at his bleeding foot. "Let's leave the shoe on till then."

Tears streamed down his face as the pain intensified. "You broke my wrist." The words tumbled out in an agonized whisper.

"The wages of pulling a gun on me."

"Not you."

"And I was supposed to know that how?"

The man didn't answer. Instead, he gritted his teeth and clutched his injured wrist against his chest. "Mr. Diamond said you'd be trouble."

"He doesn't know the half of it, hon. Lie still while I pat you down in case you're more than a one-gunner. You can relax. I'll be respectful. You're not my type."

He winced as she pushed his arms aside and ran her hands over and down his body. She pulled a wallet from his inside pocket.

"You have a permit to carry concealed?"

"Yes."

"But you're not with the hotel, are you?"

The man said nothing.

Ethel flipped open the billfold. On one side behind a plastic window was a Maryland driver's license for Brad Gordowski with a photo matching the man lying beside her. Behind the matching window on the other side was a company photo ID card in the same name with the title SPECIAL OFFICER.

"Well, well. Very interesting." Ethel looked up at Jesse. "Meet Brad Gordowski, a special officer for OmniForce Protective Services."

Diamond led Hathaway to the lobby. He and the senator saw a group in front of the hotel.

Hathaway stopped. "What's that?"

"I don't know. Just keep your head down, and we'll walk around them."

Ten feet out of the hotel, Senator Hathaway heard someone call his name. Then he saw the circling protesters. Reporters headed his way, their cameramen in tow.

"What do I say, Roger? For God's sake, what do I say?"

"As little as possible."

Chapter 28

"He pulled out a damned gun. What was I supposed to do? Watch him shoot the senator?" Ethel stretched out her arms in a dramatic gesture as if imploring Glenn Meadows to answer her question.

She and the DC detective stood in the middle of her hotel suite's living room. A uniformed officer posted by the door tensed as if Ethel might try to flee. Jesse sat calmly on the sofa, watching the scene like he was at the theater.

Glenn Meadows admonished Ethel with the wave of a finger. "What were you doing in that room?"

"Attending a meeting I'm registered for."

"And these protesters just happened to come in behind you."

"Came in peacefully and stood quietly in the back. They only spoke when spoken to."

"And disappeared before they could be questioned."

Ethel shrugged. "Maybe they simply ran for safety like everyone else did. Jesse and I were too busy tending to a wounded man."

"And taking his gun."

Ethel sat down in an armchair. "Which I handed over to

your officers before it could mysteriously disappear, thank you very much."

Glenn glared at her. "I'll say it again. I know it was no coincidence you were in that room."

"You mean it's no coincidence that a paramilitary team was in that room. A team from OmniForce Protective Services—the former employer of Ronald Drake, the alleged killer of Robert Finley. That's your line of inquiry, Detective. That's what my coincidence of being in the room flushed out into the open."

Glenn looked at the patrolman and shook his head. "Come on, Blake. There's no point in hanging around here."

Ethel and Jesse stood. As the detective walked past her, she grabbed his arm. "Some unsolicited advice. Use Rudy Hauser to get to Hathaway and Diamond. Your own department might not have the clout."

"None of us seems to have your clout, Ms. Crestwater. Just don't shut me out. We're after the same goal."

She released his arm and smiled. "Yes, but we have different methods."

When Detective Meadows and the patrolman had closed the door behind them, Ethel let out a long sigh of relief and plopped back into the chair.

Jesse hurried to her. "You all right? Can I get you some water?"

Ethel waved him away. "Just tired. Things got tense and stayed tense when that gun went off. The damned fool. OPS must have low hiring standards—at least at this level of operation. Surely their overseas paramilitary contractors aren't so inept. We're lucky someone wasn't killed."

"Do you want me to check on Henry and Bud?"

"Good God no. They're staying the night, but we're not to go near one another. Hopefully, the police think all the protestors left in the vans and both couples can check out tomorrow with no one the wiser."

Jesse walked to a window and looked out at the Potomac. Afternoon shadows lengthened. His stomach growled. He'd skipped breakfast and then spent lunchtime giving statements to the police, culminating with the confrontation with Glenn Meadows. Jesse thought about Ethel's final statement to the detective. *Use Rudy Hauser to get to Hathaway and Diamond.* Use him how? And where did General Corbin and Senator Mulberry fit into the picture?

Dark clouds gathered, accelerating the advent of evening and promising a downpour. Not the night to eat out. Not the night to eat in the hotel restaurant either. Ethel wouldn't want to risk crossing paths with Helen Hopkins or anyone who might have remembered her from the morning. Room service would be the best choice. And delivered to his room, not hers.

On second thought, why didn't they just check out?

"You hungry?" Ethel asked.

He turned from the window. "My stomach that loud?"

"For a second, I thought maybe it was a thunderstorm. Why don't we order room service?"

"Would you rather check out and eat at home?"

"No. We paid for the suites, so we'll stay here tonight. But I think we should alert Lanny that we might have visitors dropping by."

Jesse crossed the room and sat on the sofa. "What visitors?"

Ethel shrugged. "Not sure. Roger Diamond now has our names, which means Senator Hathaway does also. I'll bet Brooke has managed to alert Senator Mulberry that I recorded their conversation, so he's in play."

"Do you think we're in some kind of danger?"

"I certainly hope so. It means we're on the right track. Now order us some food to your room. I'll take a Caesar salad and bottled water."

"What else can I do to help?"

Ethel looked at her watch. "It's four thirty here, so London is nine thirty. Check in with Tracy. See if she's uncovered anything."

Jesse's face brightened at the prospect of calling his girlfriend. "Can I tell her what happened?"

"Yes. See if she can find any unusual activity by our cast of characters in the past few hours."

"Like what?"

"That's for her to assess. Now go on. I've got calls to make. And ask for the dressing on the side."

She pulled her personal cell phone from her handbag and scrolled through the list of numbers until she found the one she wanted.

Lanny Childress heard the buzz and grabbed his phone before it could vibrate off the top of his desk. He recognized the caller. "Ethel?"

"Yes. Where are you?"

"Up in my room."

"Have I had any visitors?"

"No. Were you expecting someone?"

"There's a chance. Jesse and I are out again tonight, but someone could drop by."

"What do you want me to tell them?"

"That I'm at the Mandarin Oriental."

Lanny took a sharp breath. "That's where a shot was fired. I saw internet clips of Senator Hathaway being grilled by protesters."

Fired and grilled, Ethel thought. Appropriate treatment for the senator.

"Were you and Jesse involved?"

"No, no. Strictly on the sidelines. But we had some meetings canceled because of it. We'll be home tomorrow morning."

"Brooke might be released tomorrow. I talked to her at lunch, and she said her mom and uncle would be by to pick up some things."

"Wonderful," Ethel exclaimed. "How's her memory?"

"Improving. She remembers leaving the Supreme Court with Robert Finley after sharing the elevator with the chief justice's secretary."

"Nicole Cramerton?" Ethel asked.

"She didn't say. Should I ask?"

"No. It's not important."

"Okay, I'll—" Lanny stopped mid-sentence. "Wait. Someone's knocking at the front door."

"Leave the phone on, but put it in your pocket. Don't tell I'm listening in."

"Right." Lanny's voice dropped to an excited whisper.

Ethel heard the scratch of fabric and then the muffled footsteps as Lanny hurried downstairs. The knocks sounded louder as Lanny drew closer.

"Coming," Lanny shouted.

Ethel heard the front door squeal on dry hinges.

"Can I help you?" Lanny asked.

Ethel tried in vain to recognize the voice as a man said, "Is Ethel Crestwater here?"

"No, she's not. Can I give her a message?"

"When do you expect her?" His tone was curt and flat, more of a command than a question.

"Tomorrow. She's in the District staying at the Mandarin Oriental for the night."

A few seconds of silence followed. Ethel wondered if the man had left without saying anything more.

"Sorry to bother you," he finally replied.

"No problem. Have a good evening." Again, the phone went quiet. Then Lanny said, "He's walking to a black SUV double-parked in front of the house. The windows are tinted so I can't see inside." Lanny pulled the phone from his pocket and put it to his ear. "He's getting in the driver's side."

"Describe him," Ethel said.

"African American. About six feet. I'd guess in his thirties. Dark suit. Red tie. Could be a fellow agent, given the wardrobe."

"Try to catch a plate number."

Lanny read the tag aloud as the SUV drove away. Ethel repeated it back to him.

"Should I do something with it?" Lanny asked.

"No. You did great. If anyone else comes by, handle it the same way."

Ethel disconnected, set her phone on the coffee table, and retrieved her burner from her handbag.

FBI Director Rudy Hauser answered. "I recognized your new number, so I assume this is off the record."

"Yes. How's Clarissa Baxter?"

"Safe and sound. The remote work has gone smoothly for all the justices, and we'll bring her back to Washington by the end of the week."

"Guards around the clock?"

"For the immediate future until we get further along in the Ventana murder. Now, before you ask for whatever favor I know you're going to ask, tell me you weren't involved with the debacle at Senator Hathaway's speech this morning."

"I happen to be staying at the Mandarin Oriental, if that answers your question."

"Eth-el." Rudy stretched out the two syllables in mocking disapproval.

"And the debacle was literally triggered by OmniForce Protective Services. The former employer of dead murderer Ronald Drake. I think it's worth a hard, deep look into OPS's relationship to Senator Hathaway and Roger Diamond. Anyone, for that matter, who could be in your suspect pool."

"If you're tangling with OPS, you're playing with fire. They have a sketchy history in the Middle East of using indiscriminate force that would land a regular soldier in a court-martial. If they are involved and you pose a threat, then all bets are off."

"Jesse and I have our bags packed."

"All right," Rudy said. "I'll make OPS a priority. Is that why you called me?"

"No. I need you to run a plate for me. Lanny got it off what looked like a government vehicle outside my house. I think it's fallout from the adventure this morning."

"Okay. Give it to me."

Ethel repeated the tag number twice.

"I'll get back to you soon," Rudy promised. "I'm also going to call Lanny and tell him to stand by."

"Stand by for what?"

"Stand by to get you and those packed bags. You could now be a target as much as anyone."

—

The photos came through the secure link. They were grainy and a little blurry, but Ethel Fiona Crestwater was easily identified as the woman seated in the rear of the car stopped at the gate of the chief justice's house. The woman whose prying had forced the killing of Daniel Ventana. The woman whose meddling had brought national attention to lithium mining and threatened to split the coalition in two.

The woman was proving to be a problem with too many friends in high places.

What had Stalin said? *Death is the solution to all problems. No man—no problem.* No reason that didn't hold true for a woman.

Chapter 29

The sun was setting over the skyline of Miami, igniting the wispy clouds into brilliant shades of red and orange. The man had changed into cream linen trousers and a salmon cabana shirt before heading for the hotel bar. The mojitos were excellent, the waitresses beautiful, and Washington DC was a thousand miles away, both physically and mentally.

He eyed his fellow drinkers, looking for a single woman whom he might entice to join him for dinner at Joe's Stone Crab and maybe a nightcap from his room's minibar. The evening was filled with possibilities. He noticed a brunette at the bar checking him out. Hooker, probably. That was okay. He had money to burn.

He picked up his glass, preparing to introduce himself, when he felt the phone vibrate in his front pocket. His burner, which meant if not a wrong number, then someone must have an immediate problem. Not his problem, he thought. Or maybe it was. It could be an alert that something had gone awry after that last hit. He couldn't see what that could be, considering it had been executed so quickly and he'd been in Miami less than twelve hours later. Had his escort team been picked up?

He set the mojito back on the table and retrieved the cell. "It's me. What's up?"

"I need you back here for a job."

"Back to DC? I thought you wanted me out of town?"

"Things changed. We need a problem taken care of."

"When?"

"As soon as possible. There's a late-night flight. Your ticket will be prepaid, and I'll send you the e-ticket."

"Another rush job?"

"Yeah, but don't be greedy if you want to stay in our good graces. Fifty thousand is plenty. It's easy money. If that's not satisfactory, I'll move on."

"No," the man answered quickly. Moving on meant they might never come back to him. "I'm just concerned about prep time."

"Don't be. I'll text you the details. The first half will hit your account tomorrow morning."

"Who?"

There was no answer. The caller had already disconnected.

The brunette hopped off her barstool, clutched her white wine, and headed for the man's table, confident she'd read his intentions correctly. He gave her a shake of his head, rose from his chair, and turned his back to her. He quickly walked away.

She stopped mid-stride, color flushing her high cheekbones. *Men,* she thought. Well, good riddance to that one.

Up in his room, the would-be Casanova downloaded photos to his phone. He stared in amazement. Were they serious? The picture showed somebody's grandmother.

He texted:

LET HER DIE OF OLD AGE. WILL BE QUICKER

The quick reply:

DO YOU WANT THE JOB OR NOT???
YES
THEN YOU PLUS TWO. NO ARGUMENT. UNDERESTIMATE HER AT YOUR OWN PERIL

He took one final look at the elderly woman in the backseat of a car. He didn't know what she'd done, but she'd really pissed off the wrong people. He started packing.

—

Ethel and Jesse ate at the small table in her suite. Conversation ebbed and flowed as they took their time with the meal.

Jesse swallowed a bite of burger and exhaled a satisfied breath. "Good. How's your salad?"

"Same as yesterday. It's my safe restaurant choice."

"I'm all for being safe," Jesse said. "You'll be glad to know Tracy set up a flag in all the sites where she discovered your name."

"How many's that?"

"She said not many. Ethel Crestwater isn't exactly as common as Jane Doe. She searched the way she suspects someone else might. She accessed property tax records, driver's license, home address. Things relatively easy to find outright or hack into."

Ethel laid down her salad fork and gave Jesse her full attention. "So, how's this flag thing work?"

"The easiest way to explain it is she placed little trip wires along the paths she followed. If someone enters your name in a search, she'll be notified of the inquiry. The data should also identify the searcher. Her computer will run all night with an alarm programmed to sound loud enough to wake her."

"And can she do other things while this program is running?"

"Yes. She's diving deeper into OPS and Crane and Weston, as well as Hathaway, Mulberry, and Diamond."

"I think we can now add the general and everyone Rudy said Ventana was checking."

"All the clerks?" Jesse shook his head. "That's nearly forty people."

"We'll ask Rudy where that stands, but Lanny said Brooke now remembers riding down in the elevator with Chief Baxter's secretary, Nicole Cramerton. I'd like to know a little more about her."

Ethel's burner buzzed. "Speak of the devil." She accepted the call. "Hi, Rudy, tell me you have news."

"Tell me why the Defense Intelligence Agency is interested in you."

"Defense Intelligence? That's where the vehicle trace led?"

"Yep."

"The driver wore civilian clothes. What does that tell you?"

Rudy thought a moment. "Either the driver is using the SUV as an Uber or the military doesn't want to be seen with you. Which do you think?"

"I think maybe I've meddled where Lieutenant General Corbin doesn't want me."

"That's the understatement of the year. Seriously, about those packed bags. I can have Lanny bring them and we'll get you moved tonight. I've spoken with Curt Foster. He has ample room, and I've got men in place already guarding the chief justice."

"Let me discuss it with Jesse," Ethel said. "We'll get back to you."

"What's to discuss?"

"I said we'll get back to you."

Rudy groaned. "Ethel, you're the most pigheaded, mule-stubborn—"

"Love you too, Rudy." She disconnected.

Jesse's mouth dropped open. "You just hung up on the director of the FBI."

Ethel went back to her salad. "No, I didn't. I hung up on my good friend who happens to be the director."

"What do we have to discuss?"

"Whatever our guest wants."

"What guest?"

"The one I'm expecting to make an appearance before we check out tomorrow."

"Who?"

"We'll see. Remember patience is a virtue. Now why don't you figure out how to use the coffee maker?"

Twenty minutes later, two sharp knocks sounded from the door. Ethel got up from the sofa. "I'll get it." She stopped a foot in front of the door. "Is that you, General?"

"What?" came the startled reply. Then, in a voice of resignation, "Yes, Ms. Crestwater. May I come in?"

"Only if you promise to call me Ethel." She winked at Jesse. He stared at her in bewilderment.

"May I come in, Ethel?"

She opened the door and stood to one side. The general entered. Out of uniform, he looked like a corporate CEO in his dark, smartly tailored suit, crisp white shirt, and deep blue tie. His steely gray hair was short but not in a buzz cut. He carried himself with a military bearing that kept his spine ramrod straight.

His eyes swept the room, lingered on Jesse a few seconds, and returned to Ethel. He held out his hand. "I'm Alan. I've heard a lot about you."

Ethel matched his firm grip. "Don't believe half of it." She closed the door. "And this is Jesse, my double-first-cousin-twice-removed."

The general laughed. "Sounds like something you'd hear spoken at Buckingham Palace." He crossed the room to shake Jesse's hand. "A pleasure to meet you."

"You as well," Jesse replied. "We have coffee."

"Thanks. Black, please." He looked back at Ethel. "Can we talk in private?"

She gestured for him to sit on the sofa. "Sure, but private includes Jesse."

The general nodded. "All right. Obviously. you were both expecting me." He sat on a spot on the sofa closer to the armchair Ethel took.

Jesse brought him a mug of coffee and then eased into the remaining chair.

"I guess the man at your house saw me," the general said.

"No, the visit just confirmed what we'd expected. I knew my conversation with Brooke would spur her to contact Senator Mulberry and that he would alert you. I figure our investigation is running afoul of whatever you and Mulberry are doing. The fact that you came first to my house and then here suggests the little demonstration this morning accelerated the need to talk. So, what's going on, Alan?"

Lieutenant General Alan Corbin took a deep sip of coffee and set the mug on the table. "I understand you want to find out who attacked your friend's niece. That this is personal for you."

"Not as personal as it was for Brooke, Robert Finley, and Daniel Ventana. You know and I know they were all victims of a criminal scheme. I just want to hear that the project involving you, Senator Mulberry, and Brooke isn't tied to assault and murder. Otherwise, I go to Rudy Hauser and tell him your visit wasn't to illuminate but to intimidate. I'll also give him the recording you know I have of Senator Mulberry coaching Brooke on what to say. Rudy will be very interested in that. Do I make myself clear, Alan?"

"Crystal clear. And let me make myself clear. I expect you to keep what I tell you confidential. It's sensitive and deals with national security. We are not covering up a crime but are working in our own way that will serve our purpose and possibly uncover the criminal conspiracy you're investigating."

"You swear no cover-up?"

Alan Corbin raised his right hand. "On my honor as an officer."

Ethel leaned back in the chair. "Then let's hear it."

The general rubbed his palms across the tops of his thighs as if suddenly nervous about what he had to say. "I've known Senator Joseph Mulberry for many years. He has long sat on the Senate Armed Services Committee. When I was appointed director of Defense Intelligence six months ago, Joe was one of the first to congratulate me. Two months later, he contacted me through my personal phone saying he had something important to share. He wanted to meet somewhere outside Capitol Hill or DIA headquarters. I suggested a small cottage I have on the Eastern Shore. We could make it a weekend outing. He agreed but insisted we drive separately."

"So, this was last summer?" Ethel asked.

"Yes. Clarissa Baxter had just received senate confirmation, and the court was in recess. I suspected Joe wanted to alert me to some upcoming issue on the Armed Services Committee. Maybe funding cutbacks or something in the wind impacting legislative oversight. But that wasn't the case. He told me he was acting as a member of the Senate Ethics Committee. He had received a tip that Senator Hathaway was engaging in insider trading, not directly, but through accounts set up for his wife and children."

"There are clearly laws against that," Ethel said. "Doesn't he have to disclose stock transactions by his family?"

"Yes, but it applies to insider knowledge acquired through congressional activities like private hearings and briefings. Like congressmen who dumped stocks after receiving advance information about the likely impact of COVID-19. But although the laws are on the books, penalties are minor. And congressmen claim the fault was that of an accountant or their broker or that the suspect trade was a coincidence."

"But Hathaway is more than that," Ethel stated.

The general leaned forward, elbows on his knees. His face grew grave. "Yes. The leaks weren't from Congress. They were from the Supreme Court. Someone, possibly a political opponent, had accessed information showing a pattern of trades that happened shortly before the release of a ruling, a ruling that favored or hurt some company or industry. A ruling that would affect their stock price."

"So, these weren't leaks like the *Roe v. Wade* debacle," Ethel said.

"No, just the opposite. A public leak would undercut the value of the inside information."

"Did you suspect one of the justices?"

"The justices, the staff, the clerks. But if word leaked of our investigation, it was feared everyone involved would go to ground."

"Did the entire ethics committee know about the potential scandal?"

"No. The tip only came to Joe. He knows Washington leaks like a rusted-out bucket. So, he contacted me to see if I could help. The justification in his mind was since Hathaway chairs the intelligence committee and handles extremely classified and sensitive information, he's in a position to be blackmailed. That's a national security risk that can't be tolerated. But we needed more than just a few past questionable transactions."

"The mining case," Ethel stated. "Four justices had agreed that the Supreme Court would review the lower court's support of the Lithium USA federal lease. The consequences are huge, aren't they?"

"Yes, if overturned based on ecological impact, open-pit mining could be severely limited everywhere. The stock value of Lithium USA and similar companies would crater. If the lower court's ruling is affirmed, then it's likely the stock prices will soar. It's the perfect opportunity to tempt Hathaway and his accomplice into an insider trade. Then we'd bring Rudy and the FBI up to speed to conduct a criminal investigation."

Ethel got up from her chair. The general started to stand but she waved him down. "I think better when I'm moving. Go on. I'll restrain myself from interrupting." She began pacing the floor.

"Well, we ruled out the chief justice because she hadn't been on the bench. But if we alerted her, she might have felt obligated to tell Supreme Court Marshal Ventana, and we'd risk exposing ourselves. New clerks were starting, and Joe approached me with the idea of using Brooke. He knew her and thought she might be useful. We weren't asking her to tell us the ruling. We only wanted to know when a ruling had been finalized so we could benchmark transactions that might occur before the public release."

"A leak of the progress, not of the content," Ethel said.

"Exactly. Not nearly as egregious as the *Roe v. Wade* leak of an actual opinion."

"But how would that tell you who was the inside source?"

The general sighed. "It wouldn't. But if Hathaway got trapped, we felt there was a good chance he'd give up his source. The man wouldn't hesitate to save his own skin."

"And last Friday you expected a decision to come out of the conference."

"No. Brooke had told us the chief justice and her clerks were extremely closemouthed. Baxter held her own opinions tightly guarded, and none of her clerks would even discuss which way she might be leaning."

Ethel stopped her pacing and looked down at the general. "But if someone figured the discussion would be on the agenda last Friday, an inkling of how the chief justice was leaning could be all they needed if they knew the other eight were split."

"Which is why we think this attempt to get documents was planned for Friday."

Ethel looked unconvinced. "How could they count on Robert Finley carrying documents home?"

"They couldn't. But they were covering all their bases. Maybe Ronald Drake was just one option they were ready to play if the opportunity presented itself."

"Sounds like a pretty sophisticated operation," Ethel said. "You think Hathaway conceived it?"

"Hell, no," the general nearly shouted. "He's not smart enough."

Ethel's eyes brightened. "But Roger Diamond is."

"Exactly. And your stunt this morning poked him right in the eye. A public humiliation."

"Which was my intent," Ethel admitted. She sat back in her chair. "You know his extra security at the hotel came from OmniForce Protective Services. They're tied into this, aren't they?"

The general nodded his approval. "Very good. OPS is a client of Crane and Weston."

Jesse sat straight up in his chair. "Really? I missed them on their client list."

"That's because Crane and Weston works behind the scenes, targeting key lawmakers like Hathaway and Joe Mulberry. And people like me who would have a say."

"Have a say in what?" Jesse asked.

The general turned to Ethel. "You know what I mean, don't you?"

Ethel shrugged. "I suppose you're talking about contracts for private forces to augment the U.S. military. Companies that hire trained veterans to work security in hostile areas."

"Right," the general confirmed. "We're talking millions, even billions, of dollars paid to a third party that operates outside of the military chain of command. And when things screw up, as they always do, the private contractors aren't necessarily bound by the laws of either the military or the host country. In my opinion, military operations including diplomatic security should be handled by the U.S. military."

"Have you voiced that opinion?" Ethel asked.

"Oh yeah. But to no avail. We've depleted our own security forces to the point where we have to depend on private firms. At least that's the argument made by lawmakers like Hathaway and some of his cronies on the Armed Services Committee."

"Did Hathaway and Diamond invite you to last Saturday's round of golf to lobby you?" Ethel asked.

"Definitely. We're certainly not bosom buddies. But I wanted to get close to them. Learn what they hoped to get from me."

"Which was what?"

"My recommendation that contracts with OPS be renewed."

"Nothing about lithium mining?"

"No. Just as well. I don't want them thinking I have an interest in the court's ruling."

The room fell silent for a moment as Ethel gathered her thoughts.

Then she asked, "Did you know Rudy Hauser had been invited at the last minute to complete your foursome?"

"No, but I welcomed the opportunity to be with him. You see, I anticipated needing to approach Rudy if we ever got anything on Hathaway's insider trading. It turned out Hathaway was interested in Rudy's take on the assault of the law clerks. It was the first thing he mentioned when the FBI director arrived at the course. And it was the first I'd heard of it."

"Did you know the legislative aide who was supposed to play golf wasn't really sick?" Ethel asked.

"No. Did Hathaway bump him?"

"Yes. Which gave him and Diamond firsthand access to the man who would likely investigate the attack."

"Rudy wisely left after two holes. I got stuck playing the whole round. Joe Mulberry called me on the back nine with news that Brooke was in a coma. He was distraught, both for her health and that our scheme might become public."

Without thinking, Jesse blurted out, "You broke into Ethel's house. You stole Brooke's computer."

The general offered no apology. "What would you expect? I couldn't trust that the young woman hadn't put something in a document or on her calendar app that would have compromised what Joe and I were trying to do. Surely you can understand that."

Ethel held up her hand, signaling Jesse to keep quiet. "I do, General. But you could have just asked me. I know how to keep a secret. However, I will tell you this. Go deep as you can into the ties between Diamond and OPS. Remind me who's the CEO."

"Matt Geyser. A man who never met a war he didn't like. We'll give him a hard look."

"Good. So, what do you want from us?" Ethel asked. "You didn't just come here for coffee and conversation."

The general took a deep breath. "Like I said at the beginning, I'm asking you to stand down and lie low. For your own safety. I'll admit that you've made headway in your investigation, but we don't want Hathaway and whoever else might be involved scared off. Let us proceed with our plan."

"How's it going to work without Brooke?" Ethel asked. "She's supposed to tip you off when a decision has been reached."

"Joe thinks he has a backup possibility. Or we might have to see a suspicious trade happen and then, after the ruling is officially released, ask the chief justice to share the timing of the decision process so we can establish a correlation."

Ethel frowned. "Which might not give you the source of the leak. You have no guarantee that Hathaway will flip. He might be more afraid of talking than not talking."

The general threw up his hands in frustration. "Well, Ethel, do you have a better plan?"

"I do. Would you like to hear it?"

Chapter 30

Lieutenant General Alan Corbin left after promising that he would keep his visit a secret, even from his friend Senator Mulberry. For the time being, neither of them needed to be involved any further. However, Ethel's next step meant risking a rebuke, not only from Rudy Hauser, but from the chief justice. Ethel would be asking both of them to dance along a narrow path of murky legality.

"Do you trust the general?" Jesse posed the question as he poured the last of the coffee into his cup.

"Yes," Ethel said. "If he were involved in the attempt to gain inside knowledge about a Supreme Court ruling, he wouldn't have contacted us. Why draw attention to himself and Mulberry? If there's no truth to their plan to expose Hathaway, then why tell us to back away?"

"So, what do we do tomorrow?"

"Not tomorrow, Jesse. Tonight. The situation has changed. Go pack your things." She picked up her burner phone. "I'm going to shock Rudy."

"Shock him how?"

"By taking his advice."

"Wait a minute," Rudy said. "What's the date and time? I want to record the moment Ethel Crestwater actually did something I wanted her to."

"You have a good idea once in a while," Ethel said. "I agree both Jesse and I should lie low, at least for a few days."

"At Curt Foster's?"

"Especially at Curt's."

Rudy thought for a moment, wishing that they were talking in person so that he could read Ethel's body language. He sensed she wasn't telling him everything. "What changed your mind?"

"Off the record, Lieutenant General Alan Corbin stopped by my hotel suite tonight. He seems to think that I had something to do with the anti-mining demonstration this morning. He and Senator Mulberry have been quietly looking for evidence that can prove Senator Hathaway has been engaged in insider trading."

"And he's afraid your renegade activities might scare the senator off," Rudy asserted. "Nix him from trading on any advance information he might get on the mining case."

"Yes, but he doesn't think the senator has a direct connection to the Supreme Court."

"Hathaway does have a contact there," Rudy said. "The chief justice's secretary Nicole Cramerton. Ventana had tagged her as someone to investigate before he was killed. We reviewed her personnel file. Senator Hathaway wrote Cramerton a glowing recommendation when she applied for the job."

"Maybe," Ethel conceded. "But the general told me something interesting. Roger Diamond's firm handles lobbying for another client whose name has popped up. OmniForce Protective Services."

"OPS," Rudy said with disdain. "That explains why Diamond hired them for the meeting of the Progressive Mining Coalition. He could stroke two clients at once. OPS gets a hefty fee, and the heightened security makes his attendees feel special. Instead, you blew up his coalition's brine-extraction/open-pit fault lines and publicly embarrassed a company filled with global combat-ready mercenaries. Congratulations, Ethel."

"Thanks. All in a woman's workday. Now here's how we'll get to Curt's. Jesse and I have each left a packed bag in our respective bedrooms. Lanny should bring them in his car to a service entrance behind the hotel. Tell him not to drive straight here but to assume someone is following him. Only if he's sure he doesn't have a tail should he come here. He can text me when he's about ten minutes away. Jesse and I know how to avoid the front desk, so if we're lucky, no one will see us leave."

"Okay," Rudy said. "Got it."

"That's not all. Tell him we're going to swap cars. I'll give him my room key so he can stay the night. I'll also leave my valet parking ticket and my personal cell phone in case someone tries to ping its location. Lanny can leave the hotel tomorrow morning. Warn him that my house might be under surveillance. I suggest he be armed at all times."

"Let's just hope all of these precautions are unnecessary. How long do you plan to stay out of sight?"

"Until Hathaway or Diamond makes a move."

"What makes you think they will?"

"A timeless incentive. Greed."

—

Roger Diamond was as angry as he'd ever been. He paced around his home office like a caged lion. The mining coalition was in tatters as the brine extractors used the demonstration to tout their eco-friendly process. As a result, the open-pit companies were threatening to quit the coalition and blaming him for the PR disaster. And he'd just gotten off a heated phone call with Matt Geyser, the CEO of OmniForce Protective Services, who had ripped into him for letting an elderly woman create such havoc. Diamond didn't hesitate to point out that the OPS operative who pulled his gun had been the real culprit. The idiot made Barney Fife look like Eliot Ness.

"I'm taking care of it, Matt," Diamond had assured the CEO. "Our messaging hasn't changed. Our country needs lithium, and we can't have energy independence without domestic mining. Otherwise, we'll become vulnerable to the battery equivalent of OPEC."

"To hell with your messaging," Geyser had snapped. "I've learned this Ethel Crestwater has the ear of important people in this town. We can't have her snooping around."

"Then lend me some technical help. Have your cyber team go over her life with a fine-tooth comb. If we can't quickly find some dirt that we can leverage against her, I'll take it to the next level. Right now she's still at the Mandarin Oriental, but I have watchers in place. We're ready to act."

"All right. Just make sure the investigations hit a dead end." Then, in an ominous tone, the CEO had added, "As dead an end as necessary."

Diamond replayed the conversation in his mind. Matt Geyser couldn't order him around. He wasn't Geyser's employee. Besides, they had too much history going back to Afghanistan twenty years earlier. But Geyser wasn't the kind of man you crossed unnecessarily. Not if you valued your life. Diamond knew he couldn't afford another screwup.

He stood at his desk and looked at the photos and research

documents spread across its surface. There were the grainy pictures of Ethel Fiona Crestwater in the car at the chief justice's gate, plus a Virginia driver's license photo, an FAA pilot's certificate, and her property tax records, all of which he'd paid a hacker to access.

Most concerning was the information he'd learned from sources inside various law enforcement agencies. Crestwater didn't just have the ear of top officials, it was rumored she received their cooperation. Diamond didn't like that the woman appeared to be the nexus of investigatory inquiries—the FBI, the DC police, the Arlington police, and perhaps the Supreme Court police, if Ventana had been following her last Saturday when he was killed. That was an unforeseen complication. The whole damn mess was one big unforeseen complication.

Diamond picked up the clearest photo of the woman in the back seat of the car. She was looking at the camera, which eliminated any doubt as to her identity. It also eliminated any doubt that she'd spotted the photographer's car. Another loose end that might have to be dealt with.

He opened his desk drawer and retrieved one of several burner phones. He texted a single sentence:

wait for instructions

Now, he had to wait for word that Crestwater had left the security of the hotel. Then the hunt would begin in earnest.

—

The plane touched down at Reagan International Airport at ten forty-five at night, eleven minutes ahead of schedule. A symphony of bells and buzzes sounded as passengers immediately turned on their cell phones. One man in first class felt a single vibration. He pulled his phone from his pocket and angled the screen away from the woman seated beside him.

wait for instructions

Of course he'd wait for instructions. The message disturbed him. It sounded like things weren't nailed down. How complicated could it be to take out an elderly woman?

Complicated, he decided. And that's why they'd given him the contract. He wouldn't make the mistake of underestimating the target. He was a professional.

Chapter 31

The two men were parked where they could watch the entrance to the hotel. They had the photo of Ethel and the description of her Infiniti, including the Virginia plate number. So, when Lanny Childress stepped out onto the sidewalk at eight Thursday morning and handed his ticket to the valet, the watchers thought nothing of him. Then, when Ethel's car pulled up, they stared in confusion as Lanny took the keys, tipped the attendant, and drove away. They had no instructions other than to follow the woman, not her car. Was she still in the hotel? One of the men quickly sent a text, dreading the response.

—

At eight o'clock, FBI agent Ed Tucker also wasn't happy. He didn't like his authority being challenged, even if the woman had the support of Director Hauser. He'd been unpleasantly surprised when Ethel had come to the stables an hour earlier with Curt Foster and announced she would be riding with the chief justice and that there was no need for Tucker to accompany them. When he'd refused, the woman had the audacity to call the director at home and insist she accompany Chief Justice Baxter alone. She'd listened to whatever Hauser was saying, and then replied, "All right. You can bet I will be." With an undisguised frown, she'd handed him the phone.

"Agent Tucker here."

"Look, Ed. I know this is highly unusual. So are the circumstances. I've told Ethel you will accompany them."

"Yes, sir," Tucker replied, feeling vindicated.

"But you are to distance yourself just enough so that any conversation between the two of them cannot be overheard."

"Sir, that might limit my response capabilities."

"I understand. But you won't be going solo. Ethel will be armed, and believe me, she's a damned good shot."

So, here he was, trailing the two women by a good fifteen yards while they rode side by side along the forest path. Leading them all was the German shepherd, who constantly sniffed the breeze. Tucker thought the dog made an excellent scout. Max would sense danger far sooner than he would. He relaxed. Things could be worse, he conceded. At least he wasn't stuck in a car on an all-night stakeout, drinking stale coffee and peeing behind a bush. His spirits brightened. He patted his horse's neck and took in a deep breath of cool, fresh air. The slanting rays of sunlight streamed through the tree branches, illuminating the drifting ground fog. Yes, despite Ethel Crestwater, this was a good assignment. A good morning.

Ethel looked over her shoulder at Agent Tucker. He gave a nod and continued his careful scrutiny of the trail. She judged he was far enough back that he couldn't hear them. Clarissa had been sharing stories of her life on the ranch back in Wyoming. Ethel sensed her appointment to the court was exacting a personal price that she had underestimated.

"Will you get back to your ranch for Thanksgiving next week?" Ethel asked.

"I hope so. Jackson's sister lives close by, and she's invited me to join her family for the holiday. The court's hearing arguments Monday and Tuesday, but then we're off for a long weekend. Assuming we're allowed to travel. And there's Daniel Ventana's funeral."

"It's been scheduled?"

"Not yet. His brother's making arrangements. I'll be there, even if it's on Thanksgiving Day." She choked back a sob. "This whole business is so terrible. Robert Finley's service is this afternoon in Michigan. I should be there instead of hiding from public view."

"Rudy Hauser knows what he's doing." Ethel leaned sideways in the saddle to get closer to the chief justice. "I have an option for you to consider that might give us a break in the case."

"Sure. What is it?"

"First, promise to hear me out."

Clarissa cocked her head and studied Ethel. "As long as you're not asking me to promise to do anything."

"No. Just listen."

"All right. I'm listening."

Ethel took a quick glance over her shoulder. Agent Tucker was still fifteen yards behind. She lowered her voice. "The lithium mining case. We want to leak a decision."

"What?" Clarissa exclaimed. "But you asked me to delay deliberations. To delay a decision."

"And that's what I still want. I'm not talking about the actual decision or any written drafts. Just well-placed rumors. The FBI believes we're dealing with insider trading based on leaks of confidential information before a ruling is posted. Uncovering the source can lead us to whoever is behind three murders. When's your next conference with the other justices?"

"Tomorrow."

"Good. Would you request that the conference be held in person?"

"I can. Why?"

"To add to the appearance of its importance. But don't discuss it. We want the rumor to be totally baseless. Can you do that? You'll be serving the cause of justice. And that's what drives you, isn't it? Serving the cause of justice."

Clarissa looked at the trail ahead with Max faithfully in the lead. "Good closing argument, Ethel Crestwater. You should have been a lawyer."

Nicole Cramerton hurried to the elevator. Not that she was late. With the chief justice sequestered somewhere, she felt an extra responsibility to be at her desk ahead of time, ready to handle anything that her boss might need.

"What's got you in a panic?" Jake Simmons asked, keeping the elevator door open until she was safely inside.

"The chief justice usually calls in first thing. She'll be prepping for tomorrow's conference so I need to be ready to enter any data or documents she wants to share. I like to respond quickly in case she asks for last-minute changes."

Jake started the elevator's ascent. "Any idea when she might return?"

Nicole shook her head. "No. I guess not until the FBI decides it's safe. That might not be until after Thanksgiving." She sighed. "That's why tomorrow's conference is important. They won't meet next Friday, and cases are getting backlogged."

Jake eased the elevator to a stop and opened the door. "Well, they shouldn't return till the FBI's caught the bastards. I just hope to God they're not inside our court. That would be a betrayal of this country, and I'd deal with the scumbags accordingly, leg or no leg."

His mini-rant surprised Nicole. At a loss for a response, she simply nodded and left.

Jake watched her go down the hall. She'd seemed frightened by his comment. Could it be interpreted as guilt? Maybe it was something he should share with FBI Director Hauser.

When Nicole reached her office, she logged on to her computer and checked for any internal messages. There were none. Nicole busied herself with the dictation the chief justice had sent the day before via an encrypted link. Mostly short replies to correspondence involving requests for the chief justice to speak at graduations or conferences. The majority were declined, but with an expression of regret. Those she did decide to consider were put on hold a few days until the chief justice could evaluate the invitations more thoroughly.

Nicole's desk phone rang. She glanced at her watch. Nine o'clock. Chief Justice Baxter was right on time.

"Office of the chief justice," Nicole said with precise pronunciation.

"Nicole, it's Stuart Hathaway."

"Senator Hathaway?" she awkwardly asked, her mind momentarily confused by the unexpected caller. "Good morning, sir."

"Good morning. How are things going?"

"As well as can be expected. We're all anxious to return to normal."

"Yes. I couldn't agree more. But I'm sure you're doing a great job holding down the fort."

"Thank you, sir."

Hathaway cleared his throat. "Listen, Nicole, I have a personal favor to ask."

"Yes, sir?"

"I don't know if you saw the news yesterday, but I was ambushed by a group of hostile demonstrators protesting the lithium mining lease. Someone even fired a handgun, and I could have been killed."

"I saw that. I'm so glad you weren't hurt."

"I don't mind telling you I was scared," Hathaway said. "And I'm afraid I won't be so lucky the next time."

"Next time?"

"If the ruling comes down against them, they could take it out on me. I'd just like a little advance warning."

"You mean if the lower court ruling is affirmed."

"I don't intend to put you in an awkward position. We've always had a great working relationship. Just tell me not to worry or to be on the alert. That's all I need."

"All right. I guess I can do something like that."

"Thanks, Nicole. You'll always have a home on my staff."

A guaranteed job in the U.S. Senate was no small thing, she thought. Nicole continued to think about it for thirty minutes until she wondered why the chief justice hadn't called.

Clarissa Baxter listened as FBI Director Rudy Hauser outlined Ethel's plan. He, Clarissa, Ethel, and Jesse sat in Curt Foster's den. Curt had taken his wife for two days of appointments with her Parkinson's medical team at the Inova Fairfax Medical Campus, which worked out well because Rudy didn't want the discussion to go beyond the four of them. He even kept his agents outside.

Max lay beside Clarissa's chair, content as she rubbed the dog's side.

"The leak will be of a nonexistent decision," Rudy reiterated. "We just need to prioritize who gets the leak in what order. We're agreed the initial pool is anyone who saw or spoke to Robert Finley after his basketball game with Brooke. When he had his full backpack." He turned to Clarissa. "I hate to suggest it, but your secretary Nicole Cramerton is ideally placed to have advance knowledge of court rulings. And Hathaway knows her."

"She knows a lot of senators from her years as a stenographer."

"Yes, but we have reason to believe Hathaway's the one receiving the information."

"All right. We'll have the in-person conference tomorrow, and afterward I'll mention to her that I'm leaning a certain way. Only I will know whether I'm really leaning one way or the other."

"Good," Rudy said. "Then we'll wait a few days to see if any stock transactions occur."

"Let's cut the time in half," Ethel said. "Give one suspect one leaning and another the opposite leaning. If there are any stock transactions, they should reveal who leaked which version."

"Makes sense," Rudy agreed. "Clarissa, can you pull it off?"

The chief justice looked grim. "For the integrity of the court, I have no choice." Her phone buzzed. "It's Nicole. I'd better take it. We need to tell the other justices that we're in person tomorrow." She stood up and took the call in another room.

Rudy also rose. "I need to tell the men to escort the other eight into the court building in the morning. I'll release the communications team placed here, since we won't need them." He left.

Max got up and shook himself. Then he lay down at Ethel's feet. She leaned forward and gave him a gentle scratch behind the ears.

"He likes you," Jesse said.

"Then he's in a rare club."

Jesse's phone vibrated. "It's Tracy. She's texted she needs to talk with me."

"Take it up in your room where you won't be overheard. You can brief me later."

Ethel closed her eyes, not in sleep, but in concentration. Her plan was fraught with pitfalls. Foremost was the chief justice's ability to convincingly play her role. Leaking information or rather misinformation went against her nature. And how could Ethel be sure they even had the right suspects? Ventana had just started tagging them. Rudy said the FBI background checks had yielded nothing suspicious.

"Ethel?"

Ethel opened her eyes.

Clarissa was standing in front of her. "You need to change your plan."

—

"Well, damn it, where the hell is she?" Roger Diamond stood behind his desk in his K Street Crane and Weston office and yelled into his cell phone. "She must have left the hotel during the night. Either someone picked them up or they swapped vehicles."

"What's the big deal?" a man asked. "She's just an old lady."

Diamond squeezed the phone, wishing it was the neck of the idiot on the other end. "That old lady organized the protest that's practically destroyed the coalition and unnerved Hathaway. That old lady may have spotted one of our cars outside the house of the chief justice, and she's got an inside track to the chief justice and the FBI. If that isn't enough to worry about, the old lady's ex-FBI herself, sharp as a razor and as cunning as a fox. I want her found." He ended the call and barely restrained himself from hurling the phone against the wall. As his rage subsided, he wondered if Ethel Crestwater really was such a threat. Was he making this personal? There had been too many mistakes already and reacting out of anger raised the prospect for more. He wouldn't do anything rash, but any action would be moot until he knew her location.

Diamond sat down at his desk and looked at the documents OPS had delivered. He was impressed that Ethel had a pilot's license. Maybe she'd flown away. Sabotaging her plane sounded like a promising option if he knew when she might be flying. He turned to the listing of her taxable property. The house was valued at one-point-two million. Jesus, he thought. That old place? Washington real estate was insane. He had the house under surveillance. There was the tax assessment for a 2022 Infiniti, a car he knew was parked in her driveway. Then there was the plane, a Cessna 172, that listed Crestwater as a part owner. The FAA registration number was also on the tax document.

Diamond turned to his computer and called up the FAA registration website where he found a link where he could match the number to the owner. Two were listed: Ethel Fiona Crestwater and Curtis Foster. The address was Foster Stables, Manassas, Virginia. Diamond rubbed his palms together. Just maybe this was the break he needed.

Chapter 32

Ethel and Jesse took a stroll out past the stables where they could watch the horses graze. Leaning against the fence, Ethel said, "I didn't want you saying anything in front of the others, but did Tracy have any news?"

"Yes. She said trip wires had signaled searches for your name in places like the DMV, Arlington County tax records, and voter registration."

"Things in public records?"

"These weren't Google searches. She strongly suspects they were very sophisticated hacks."

"Was she able to determine a location?"

"No IP addresses. And she thinks the probe was relayed through multiple VPNs, masking the true address."

"Tell me again what's a VPN?"

"Virtual Private Network. It hides your IP address and encrypts your data. Tracy got the search alerts but that's all."

"Would she know if she had hit a trip wire herself? Something that could trace back to her?"

"She wouldn't know. But if someone got an alert, they wouldn't find her IP address because of her VPN protection."

Ethel turned to face him. "IP addresses...VPNs. I feel like a dinosaur."

"Yeah. A T. rex. I don't think you have to worry about becoming extinct."

Ethel threw back her head and laughed. She grabbed Jesse by the arm. "Come on, Cousin. Let's walk to the end of the road and back. I missed my RBG workout this morning." She pulled him alongside her. "I suspect we'll have a meeting with Rudy and Clarissa soon."

They were halfway back when the FBI communications van and the RV came toward them. Ethel and Jesse stepped to the shoulder and waved as they passed.

"Well, I guess it's official," Ethel said. "Clarissa's heading back to DC. Let's go hear the details."

They found the chief justice and Rudy in the den, each in the chair they'd claimed since the first gathering. Ethel and Jesse took their customary places.

"We've got the logistics worked out to have the protection of the justices turned back over to the U.S. marshals and the Supreme Court police. However, I've insisted the FBI continue to provide protection for Clarissa."

"So, agents will remain in place?" Ethel asked.

"In place with Clarissa, not here." Rudy looked to the chief justice.

"I've agreed to go back tonight and stay in a hotel," Clarissa said. "We won't have to worry about the long commute in the morning. And Rudy wants me there for the encounter with Nicole."

"Face-to-face tonight?" Ethel asked.

"Tonight," Rudy confirmed. "I have her apartment under surveillance, so we'll know when to make the approach. I hope she's staying home tonight so we're not knocking on her door at ten o'clock."

"Sounds good," Ethel said. "And Max?"

The German shepherd lifted his head and thumped his tail on the floor.

Clarissa turned to Rudy. "We haven't discussed that. I suppose we could swing by my house and drop him off."

Ethel leaned forward and snapped her fingers. Max took the cue and came to her, his tail still wagging.

"What if he remains here with Jesse and me? I promised Curt we'd take care of the horses, so we're staying." She focused her gaze on Rudy. "Wouldn't that save time?"

"Yes. And, Clarissa, I could bring you back here tomorrow afternoon. The Fosters told me not to hesitate to keep you here."

"Or we could bring Max to your home," Ethel offered. "But you know he'd love another day on the farm."

Clarissa laughed. "Well, how can I say no now that Max has heard the invitation?"

—

Lieutenant General Alan Corbin stared out the window of his Defense Intelligence office. Five o'clock and the expressways were a parking lot. No question the thousands of idling cars were pumping poison into the atmosphere. He accepted the conversion to electric vehicles couldn't come fast enough, but without the domestic mining of minerals needed for batteries, the United States would be forced into depending upon countries like China, Russia, or other adversarial states. It didn't take military intelligence to foresee the national security implications. Global demand for lithium, cobalt, and nickel could pit the industrial nations against one another in the race for resources. And yet the demonstrators had a point—the mining was dirty and toxic, creating long-term consequences that could last for centuries.

A knock sounded from his office door and he turned from the window. "Come in."

His aide entered carrying a file folder. "Sir, I have the information you wanted."

"Thank you, Dawkins." The general took the folder but didn't open it.

"Will there be anything else, sir?"

"Were their service records easy to access?"

"Yes, sir. No flags or classified material."

"Then that will be all." He glanced over his shoulder at the window. "Why don't you call it a day and join the crawling throng?"

"Thank you, sir."

When his aide had left, the general sat at his desk and opened the folder. Inside were the Marine Corps service records of two men—Roger Diamond and Matt Geyser. He scanned the lobbyist's records first, zeroing in on his time in Afghanistan. Then he turned to the CEO of OmniForce Protective Services. The tour dates not only matched but they were in the same platoon. The two men had been decorated for heroism. In the face of heavy Taliban fire, they'd retrieved a wounded comrade.

Matt Geyser and Roger Diamond had forged a bond like tempered steel. It explained their connection and told the general there might be no limit to what they'd do for each other. Matt Geyser at OPS, Roger Diamond at Crane and Weston, and Senator Hathaway on the Intelligence and Armed Services committees. An unholy alliance. Ethel Crestwater had pushed him to investigate them. The woman had been right, but she wasn't the one to take it further. He had an ally who could. He reached for his phone, glad to have shared personal numbers.

Ethel led Suzy Q, the last of the horses, into her stall where she'd already prepared fresh hay and water. Max sat outside the open gate and watched her.

"Don't worry, boy. You'll get fed next."

"I would hope so," Jesse said, as he walked inside the barn.

"You know I meant the dog, unless you'd also like a bowl of Purina."

"What's the other option?"

Ethel gave Suzy Q a pat and closed the gate.

"I saw pancake mix and Vermont maple syrup in the pantry. There's Canadian bacon in the fridge. Sometimes the best-tasting breakfast comes at suppertime."

"Well, it's a tough choice, but I'd hate for you to eat pancakes alone."

They walked outside, and Jesse closed the double barn doors. Dusk cast everything in muted colors and the breeze grew colder.

Ethel wrapped her arms around herself. "I swear my blood must be getting thin."

"Just old age."

"Listen, youngster. Hold your tongue if you want to make it to your old age. That said, how about building your broken-down cousin a fire while I feed Max and mix the—"

Ethel's burner phone vibrated. She checked the screen. "It's Rudy. I hope nothing's gone awry." She accepted the call. "What's up?"

"I just had an interesting talk with Corbin. He went deeper into Diamond's military career. He also reviewed the records of the OPS CEO Matt Geyser. Guess what?"

"They knew each other in the service," Ethel stated.

"Not only knew each other but were in the same platoon. Together they saved a wounded comrade and earned commendations for their bravery."

"Isn't that in their bios? It's great PR."

"Yes," Rudy agreed. "But no one tied their service records together. They're clearly more than business associates."

"And they could both link back to Ronald Drake, former OPS employee and overzealous mugger. Tell me about the third man."

Rudy was quiet a second, and then asked, "What third man?"

"The man they saved. The man who was wounded. That's someone with a lifelong bond, a lifelong debt."

"Jesus," Rudy whispered. "An invisible man."

"What do you mean?"

"The court's elevators are still manned. One operator's a wounded vet. Jake Simmons. I met him. Ventana tagged his file because he must have been on duty Friday afternoon. But Ventana wouldn't have known about a connection to Diamond and Geyser."

"And we don't know that their tours of Afghanistan overlapped. Find that out first. I'll call Frank."

"Why?"

"Because he said Brooke now remembers riding down in the elevator with Nicole Cramerton. Someone had to be operating it. Someone who overhears hundreds of conversations a day. Like you said, Rudy, he's an invisible man. People forget he's there, listening to every word. Clerks, administrative staff, even the justices. Piece together enough bits of information and you can fill in the blanks. So, forget prioritizing the other clerks. He's your target."

She disconnected. Jesse, wide-eyed, immediately peppered her with questions. "Who's the target? Who's an invisible man? What about Nicole Cramerton?"

"Patience. All in good time." She stepped up on the porch and entered the farmhouse with Jesse close behind.

"I'll tell you after I talk to Frank. Why don't you feed Max and build that fire?" She went upstairs to the bedroom she was using, turned on the light and sat in a chair by the window. *Brooke should be at Frank's house,* she thought. He might not recognize this number, but she'd keep calling until he answered.

He did so on the third ring. "Yes?" he asked without giving his name.

"It's Ethel. I'm using a different phone."

"Where are you? I've been calling and leaving you messages."

Ethel became alarmed. "Everything all right?"

"Yes. Brooke's been discharged but has been told to take it easy. I went by your house to pick up some of her things. Lanny told me you and Jesse had gone into hiding. He didn't know where."

"Not hiding, just staying out of sight. We kicked a hornet's nest yesterday."

"So I gathered. I've been calling to see if I can help in any way, now that Brooke's out of danger."

"Actually, that's the reason for my call," Ethel said. "We're looking at one of the elevator operators at the Supreme Court who was on duty last Friday afternoon. Brooke told us she rode down the elevator with the chief justice's secretary, but said nothing about the operator. I'd like to know what interaction if any might have occurred with him."

"All right. She's sleeping now. Can it wait?"

Ethel's first response was to say no. She reconsidered. The young woman would probably be thinking more clearly if she awoke naturally. "Yes. But ask her as soon as she wakes up. Call me on this number regardless of the hour."

"Anything else?"

Ethel thought a moment. She understood Frank's desire to help. "Drive your car by my house and check for surveillance."

"And if I find you're being watched?"

"Run the plates, and we'll see where that takes us."

"Got it," he said, clearly happy to have an assignment. "Promise me one thing, Ethel."

"What's that?"

"You'll stay out of sight till we figure out what the hell's going on."

"Frank, I'm perfectly safe."

She disconnected and looked out at the dark landscape. Stars emerged as the sky turned black. She never saw the drone hovering over the barn.

Chapter 33

Roger Diamond studied the footage on his cell phone with more intensity than a doctor examining an X-ray. The drone had been a risk, but when his scout team reported that a stealth search of the open hangar confirmed the location of the Cessna, Diamond decided to order an aerial pass to assess the ground conditions for himself. In the fading light, details were hard to make out. He saw the large farmhouse was at the end of a long, single-lane road that ended behind the barn. *Good,* he thought. The house wasn't visible from the main road, and the road wasn't visible from the house. A car without headlights could approach noiselessly. Had the driveway been gravel, the crunch of stones might have awakened a light sleeper.

Only one vehicle was parked by the house. Although the plates on the compact SUV were too dark to read, they didn't appear to be Virginia's white background. Diamond thought there was a good chance the SUV had brought Crestwater and her young accomplice to the farm from the hotel. If they'd driven themselves, they could be the only ones there. That would be ideal.

The drone rose above the barn and flew closer to the house.

A woman sat behind a window. She had a cell phone pressed to her ear, obstructing her profile. After about ten seconds, she lowered the phone and stared out the window.

Diamond hit pause. "Gotcha, you old biddy." Then he continued watching as the drone flew a three-sixty around the exterior of the house. The only other sighting was through a kitchen window. The young man was preparing something, but could only be seen from the waist up. The drone retreated and the footage ended. Diamond watched it three more times. Confident there were only the two of them, he formulated his plan.

No man—no problem. Diamond thought of another Stalin tactic. The dictator allegedly rounded up political opponents and perceived enemies at four in the morning, a time when they would most likely be in deepest sleep. A time when a sudden, aggressive awakening would be disorienting and confusing. It would be like shooting fish in a barrel.

—

The text came through shortly before nine pm:

Be ready for pick up at 2. Ninja show at 4. Details to follow

Ninja. Black clothing for night-stalking. He was expected to get close to the target. A few minutes later, he received two more texts. One contained drone footage of some farmhouse. Another showed two freeze-frames lifted from the video—the woman at a window on the second story and a young man at a window in the kitchen. The young man was a surprise. He didn't like surprises.

He texted back:

Who's the man Not going in outnumbered

Consider him a 25% bonus Outnumbered by old lady and college kid?

OK Will text when done

—

At ten thirty, Ethel had just closed the bedroom curtains and was unlacing her shoes when Frank called.

"You were right," he said. "Someone was staking out your house."

"Was or is?"

"That's the interesting part. Two men were in a dark green Chevy Malibu parked about two blocks away. I saw them through their front windshield as I drove toward them. I turned on Ninth and stopped out of sight, waited ten minutes, and went back down North Highland. As I was approaching from the rear, they pulled out from the curb and drove away. I circled back five minutes later to see if another team had taken up watch. No further sign of surveillance."

"Did you run the plate?"

"Yeah. It's a company car."

"Crane and Weston?"

"No. OmniForce Protective Services."

"Good."

"How can you say that? Those people don't fool around."

"Because it ties them further into the conspiracy."

"Why do you think the watchers left?" Frank asked.

She didn't have a good answer. "I guess because they were told to."

"Where are you, Ethel? I want some reassurance that you're safe."

Ethel decided there was no reason to keep him in the dark now that the chief justice had gone. "If you must know, Jesse and I are at Curt Foster's. Curt and Connie are away, and we're house- and horse-sitting. No one outside of you and Rudy knows we're here." She shifted the conversation. "I guess you haven't spoken with Brooke yet."

"Just finished. She does remember the conversation with the elevator operator. Jake Simmons."

"That's the man," Ethel interjected.

"He was teasing Robert Finley about his heavy book bag. Told him not to drain his batteries. Brooke now thinks he guessed that the mining case was the one Robert planned to work on over the weekend. Robert also mentioned that he and Brooke were going to the Dubliner."

"Which would have given Ronald Drake time to get in position to either follow Robert or wait near his house."

"Simmons could have reported to someone," Frank said. "Fits the time line. What's your next move?"

"Let Rudy do his job. Thanks, Frank. You've been a big help."

"You can thank me by staying put." He disconnected.

Ethel sat on the bed, one shoe off, one shoe on.

Her mind went back to the surveillance of her house. Not that she was being watched but that now she apparently wasn't. She trusted Frank's ability to have spotted any replacements. Did that mean she was no longer a target or that they knew she was elsewhere? Knew she was here?

She was still sitting on the bed fifteen minutes later when Rudy called.

He got right to the point. "Diamond, Geyser, and Simmons were in the same platoon the day it was ambushed. Chief Justice Baxter and I also met with Nicole Cramerton, and I heard firsthand what she'd told the chief justice over the phone. Senator Hathaway had asked her for advance knowledge of the mining decision."

"Did she record it?"

"No. She had no idea the request was coming."

"Damn," Ethel said under her breath.

"Yeah," Rudy agreed. "It will be her word against a U.S. senator's. But I did wake up a friendly judge who issued an approval to put a tap on the cell phones of Simmons, Geyser, and Diamond. I then had the chief justice tell the judge of Hathaway's alleged request for inside information. He went out on a limb and included Hathaway's cell."

"Anything incriminating will be on burners."

"Probably," Rudy said. "But Hathaway could be the careless one. I can see him just using his personal cell and saying something he shouldn't. I've got agents contacting the service providers and putting teams in place for monitoring. I hope everything's operational by midmorning."

"And the chief justice's secretary?" Ethel asked.

"She proved herself by reporting Hathaway." The FBI director let out an audible breath. "She's shaky as an actress, but we're coaching her. She's our best shot."

"I heard from Frank." Ethel reported Brooke's memory of the elevator conversation with Simmons.

"That certainly gave him enough information to act on," Rudy said. "We need to link him to Diamond and OPS by more than just the service records."

"OPS had my house under surveillance till around nine thirty tonight."

"What?" exclaimed Rudy so loudly that the sound distorted.

"I guess they decided we weren't coming home tonight."

"I don't like it, Ethel. I can send an agent to you."

"You've got an agent here. A damn good one. Me. Use your resources where you really need them."

After the call, Ethel wondered if she shouldn't have accepted Rudy's offer to send an agent. Maybe she and Jesse should leave. They could even take her plane and avoid any chance encounters on the ground. She was instrument-rated and knew the airstrip well enough to take off blindfolded. Max could lie across one of the rear seats. The dog looked up at her from where he lay on the floor as if reading her mind. *No,* she thought. She couldn't leave Curt's house and horses, and the likelihood of something happening was small.

Her thoughts of the Cessna triggered a memory. Tracy had said someone had searched her property tax records. She hadn't been concerned about her house and car because they could be identified easily. But the tax on the plane would lead to the FAA registration. *What an idiot,* she thought. That would lead here. The connections had been staring her right in the face, and her missing it was inexcusable. So much for being a damn good agent.

She put her shoe back on. She and Jesse had work to do.

—

The hinges on the steel door squealed as he pushed it open. He made a mental note to oil them himself. As the back door to the dumpsters for his condo building, it was a useful exit to avoid being seen coming and going. At two in the morning, he didn't want anything drawing attention to himself. In black sweater, black slacks, black gloves, and dulled black shoes, he wanted to be a walking shadow within the shadows. That meant no reflections—no watch, no rings, no bracelet, no glasses, no belt buckle. The only thing he carried was a black pouch containing his lockpicks and glass cutter.

He emerged from behind the dumpsters and found the black Lexus already in the alley. He glanced at the plate. If it was the same car, the plates had been switched. Good move. He appreciated professionalism.

He slid into the back seat. The men in the front were the same two who had driven him before.

The one in the passenger seat turned to face him. "Here's a Glock with suppressor attached. Magazine's full, none in the chamber." He handed over the semiautomatic. "And here is a pair of night-vision goggles. They're antiglare so no reflection. We thought they'd be needed to move through the house."

"All right. But this is my operation. Understood?"

"Understood," the men answered in unison.

"Good. Then let's get her done."

Chapter 34

A new moon and no light pollution meant only starlight illuminated the landscape. Not a single light burned in the dark farmhouse. Ethel sat in the chair by the upstairs bedroom window with a Remington twelve-gauge pump shotgun across her lap and her .38 revolver tucked in the waistband of her jeans. Max lay on the floor at her feet, his faint snores indicating at least one of them was getting some sleep.

Ethel watched the driveway through a narrow gap in the curtains. If they came, she was ninety percent certain it would be on the pavement. Even if they approached on foot, the asphalt would be easier walking than uneven ground.

She hoped her vigilance proved to be wasted effort, but she believed the old adage "prepare for the worst, hope for the best." She felt no fear for herself. Her concern was for Jesse. She'd made it clear he was to play his part and then retreat to the horse trail. If she could, she'd join him. If the odds were too great, they'd abort everything before a confrontation occurred and simply disappear off the trail and into the forest.

Jesse sat in the dark on the one chair left in the kitchen. A twenty-gauge Weatherby leaned against his knee. Ethel's familiarity with the Fosters' home included knowing where Curt kept the key to his gun safe. Ethel told Jesse the shotgun was Connie's and had less weight and kick than the twelve-gauge. "Don't hesitate to use it," she'd ordered. "Point at the chest, pull the trigger, and the fired shell ejects and a new shell is automatically loaded. Fire again if there's any doubt he's down." Jesse would have felt more comfortable if she'd given him a pistol. That's what she'd been teaching him to use at the practice range. But Ethel told him in the heat of the moment he probably couldn't hit the broad side of the barn, a barn that was only thirty yards away. They'd both laughed and the tension had eased a little. Only a little.

He patted his cell phone in his chest pocket. Ethel had instructed him not only to have it silenced, but to keep the screen turned against him so that if it lit up, he wouldn't become a target.

The hours ticked by. Several times he dozed just long enough for his chin to fall on his chest. He hoped Ethel was more alert.

She realized she not only had to be alert, but she also had to be limber enough to move fast. Sitting in a chair for hours stiffened her muscles. Holding on to the shotgun, she paced the clear path from the chair to the door and back. Every second or third short lap, she checked the window. After ten minutes, she laid the shotgun in the chair and did a few standing stretches. Her head was clearer and her muscles looser.

Then Max growled.

"Easy, boy." Ethel peeked out the window. A black sedan with no lights crept around the curve in the driveway.

"Quiet, Max. We practiced this." She pulled her phone from her pocket and sent the pretyped message:

visitors be ready

"Looks like everyone's asleep," whispered the driver. "Do you want us to wait here?"

"I want you to turn off the engine and not say another damn word." He slipped the strap of the lock-picking pouch over his shoulder, grabbed the Glock, pulled back the slide, and chambered a cartridge. "You can flank me ten yards either side. If something goes wrong, I don't want to be caught in the crossfire. Keep your guns tucked by your side. You'll only shoot if one of them gets by me. But that ain't going to happen. We'll open the doors on my count of three and leave them open. I don't want to hear so much as a squeaky shoe." He slipped on and activated the night goggles. "One, two, three."

Ethel saw the doors open simultaneously. No courtesy lights came on. The men looked like shadows as they moved away from the car. The one from the rear seat adjusted something around his face. *Night goggles,* Ethel thought. He would be the leader. The one to take out first. She wished she could will him to the front door.

"Heel, Max." Ethel picked up the shotgun, loosened the revolver in her waistband, and headed for the stairs with the German shepherd close to her side.

Jesse had felt his phone vibrate and took a quick look at the screen. It was the code word. Adrenaline poured into his bloodstream. He headed down the dark hallway to the back porch and eased the rear door open. He went to the far corner where the electrical panel was attached to the house. The cover was already open. He put his hand on the main breaker and focused all his attention to listen for one thing—the sound of Ethel's voice.

The assassin held his pistol tight against his side as he stepped up on the front porch. The planks creaked under his weight. He looked to his left and right, signaling with a headshake for the two to stay on the ground. His pains for silence might be for naught if he couldn't pick the locks and had to force a window. He saw a Yale dead bolt, a model he'd practiced on. He relaxed. Five minutes max. He'd have to set down his gun, which couldn't be helped. He didn't have confidence in the men with him. They struck him as nothing more than cheap muscle.

He started to lay down his pistol when he thought, what the hell, try the door first. The handle turned, and the door inched open on its own. Country people, so trusting. Slowly, he swung the door wide and stepped over the threshold.

At first, he didn't understand what he saw. In the greenish glow of the night goggles, it looked like a wall of jumbled shapes. Then his brain sorted them out into chairs, sofas, tables, and other furniture spread in an arc in front of him.

"DROP THE GUN NOW!"

Jesse heard Ethel loud and clear. In less than a second, he threw the main breaker.

Instantly electricity flowed through the circuits of the house, turning on every light inside, the spotlights under the eaves of the house and barn, and portable work lights spaced among the upended furniture and throwing their bright beams directly at the front door.

The intensity of the sudden luminance exploded the night-vision goggles into a blinding brilliance. The assassin instinctively fired in the direction of Ethel's command. She moved from her hiding place on the upper stairs to the mid-landing. The shotgun was already braced against her thin shoulder, and her finger was on the trigger. Her attacker desperately grabbed at the goggles.

Ethel fired.

The lethal load of buckshot slammed into the killer's chest, knocking him back through the front door like gravity had suddenly ceased to exist.

"FOE! MAX! FOE!"

The German shepherd launched himself from the landing, bounded over the makeshift barricade, and charged onto the porch.

The two men stood frozen in the light, their own eyes adjusting to the glare. One of them raised his gun, and Max went for him so fast the man didn't have time to aim. The shepherd's powerful jaws latched onto his wrist as Max knocked him to the ground. The pistol flew wide, and the man screamed, "Get him off me."

His partner fired a shot and Max yelped.

Ethel hurried through the narrow gap she'd hidden in the barricade and ran crouching onto the porch. Her eyes went first to the man and dog lying on the ground. Then she sought the third gunman. He was in a shooter's stance, his pistol already leveled at her. Ethel tried to wheel the shotgun around as she kept moving.

A shot rang out. The man fell on his back and lay still. Jesse stepped from the corner of the house, his shotgun at his shoulder, his eyes wide with a combination of fear and excitement.

"Kick his gun farther away," Ethel ordered. "Keep him covered." She gave a quick glance at the man she'd shot, saw his chest was mincemeat, and hurried to where Max was struggling to stand. Blood seeped from a wound on his right haunch. The bullet appeared to have grazed the muscle. Max made it onto three legs and sniffed the man's face before limping to Ethel.

"Good boy, Max. Lie down. We'll get you patched up."

The dog gave a soft whimper and settled on the ground. Ethel kept her eyes on the supine man beyond him. Blood stained his right forearm where Max had clamped down on his wrist. That wound wasn't fatal. The hole in his temple was.

Ethel looked across the yard to Jesse. "The dumbass killed his own partner."

Jesse didn't reply. His gun barrel wavered as his whole body trembled.

He's going into shock, Ethel thought.

"Stay, Max." She ran to her cousin. "Lower the gun, Jesse, and take deep breaths." She looked at the man Jesse had shot. Lifeless eyes stared up at nothing. "It's over. Max is hurt. Nothing serious, but there's a first-aid kit in a cabinet over the sink. We'll need tape and bandages."

Jesse took a few more deep breaths and pointed the barrel at the ground. "Shouldn't we call the police?"

"No. That would screw up things that have been set in motion." She took his free arm and walked him to the porch steps. "Let's sit down a second."

They sat, each with a shotgun in one hand.

"We'll call Rudy. He'll know what to do. But before we treat Max, I want to search the bodies and the car."

"For what?"

"Phones. They might provide a harvest of intel, like who hired these jokers."

"Even if you find them, they'll be locked."

"And if unlocking is by fingertip or face recognition, no problem. They've still got their hands and faces. If the phones are locked by numeric code, then Rudy's techs will have to crack them. But first we've got to find them. You sit, I'll search."

Leaving her shotgun on the porch, she went to the man Jesse had killed and found a phone in the front pocket of his pants. The man shot by his partner also had his phone in his front pocket. She gave the third man, the one she decided had been the leader, a frontal pat-down but his pockets were empty. She reached under his butt. "Pardon me," she whispered. "Nothing personal. I only date men with a pulse." No phone.

She left the porch and walked to the Lexus. With the doors

still open, she could reach in without leaving prints. She was sure the vehicle would be a DNA treasure trove. A phone lay on the back seat. She picked it up but nearly dropped it when it vibrated. A text message appeared on the screen:

DONE?

She quickly replied:

DONE!!

Then she read back through the incriminating text thread. "You'll be done, all right," she said to the phone. She returned to Jesse. "This one's unlocked. I didn't try to open the other two."

"Let me see them." He pressed the home button on each. The screens lit up. "They must have turned auto-lock off. Guess they didn't want to bother with a password if they needed to communicate while trying to kill us. You might want to open and close an app every ten minutes just to make sure they don't lock up."

"I'll leave that to you. But first see if you can get me the phone logs on each of them. Actual numbers. Then see what you can do for Max. Oh, and kill most of the lights. We're probably visible to the International Space Station."

When Jesse had found the call logs for Ethel to scroll through, he went back in the house, giving wide berth to the body in front of the door.

Ethel called Rudy.

"What now?" he asked, failing to hide his annoyance. "Are you lonely?"

"Not in the least. We had some company drop in about fifteen or twenty minutes ago. I'm calling you to come to the party. It's BYOS—Bring Your Own Shovel."

Immediately Rudy's sarcastic tone transformed into urgent concern. "Ethel, are you safe?"

"Yeah, but it's my own damn fault. You offered an agent. Now I'm pretty sure I was traced here through my plane registration."

"Did you kill the attacker?"

"One of them. Jesse took out another. Max earns an assist for the third."

"Good God, Ethel," he shouted. "You took out three men? What are you going to tell the police?"

"Nothing. They've not been notified. You're going to come clean up and keep this under wraps for a while. I used one of the killers' phones to confirm that Jesse and I are dead. I also collected two other phones, all unlocked. I'll give you the numbers so you can wake up your friendly judge and add them to your tapped list."

"Did you recognize any of the men?"

"No. But they came in a black Lexus sedan, and I've got a plate number. A full forensics exam might yield DNA and other hard evidence."

Rudy took a deep breath. Ethel let him have a moment or two to process everything she'd dumped on him.

"Then we'll proceed as planned," he said. "I'll get a team down there as soon as I can. Certainly before dawn. Do you or Jesse need anything else?"

"No, but Max needs a vet. He has a flesh wound. Maybe someone from the K-9 unit."

"That can happen. Now give me the phone numbers so I can get moving."

Ethel read off what Jesse had found on the three phones and the plate on the Lexus.

When Rudy had finished repeating them back for confirmation, he said, "Ethel, I'm really upset about what went down tonight. You came damn close to getting you and Jesse killed."

"I know," Ethel said softly. "I guess I'm not immune to hubris." She looked at the three bodies surrounding her. If Jesse hadn't disobeyed her order to throw the main switch and run, she might not have survived. "It could have gone the other way. But I hope what I've given you breaks the case. And I do need something else?"

"What?" Rudy asked warily.

"To be there at the takedown. A ghost who comes back to haunt. It might get an interesting reaction."

Rudy couldn't suppress a chuckle. "It might indeed. And I need something from you."

"What?"

"Promise you won't shoot anybody else until my people can get there."

Chapter 35

Nicole Cramerton buttoned up her blouse. She had been assured by the female FBI tech that the tiny microphone clipped to her bra would clearly pick up the conversation. Her job was to act naturally and not overdo it. The last time she'd had to act was in an elementary school play. She'd been a talking tree.

"Turn your nervousness into exasperation," the FBI woman had coached. "You're worried about getting all your work done. Share that a lot was decided in the morning conference, and you're only getting a quick lunch break."

The elevator door opened. Jake Simmons gave Nicole a big smile. "Taking the afternoon off?"

"I wish." She felt perspiration under her arms.

"You look stressed."

"I was supposed to meet friends for lunch, but instead I'm grabbing takeout to eat at my desk."

Jake closed the door but hesitated in starting the descent. "You had in-person conference this morning, didn't you?"

"Yes. A lot was decided, and the chief justice is writing the majority opinion for one of the cases. I'll take dictation as she outlines key points."

"What about her clerks?" Jake asked.

"They'll use the outline for a preliminary draft. The chief justice wants one ready to circulate as soon as possible."

"Sounds like what Robert was working on." Jake shook his head. "His loss is a real tragedy. I'm sure the chief justice misses him."

"Yes. She said so herself. Robert would have gotten the assignment."

"You heard about the protests at the Mandarin Oriental last Wednesday," Jake said. "Should we be expecting something like that?"

"I hope not. Or that at least those same protestors will continue to be peaceful when the decision is announced."

Jake turned to the controls with just the hint of a smile. "So do I," he said. The elevator descended.

Ten minutes later, the tap on Jake Simmons's phone intercepted a call to an unknown number.

"Have you got something?" Roger Diamond asked.

Rudy Hauser gave a thumbs-up to Ethel and Jesse. They were together in Rudy's office in the Hoover Building, where the tech team could let them monitor the calls. Diamond's voice was clearly recognizable.

"The lower court ruling is upheld," Jake said.

"You're sure?"

"The secretary as good as told me so. The preliminary decision came out of this morning's conference."

"Good work. Let me know if you pick up anything else."

The call ended.

Rudy applauded. "That's one link connected. Simmons to

Diamond. And Nicole did a great job dropping information. Now we'll see what Diamond does."

"But we don't have a tap on the phone Simmons called," Ethel said. "Diamond could continue using it, and we wouldn't know."

A tech came on the secure line. "Sir, the phone that sent the texts has activated. I'll patch it in now."

Two rings sounded before the call connected.

"What?" someone asked.

Rudy shrugged. "I don't know who that is."

"The lower court's upheld," Diamond said.

Rudy pumped his fist in the air. "Yes! We've linked Diamond to the lead assassin. He's using the phone that sent the kill orders."

Diamond continued. "Jake heard it from the chief justice's secretary. You want to call Hathaway?"

"Yes, I can record the call here. I want a record of Hathaway accepting the information as insurance against his ever turning against us. Or not supporting our contracts."

"He's a greedy bastard," Diamond said. "So as long as we fill the trough, he'll do as we say."

"Have you heard any media reports out of Manassas?"

"No. But the farmhouse is pretty isolated. You can't see it from the road."

"My guys haven't checked in."

"They're probably sleeping, Matt. It was an all-night operation."

"Yeah, you're right. But I'm still not sure about that one."

Diamond's voice grew louder. "You're the one who wanted a dead end. What the hell did you think I was doing? Sending her on vacation?"

"You let the old lady get under your skin, Roger. It became too personal. I hope you haven't made things worse."

"Relax. Nothing can be traced back to us. You just take care of Hathaway and buy plenty of stock in Lithium USA for yourself. After all, what good is inside information if we don't use it?" With a laugh, Diamond disconnected.

"Unbelievable," Rudy exclaimed. "The other voice was OPS CEO Matt Geyser. That conversation just hanged both of them."

"Thanks for the color commentary," Ethel said. "But to really nail this down, I want to hear Hathaway accept."

The tech's voice broke in again. "Hathaway's phone just activated. Patching it through now."

Rudy could hardly contain his glee. "You're getting your wish, Ethel. And God knows you deserve it." He blew her a kiss.

"Hello?" Senator Hathaway said.

"It's Matt. Are you where you can talk?"

"In my office. Alone."

"The mining case. Baxter's confirming the lower court's decision. Lithium USA should surge in value. But it might be a while before the final ruling is posted. So, spread your buys over a few weeks and a few accounts. And keep the inside information tight. The more people know, the more likely the price will soar prematurely."

"I'm not stupid, Matt. It's not my first rodeo."

"I didn't say it was. Can we count on your support for my company?"

"You've got it. As long as I'm reelected, of course. And you know I'm not shy about asking for campaign contributions. Gotta go. I've got some important financial business to attend to."

Ethel got up from one of the guest chairs in Rudy's spacious office. "Heard enough? Do you need to take a cold shower?"

"Close to it. They're all so screwed. Hathaway's going to call his broker next and we'll have them dead to rights."

Ethel signaled for Rudy and Jesse to stand. "Well, what are we waiting for? Have you got teams in place?"

"Yes," Rudy said. "And arrest and search warrants. We'll hit Geyser and Diamond simultaneously so that they can't warn one another. We'll pick up Simmons as he enters his apartment. I'd like to let Hathaway dangle a little longer to see who, if any, of his cronies he contacts. That depends upon how soon the media learns about the other arrests."

"Are you still good with our approach to Diamond?"

Rudy grinned. "Definitely. If it goes down like you plan, I might need that cold shower."

—

A few minutes after five, Rudy and four agents exited an elevator and entered the lobby of Crane and Weston. Behind a chrome-and-glass desk, the receptionist, a pleasant young woman in a smartly tailored pantsuit, stood and flashed a smile of perfect teeth.

"I'm sorry. We're closing, and most everyone's gone for the weekend. Did you have an after-hours appointment?"

Rudy flipped open his FBI credentials. "We don't need one."

Her eyes widened. "Let me get Mr. Diamond. He's the senior officer still here." She reached for her desk phone.

Quick as a cobra, Rudy's hand snapped out and covered the instrument. "Here's what's going to happen, Miss—" He looked for a nameplate.

"Joanne," she said in a shaky voice. "I'm Joanne."

"Here's what going to happen, Joanne. You're going to lead us to Mr. Diamond's office. Then two of these gentlemen will escort you back to your desk. You'll not call anyone or use your cell phone in any way. Is anyone else here besides you and Mr. Diamond?"

The woman looked around the lobby like someone might materialize right in front of them. "Maybe. I don't know for sure."

"Well, if they come through here, wish them a good weekend. If they ask about my colleagues, tell them they have an appointment with Mr. Diamond. Can you do that?"

"Yes, sir."

"Good. Then lead us to where you can point out Mr. Diamond's office. No need to go any farther."

She stepped away from her desk and opened a large oak door. The hallway beyond had offices on either side and ended in a T intersection. To the right, Rudy could see a break room, bathrooms, and a supply room. To the left, glass-paneled walls enclosed conference rooms on either side with more offices beyond.

Joanne stopped and pointed down the left hallway. "His office is the last one on the right," she whispered. "Looks like his door is closed."

"Thank you." Rudy nodded to two of the four agents. "Take her back to her desk." He glanced at his watch. "Our guests should arrive in five minutes. One of you can bring them here."

Roger Diamond poured himself a Scotch and leaned back in the oversized leather desk chair. He held the crystal glass up to the light, swirled the amber liquid, and then toasted himself. Things were looking up, despite the botched mugging, Ventana killing, and Progressive Mining Coalition debacle. Simmons was still in place to pick up what tidbits he could, Hathaway was on the hook as one of the best senators money could buy, and he had the bonus to reap from a windfall of the expected surge in Lithium USA stock.

He was confident he could patch up the mining coalition as well as his relationship with Matt Geyser. So what if taking care of the old woman had been personal? No woman, no problem. He took a healthy swallow of his Scotch and set the glass on his desk. Then he opened a drawer and retrieved one of several burner phones. He'd check in with Matt and see if he'd made contact with last night's team.

The door suddenly opened. Diamond laid the phone facedown on his desk as he looked up to see FBI Director Hauser and two men standing in his office. One of the men in the rear closed the door.

Diamond forced himself to stay calm. He got to his feet but stayed behind the desk.

"Director Hauser, this is a surprise. To what do I owe the pleasure?"

"I thought I'd come here in person. You know, as a courtesy, since we'd played golf together."

"All of two holes," Diamond said, trying to lighten the exchange. "Tell you what, why don't I treat you to a round next weekend? Maybe Senator Hathaway could join us."

"I think Hathaway's going to be up to his ass in alligators."

Diamond's eyes narrowed. "What are you talking about?"

"He's the subject of an FBI investigation. Looks like he's been doing a little insider trading."

"Really?" Diamond felt his throat go dry. "I'm disappointed to hear that. If it's true."

"Correct," Rudy said. "Innocent until proven guilty. He'll have the chance to tell his side of the story. Maybe cut a deal if that's in his interest."

"And your courtesy is telling me about the senator's troubles in advance?"

"No." Rudy reached his hand into the interior pocket of his suit coat and retrieved a document. He stepped up to the desk and showed it to Diamond. "I'm here to personally present this warrant to search your office and home."

"What? This is ridiculous. I know the senator; we golf occasionally. Whatever he may or may not have done has nothing to do with me."

Rudy stood silently staring at the other man. He saw the

sweat break out on his forehead. He waited, still offering the warrant for Diamond to examine.

The buzz sounded. Diamond looked down at his open desk drawer where one of his burners vibrated with an incoming call.

"You might want to get that," Rudy said.

"It can wait."

A second buzz sounded, louder this time. The phone Diamond had laid down on his desk started moving across the surface with each vibration.

Rudy lowered the search warrant. "I can see you're an important man. We can wait while you take care of business."

"Go to hell," Diamond growled. "You've got nothing on me."

"Looks like he's not going to answer." Rudy stepped to one side, and his agents stepped away from the door.

For a few seconds, only the two phones made a sound. Then, the latch clicked. Diamond's gaze focused on the slowly opening door. Rudy's eyes never wavered from Diamond's face.

Ethel entered, a cell phone to her ear. Jesse followed with one of his own.

Ethel stretched out her arms, one hand still clutching the phone. "You missed me, Roger."

Diamond wobbled as the blood drained from his face. "But...but," he sputtered. "But you're dead."

"Like I said, you missed me."

Diamond tilted forward and then collapsed backward into his chair, dragging his arm across the desk, and sending his Scotch and phone crashing to the floor.

Ethel smiled at Rudy. "I think you should read him his rights. It's not everyone who gets arrested by the FBI director. It'll be good for his ego."

Chapter 36

Senator Stuart Hathaway was reclined back in his easy chair, mindlessly watching the Wizards and the Hornets NBA game when he heard the front doorbell. He clicked off the television and checked the time. Nine thirty. Whoever it was had better have a damn good reason for disturbing him.

Hathaway extricated himself out of the easy chair and took care with his balance. He was a little unsteady on his feet. He'd come home late to his upper northwest Washington residence, declined the casserole his wife had reheated for him, and drank two vodka martinis on an empty stomach.

His wife could read the signs that he'd fall asleep in front of the TV and leave her to take a book to bed. Fine with her. The book didn't snore.

Hathaway still wore his white dress shirt, although the tie was gone and the buttons were open at the neck. His trousers were wrinkled like an accordion. He tucked in his shirttail and looked down at his stocking feet. He sure as hell wasn't going to lace up his shoes again for somebody who might have the wrong address.

The doorbell rang again.

"Stu," yelled his wife from upstairs. "Answer the door."

"I'm coming," he shouted for the benefit of both his wife and the unknown visitor.

He threw the dead bolt and opened the door.

"Good evening, Senator."

Hathaway stared open-mouthed at the FBI director and two agents. "Rudy. What's happened?"

"A lot. I need you to come with me."

"No. Not until I know what's going on."

"All right." Rudy reached into his suit pocket and withdrew a small digital recorder. He pressed play.

The mining case. Baxter's confirming the lower court's decision. Lithium USA should surge in value. But it might be a while before the final ruling is posted. So, spread your buys over a few weeks and a few accounts. And keep the inside information tight. The more people know, the more likely the price will soar prematurely.

I'm not stupid, Matt. It's not my first rodeo.

Hathaway felt the martinis lurch in his stomach.

"This afternoon you placed orders to buy a total of two hundred thousand dollars' worth of Lithium USA stock immediately after receiving this phone call. Roger Diamond and Matt Geyser are in custody. The only question left is which one of them will sell you out first."

Hathaway started trembling. "No, no, this is all a terrible mistake."

"It is a terrible mistake. Innocent people died, Senator. Now, are you coming quietly or do you want me to light up your street with blue flashing lights?"

When Hathaway was settled in an FBI vehicle, Rudy walked half a block and called Ethel.

"Is it done?" she asked.

"He's in custody. He'll probably rat out others if he thinks it will help his case."

"Any media show up?"

"No. And nothing's surfaced yet about the arrest of Diamond and Geyser. I hope we can call a news conference tomorrow afternoon. As soon as we disconnect, I'll alert the AG, and he can inform POTUS. With the evidence we've got, no politician will go near Hathaway."

"Any evidence regarding Ventana's murder?" Ethel asked.

"Simmons had a camera that still had your pictures on the SD card. The ones showing you in the car at the chief justice's gate. That puts Simmons at the scene of Ventana's murder. Obviously, Ventana would have recognized him and started asking questions. We found the same images on one of Diamond's phones. Diamond and Geyser had drone footage of Curt's farmhouse. Their complicity in the attack on you is undeniable."

"Do me a favor, Rudy, and keep my name out of it."

"I understand. I don't want anyone questioning your methods either. Thanks for keeping me in the dark on anything that might be awkward to explain."

"What would you think about one more leak?"

Rudy hesitated, bracing himself for whatever Ethel was scheming. "I'm listening."

"I'd like to give Senator Mulberry and General Corbin a heads-up. They pointed us to Hathaway. You shouldn't because the AG and POTUS will want to control the information flow. I, on the other hand—"

"—don't give a damn about the AG or POTUS," Rudy interjected. "All right, Ethel. Leak away."

—

On the Saturday two weeks later, Curt Foster and his wife, Connie, hosted lunch at the farm. Her Parkinson's medication had been tweaked after her exams, and her symptoms were greatly reduced. She'd wanted to invite Ethel, Jesse, Rudy, and Clarissa. The goal was to enjoy each other's company without the tension of hiding out. Her real goal, Curt said, was to see Max. The German shepherd seemed overjoyed to be back on the farm, temporarily forgetting his despondency at having to wear a cone of shame to keep him from gnawing the stitches on his shaved haunch.

The weather on the last Saturday in November was chilly and damp, but a fire in the den and a bowl of Connie's homemade chili and corn bread provided all the warmth needed. After eating in the dining room, everyone took coffee in front of the fire.

Jesse and Curt brought in extra chairs from the dining room.

"I don't know why I'm doing this," Curt said. "Jesse and Ethel have proven themselves to be the best furniture movers."

"Desperate measures," Ethel admitted.

"What if they hadn't come in the front door?" Curt asked.

"I was set to text Jesse to abort. He wouldn't even have had to read it. He'd head for the trail; I'd try to sneak out the front for the woods behind the stable. I was banking that they'd at least try the door."

"What about Max?" Connie asked.

"He would have come with me. Max was our secret weapon."

"Why hasn't the media said anything about the attack?" Curt asked.

"We checked with local police," Rudy said. "No one reported gunshots, so we were able to keep control of the story."

"Can you tell us who they were?" Connie asked.

"If it stays within these walls. Two were OPS employees. The other seems to have been freelance. He had a bag of lockpicks, and we pulled prints off the metal where he got careless. His prints showed up in a military data bank. Tyler Gordon. Sends in tax returns as a freelance security consultant. I'm sure that's just a fraction of what he earned. He won't be filing taxes this year. We found his condo and multiple IDs. He used one of them to fly to Miami the day after Robert Finley and the fake homeless man were killed. We figure Gordon cleaned up after the botched mugging. Then he used the same ID to fly back the day Ethel created the chaos at the hotel."

"And then came here," Connie said.

"Sorry about the bullet hole," Ethel said.

Connie waved the apology away. "I've been after Curt to repaint that wall for years. Now he's got no excuse."

Clarissa stood up, her back to the fire. "Let me say something serious." She smiled. "As if bullet holes in walls aren't serious enough. Thank you for the role you each played in protecting the integrity of the court. We're starting deliberations on the case that caused all of this trouble, and we know it's a difficult issue weighing national security and existential dangers against the rights of those Native Americans and ranchers who need clean land and clean water without fear of toxicity. There'll be consequences either way—extreme consequences. But you protected the process. So, thank you. And thank you for welcoming me." Tears glistened in the chief justice's eyes. "I'm told I'm now a part of Ethel's Army." She looked around the room. "And I couldn't be prouder of being a fellow enlistee."

Ethel stood, her own eyes moist. "Then I accept you into what others call my army. But I propose we all be the same rank."

"And what would that be?" Rudy asked with a wicked grin.

"That we all be double-first-cousins-twice-removed."

Above the laughter, the chief justice shouted, "So ordered."

AUTHOR'S NOTE

The existential threat of our time is climate change. In response, the effort to convert vehicles from fossil fuels to batteries has become a national priority. But the critical battery element lithium is in short supply. The United States produces only two percent of the world's lithium, potentially leaving the country at the mercy of hostile nations that could control the global supply. Exploration for new domestic sources that can be mined is not only desirable but critical for national defense. However, the open-pit mining method is extremely dirty, poisoning the site for three hundred years and requiring billions of gallons of water. Mining leases have been awarded on federal land that is sacred to Native Americans and also supplies water to farmers and ranchers. The dilemma is real and ongoing. What environmental price do we pay to save the environment? What people do we harm in the process? These are questions I wanted to raise in the story because there are no easy answers—not for the courts, not for the politicians, not for the energy companies, and not for the country. The complexity of the issue requires a cooperative and collaborative approach. Working together is our only way forward.

READ ON FOR AN EXCERPT FROM *SECRET LIVES*, ANOTHER EXCITING ETHEL AND JESSE ADVENTURE!

Chapter 1

Jonathan Finch saw the dark sedan parked where he'd been told it would be—on the top level of the parking deck near Whole Foods in the Clarendon neighborhood of Arlington, Virginia. At four in the morning, the county across the Potomac River from Washington, DC, came as close to shutdown as anytime, except for the occasional snowstorm. Finch's Ford Escape SUV and the sedan were the only vehicles in sight, and with headlights off and windows tinted, they appeared as shadowy shapes illuminated by a half-moon and the ambient light from the streetlamps below.

Finch would have preferred a more crowded, public rendezvous site, but he also understood anonymity figured predominantly in any transaction. Security meant precautions, and those precautions varied from person to person, or p2p, as expressed in this world. Peer-to-peer.

As had been prearranged, Finch opened the laptop on the passenger seat, connected it to the hot spot of his cell phone, and logged in. He used the special password-protected software program to call up the private key to his anonymous account. The next steps were simple. He typed a message to the nameless address that was the destination of the transfer:

I'M READY. BRING FIRST HALF MIDWAY.

The driver's door of the sedan opened, but the interior lights stayed off. Finch cursed that his counterpart displayed more caution than he'd anticipated. It was too late for him to disable his own courtesy lights. Instead, he reached inside his nylon windbreaker and unsnapped the flap of his shoulder holster. The Beretta would slide free in a matter of seconds.

Holding a gym bag with both hands, a figure in a hoodie rounded the back of the sedan. The stranger appeared to be no more than five-foot-six in height, and the slender build suggested a lithe, muscular body. The movements were catlike, sure-footed, and agile.

The hooded figure dropped the gym bag on the concrete. The smacking sound told Finch the bag was full. Without giving him a second look, the carrier turned around and returned to the car. Finch eased out of the driver's seat, facing away as the SUV's dome light came on. He strode toward the bag, keeping his eyes focused on the back of the dark figure until it disappeared into the sedan. He knelt, still watching the car and listening for any footsteps. He grabbed the bag's straps with his left hand, stood, and slowly walked backward until he sensed his Escape was within reach. He lifted the bag to cover his face as he sat back in the driver's seat and closed the door.

Finch picked up a small flashlight lying beside his laptop and flicked it on. The narrow beam glinted off the shiny zipper. He opened it, spread the sides of the bag apart, and sucked in a deep breath as he looked at the rolls of hundred-dollar bills inside. He slid the rubber band from one roll and counted twenty-five Benjamin Franklins. He made a quick calculation that the bag was large enough to hold one hundred rolls. Two hundred fifty thousand dollars.

He re-zipped the bag and tossed it into the back seat. Then he picked up the laptop. He'd already entered the appropriate amount of cryptocurrency, clicked the transfer icon, and watched as his account balance reduced accordingly. Then he set the laptop on the passenger seat and turned back to the sedan. The faceless person was already walking toward him, carrying a second bag. Everything had worked perfectly for stage one.

Stage two carried the greater risk. The other driver, or an accomplice, had proposed Finch go first in this second exchange—transfer his remaining funds and then receive an identical gym bag holding more U.S. dollars. But Finch wouldn't agree. There was no reclamation if the recipient simply sped away, stiffing Finch out of the final two hundred fifty thousand. His coins would be irretrievably lost, whereas the gym bag of cash physically existed and could be physically recaptured if Finch tried to make a break for it. And he wasn't entirely confident they couldn't track him down.

The second bag smacked against the concrete, and the figure retreated faster this time. Finch stayed as cautious as before, this time sweeping his eyes in a wider arc across the deck as he approached the final payment. This time he kept his right hand on the butt of the holstered Beretta as he carried the bag to the car.

Again, he pulled out a roll of currency at random. Twenty-five one-hundred-dollar bills with enough other rolls to increase the total cash value of the haul to a half million. He tossed the zipped bag into the back seat with the first, and then turned his attention to the laptop. With a few keystrokes, he set up the second transfer, moved the cursor to the icon, and paused. If he'd been heading up a sting operation, he would have called in his backup. He now had a record of the transfer and the cash as evidence. On his signal, all exits to the parking garage would have been sealed, and a computer forensics team would have descended upon the car, primed to confiscate all electronic equipment before it could be wiped clean.

If he were heading up a sting operation.

He started the engine. Then he clicked the icon to initiate the second transfer, deleted his private key, and slammed the transmission into reverse. The vehicle rocketed backward so fast, the tires laid rubber. The laptop tumbled onto the floorboard, shutting the screen against the keys. But Finch wasn't taking the time to watch the balance of his account decline. He was hell-bent on getting the half-million dollars to safety. The tires continued to screech in protest as he raced down the ramps to the exit.

The crossing bar was down. If he'd been set up by the mysterious other party, the exit lane could be the ambush point. He'd checked that there were no surveillance cameras on the entrance or exit. So, without stopping, he crashed through the bar, sending it splintering onto the pavement. What was a dent or busted headlight in exchange for the untraceable windfall that rode with him?

He breathed easier as he disappeared into the backstreets of one of Arlington's residential neighborhoods. He slowed enough to turn off his phone and eliminate the hot spot used by his computer. Though the odds were slim his signal was being tracked, why take a chance? The next step would be to ditch the gym bags and then begin banking the cash in amounts less than ten thousand dollars. Multiple accounts until he could consolidate them into a trust fund. The plan would take time, something of which he had precious little.

Three blocks from the parking garage, two men sat in a black SUV. In DC and the surrounding area, the vehicles were as common as politicians. The two men inside watched a computer monitor wedged on the console. A red blip moved through a grid of streets.

"He's slowing down already," the driver said.

A voice crackled from the speaker of a cell phone. "I've lost his signal."

"Copy that," the driver said. "We've got the GPS tracer."

"Do you need me to head him off?"

"No. We'll retrieve. Good job. Check your wallet in the morning."

"You know I will. I'll wipe down the car and leave it where we agreed. Good hunting."

"Let's move," the second man said. "We don't want him to get out of range."

"I think he's going to nest close by," the driver said. "But better to intercept before he stashes the money somewhere. Let's go introduce ourselves to our new best friend, whoever he might be." He eased the SUV away from the curb and headed for the blinking red light.

Jonathan Finch found a parking place on North Highland Street in front of the house. Fortunately, his landlady and her other boarders should be asleep, but if anyone happened to see him, he would say he'd just driven in from Richmond. That was true. They were used to the odd hours of his work. He could explain the bags as heavier clothing now that autumn was right around the corner.

Carrying one of the gym bags, he walked to the rear door, where a back stairway took him closest to his room. He used his key to unlock the bolt and tiptoed up the steps. Still, the old, dry floorboards creaked beneath his feet. He opened the door to his small room. There was a dresser, an armoire, a desk, and a single bed with a nightstand. He knelt and pushed the gym bag as far under the bed as he could.

He returned to the car and opened the rear door. He reached across for the bag that had fallen behind the driver's seat.

"Back out slowly." The hoarse whisper was more growl than voice.

Finch froze.

"Do as I say. Leave the bag, and we'll go get the other one together."

"It's a boardinghouse," Finch said without turning around. "People are stirring."

"Then we'll just have to hope you're quiet. Now get out."

As Finch slowly withdrew from the car, the rear door opposite opened and a second man grabbed the bag. He looked up at Finch. The blood drained from his face. "Jesus."

Finch lunged backward, spinning rapidly and throwing his left elbow at the height where the voice had sounded. The blow caught the man in the throat. Finch kept spinning, yanking the Beretta free and aiming through the open doors. The second man had dropped the bag and replaced it with a Glock.

The two gunshots exploded as one.

Chapter 2

Jesse Cooper stopped in mid-sentence. The bang sounded like a bomb had detonated beneath his window. Gas explosion, he thought.

The young woman on his computer screen jumped. "What was that?"

Without answering, Jesse ran to his window and parted the curtains. At four thirty in the morning, houses were dark, with only streetlights casting an illuminating glow. Jesse saw an SUV parked at the curb, saw a man sprawled by the rear passenger door, and, more ominously, saw two men running away, one carrying a square object under his right arm, the other clutching a gym bag in his right hand while his left arm dangled by his side.

"Something's happened, Tracy. I've got to go." He hurried from the room, leaving the woman on the screen frantically calling his name. Clad only in a T-shirt and boxer shorts, he bounded down the stairs two at a time. As he reached the bottom, an elderly woman cinching a powder-blue robe stepped into the hall.

"Ethel, stay inside." Jesse was out the front door before she could reply.

He ran barefoot across the yard to the vehicle. An engine roared to life half a block away. For a few seconds, he heard the squeal of tires and saw a dark SUV accelerate down the street, its headlights off.

The pool of light from a streetlamp just reached the figure lying faceup on the sidewalk. Jesse recognized one of his fellow roomers. Jonathan Finch, a Secret Service agent. Blood stained his chest and flowed onto the pavement. A pistol lay at his feet.

Jesse knelt beside him and heard rapid, raspy breathing. "Jonathan, hang with me. I'll call for an ambulance."

But he had no phone and hesitated to leave the man. He turned and saw Ethel hurrying across the yard. He opened his mouth to yell for her to go back inside and phone for help, but she spoke first.

"I've called for an ambulance and police. Put pressure on his wound."

Jesse placed his palms on the spot that seemed to be the center of the injury. Blood flowed between his fingers. The man's short breaths struggled to become words. Jesse bent closer till his ear nearly touched the man's lips.

"Tell Ethel... Tell Ethel...the secret..." The last syllable was no more than a faint puff of air.

"Move." Ethel Fiona Crestwater barked the order as she slipped out of her terrycloth robe and wadded it into a ball. Wearing only a gray flannel nightgown, she nudged Jesse aside and pressed the makeshift bandage against the wounded man's chest with one hand, while feeling his neck for a pulse in the carotid artery.

Ten seconds later she whispered, "May your soul fly with angels." Then she pulled her blood-soaked robe from the dead man's chest and unraveled it until she reached her cell phone jammed in a pocket.

Lights began coming on in neighboring houses. A distant siren wailed.

"Jesse, we don't have much time." Ethel used a dry corner of her robe to wipe the blood off her phone. "I want you to observe everything you can." She activated the phone's light and video app and then ran it up and down Jonathan Finch's body.

Jesse stared wide-eyed, having trouble pulling his gaze from the elderly woman to the target of her recording.

"Come on. I want an extra set of eyes. I don't depend upon technology." She bent down and studied the pistol for a few seconds. "A Beretta. Interesting." She looked through the open rear passenger door of the SUV. The one opposite was also open. She hurried around the front of the vehicle, pausing to film damage to the grille.

Jesse followed. In the crease of the dent, he noticed white paint streaked onto the SUV's green. The driver's door stood ajar, and he looked over Ethel's shoulder to see a cable dangling from a twelve-volt socket. "Looks like a power adapter for an electronic device."

"Phone?"

"No," Jesse said. "From the type of connector, I'd say a computer. I know he has a laptop."

Ethel turned her phone camera on the open door behind the driver's. A spiderweb of cracks radiated from a hole in the window.

Jesse bent down and peered through the hole. "Someone shot him through the window. This lines up with where Jonathan must have been standing."

Ethel focused her phone on the pavement and then ran it up the inside of the rear door. "No. Although the safety glass didn't shatter, the shards made by the bullet's impact fell outside the door, not inside." She moved her phone closer to the window.

"And there are blood traces on the door's interior panel. Jonathan fired the shot and must have hit his killer's arm or shoulder. The bullet went through but created a DNA signature."

The wails grew louder.

"I saw two men running away," Jesse said. "One of them had a dangling arm."

"Brief me later. I want to check one more thing." She scooted around the rear of the Ford Escape, around the supine body, and, grasping a fistful of her nightgown to avoid leaving prints, she opened the front passenger door and popped the glove box. A black pistol and an extra magazine lay on top of the vehicle's registration and insurance papers. "There we go," she whispered. "There's the Sig."

Jesse stared open-mouthed at the petite grandmotherly woman. *Brief me later? Beretta? Sig?*

She snapped the glove box closed and shut the door.

The sirens sounded only a few blocks away.

Ethel stopped recording, grabbed Jesse's arm, and pulled him up on the sidewalk. She looked around. "The neighbors, police, and EMTs will soon turn this into a zoo until the crime scene is secured. Did Jonathan say anything before he died?"

"He whispered, 'Tell Ethel the secret.' At least I think that's what he said."

"The secret? You're sure that's what you heard?"

"Yes, although it trailed off."

"Okay, Jesse, here's what we're going to do." She stepped closer to him. "You'll give a statement to the police. So will I. They should question us separately. At this time don't tell them what Jonathan said."

"Lie to them?"

"No. If they ask, say he whispered something and you're not sure what, but he didn't say what happened or who shot him. I'll tell them I came right behind you and heard nothing. Now I'm going to leave you."

"Leave me?"

"Yes, tell the police I was overcome by what happened and went inside." She started scrolling through phone contacts.

"What are you going to do?"

"Call Cory Bradshaw."

"Who's he?"

"Head of the Secret Service."

"You know their number?"

Ethel began walking away. "Yes, but at this early hour it will be Cory's personal cell phone. So, talk to the officers and buy me a little time. I should really search Jonathan's room."

The blue glow of flashing lights pulsed across the scene as racing vehicles braked to a stop. Jesse watched Ethel retreat into the shadows, her phone already at her ear. He didn't know which stunned him more, the murder of Jonathan Finch or the actions of his seventy-five-year-old landlady.